'Nolan writes with an unpretentious, been-there-done-that eye for the details of amateur debauchery and motley student life – the late night allure of strip-lit 7-Elevens; the hastily assembled facade of decent living when parents come to visit; the half-baked ambition to get past page eight of The Satanic Verses...warmly funny and immensely readable.' *The Times*

'A hilarious, high speed first novel.' *Scene*

'it explores what is assumed to be the ultimate twenty something fantasy. With parodic echoes of Enid Blyton, the 'Four Take Cocaine' and embark on a series of drug fuelled adventures including a rather nasty S&M encounter involving a scaffold and a paddle. Nolan's sharp, satiric gaze makes this a confident and genuinely comic contribution to the Brit Lit druggie genre, but oh for the innocent pleasures of Jackie.' *Observer*

'A quietly clever insight into temptation...Nolan plays with the inevitable psychological effects of the drug... the stages of their addiction are gently and comically rendered.' *Independent on Sunday*

'Hilarious.' *Daily Mirror*

'Brighton [is] just the place for this story, with its strange mixture of innocence and sleaze, its Playtown atmosphere, which he evokes perfectly...the book has a central question to ask...namely: do we know how to enjoy ourselves anymore?...This is very much for that crowd that likes Charles Higson, James Hawes, etc. But it's less blokey than Higson, less histrionic than Hawes and, deep down wiser than either.' *Guardian*

as good as it gets
simon nolan

quartet books

First published by Quartet Books Limited in 1998
A member of the Namara Group
27 Goodge Street
London W1P 2LD

This edition published by Quartet Books Limited in 1999

A catalogue record for this book is available from the British Library

ISBN 0 7043 8108 7

Printed and bound in Great Britain by Cox & Wyman, Reading, Berks

as good as it gets

before...

ward

Summer came all at once to Brighton After weeks of dark cloud and unexpectedly cold winds, one day there were blue skies, heat, people in T-shirts and cut-offs, sweat and booming open-top cars full of ravers with non-specific expressions of pleasure plastered over their faces There had been no warning, except perhaps an odd vagrant wisp on the air at night, the instantly familiar tang of something flowering far away People paused as they locked up their cars or stepped out of pubs, raised their faces to the sky, sniffed Something coming, then it was gone again. There could never be another summer.

And suddenly there it was, a vast, all-encompassing thing, smiling a huge and puzzlingly unmotivated smile over the hot, busy, anxious town Just like last year, but who would have expected that?

For Ward, slouched in the front room, the summer resolved itself into a set of simple questions. How long could you decently delay going out into the sun? Where did you put your book? And, most pressing of all, were you going to take your shirt off?

The first to take off their shirts in Brighton were always builders or scaffolders Not the good-looking ones either, but the gingery, tripe-pallid freckled ones, with their pie-and-chips bellies and their curiously floppy chests and nipples and oddly meaningless tattoos. They stripped off, then strutted around, as if bewitched into believing themselves beautiful. Their grey, gristly, doughy skin would start to burn just about immediately, leaving them with hot red necks and shoulders, but the same curdled-cream torsos and wattly arms. Their faces would go red straight away and the wrinkles around their eyes would become exaggerated by alternating stripes of burnt red and puffy white. They would wear appalling shorts in khaki and plaid and strange, unusual shades of orange and purple. These shorts would be either disturbingly loose, suggesting all sorts of unattractive goings-on underneath, or repulsively tight, pinching up ridges of leg below and squeezing out folds and ripples of belly above – thick, wobbling chunks of meaty body slapping and sliding about over hips and pelvis

It was wise, Ward reflected, to wait until the general tone improved If you were determined to do it at all There was nothing in the by-laws of course, but nevertheless it was understood that at some point male citizens were expected to get out there and take off their shirts, irrespective of the merits or otherwise of their thoracic parts. It was a civic responsibility, like jury service

The flat was hot and quiet; Ward was the only one in The light streamed in through partly drawn curtains, taking an unseemly interest in the carpet, which was decorated with months of coagulated dust, little pieces of debris, odd, neglected pieces of cutlery and a glass with tea in it, the tea solidifying and growing up the sides Ward contemplated this for a few vague minutes Why was it there, he wondered, why was it half-full of tea? Why would that happen? He had no idea. The front room was hot already; God alone knew what would happen when the sun came round full on, as it did late afternoon. Nothing could keep it out. The television, the screen a blank dusty glare, was in the way of an intrusive

4

little dart of sunlight and made a sudden loud crack as some part of it expanded.

It was only half-ten. Ward had been up for an hour already, had gone out and bought the *Guardian*, read as much of it as he could bear and then gone straight to the television page. He had a particular horror of the International News pages, brief though they were· whatever ghastliness was going on here, they had it over there, only worse. What was the good of reading about it? What difference did knowing about it make? Did it make you a better person? And even if it did, so what? How did that help the poor bloody flood victims and police-brutality victims and all the rest of them?

He tried to wrench his mind away from these questions He could sit in this flat for days on end pondering such matters, gloom growing inside him like weeds in a ditch. It started with some business in Chile or a corruption scandal in Burkina Faso, and before you knew it you were choked up with a deadly cargo of despondency and rank, unfocused rage. What's the point, Ward would find himself muttering as he went about his business, what's the bloody point? And even if somebody could tell you what the point was, what would be the point of knowing?

Ward, as he was the first to admit, had what could only be described as 'good days' and 'bad days'. Good days meant he got down to the bank, posted a letter, did his laundry. Bad days, he didn't.

Nor was this a recent development His parents kept a photograph album of him and from age three he was, with only two exceptions, gazing straight at the camera with a kind of satanic loathing, and sitting in a chair. Ward's history was the history of soft furnishing in his parent's bungalow in Redcar knobbly tweedy oatmealy from age three to seven, murky deep-buttoned chocolaty leather age seven to twelve, when he suddenly grew by about three foot eight and started to hang bits of himself off the furniture, an arm here, a leg there. Sometimes other family members or a stray pet would sneak into the frame, but mostly it was just Ward and chair. The habit had never left him. He had made the pilgrimage from there to do a degree in modern history and politics at the newer and less prestigious of Brighton's two universities, but had found when he got there that he just didn't want to. No one seemed to understand him. Try a bit of plain speaking about the fucking Irish, for instance, or the cunt Chinese, and they looked at you snotty He had no mates. He'd always had mates before. Jessies on the course didn't know what mates were. All they wanted to do was have fucky little dinner parties and talk about how awfully clever Tony fucking Blair was. He just didn't want it, any of it. He wanted to go back North, back home. Didn't dare show his face.

So, instead of doing modern history and politics, he had settled himself on the couch in his first flat – a nice black and grey herringbone with scarred wooden bits on the ends of the arms, as it happened – and stayed resolutely put Modern history and politics would simply have to come to him. He drank They wanted the first year's grant back, also the loan. He moved twice, quickly, and lost them. He found that he wasn't fussed. It was good to be free of the worry of it.

Ward was not his real name. Neither one of his parents, expert though they might be in home furnishing, would have been capable of ever conceiving of such a non-standard thing· they had picked, with a quite breathtaking insouciance, David. If it's a boy it must be David, if it's a girl Sarah.

No, Ward was an abbreviation of the name he'd been given when he was going through a long, long succession of bad days Ward was short for 'Wardrobe'. A large, silent object which you found in bedrooms and which didn't move about very much

The sunlight outside was silently, implacably demanding that he go outside and be in it He would resist as long as he could, then he would start to grapple in earnest with the problems of footwear (not his Cats, not the Doc Martens, not the Nikes, definitely not any kind of horrible, tatty last-year's espadrilles, so what then?), with how to carry his book (*Ecce Homo*, Penguin Modern Classics edition) without it becoming a nuisance, with whether to take a towel or a pillow

Sunglasses? The issues multiplied menacingly, and at the end of them what was there? A patch of beach, the stones maddeningly uncomfortable and too hot, many of them coyly concealing little blobs of oil; sweaty bodies and hysterical children, and an hour or so of trying to get comfortable, trying to read the book, trying to keep the sun out of his eyes, trying to get a tan, trying not to burn It happened every year. It was a bloody nuisance. He would sit it out a little longer, here on the couch, he would wait until it could not be deferred any longer He picked up the paper again and, despite himself, was soon wandering mournfully round the ravaged streets of some Asian city while American-trained police shot at British-armed rebels The sun fell on to the glass of mouldy tea, illuminating it minutely from within, as if it alone amongst all things were uniquely worthy of being seen.

ben

The doorbell rang at two o'clock. Ward debated with himself whether or not he could really be bothered to answer it, whether or not it could possibly be important. It was wholly unlikely that it was anyone for him. Probably one of Marina's annoying friends, Kerry or Derry or Terry. They were always ringing up when she was out and then not leaving any message

'Is there any message?' Ward would ask, and they would say, 'Oh, no,' and Ward would think: so why did you ring, then? Hm? Weren't you going to say anything to her?

The bell sounded again, three long bursts. The kind of ringing a person might do if he was already fairly sure there was no one in Ward decided to surprise him.

'Hi,' the person said as Ward opened the door, and smiled. 'Is Steve here?'

Ward regarded him: he looked cocky and over-confident, Ward thought at once, and he'd got stupid hair. Cultivated dreds, bleached out at the tips, and an absurd piece of bum fluff under his chin. Garish baggies, the kind that weight-lifters wear, and a top that must have cost a fortune because it was so perfectly uninteresting. It had some stupid little designer patch on the front. 'Fluffy' in a heavy, slanted typeface Ward had never heard of 'Fluffy' before, it had to cost a lot of money. He was carrying an Asics sports bag

'No '

'This is the right address though, yeah? Yeah?'

'Yes '

'Brilliant. Know when he'll be back?'

'No idea.'

'Right.'

'Sorry I'll tell him you called.'

'Yeah, well, actually, you don't mind if I come in and wait, do you? Excellent.'

The person squeezed past Ward's solid bulk and made for the kitchen 'Ben,' he said over his shoulder. 'I'm staying for a day or two, yeah?' Ward, still holding the door open, glared at his back as he disappeared into the kitchen.

Ben already had the kettle on by the time Ward followed him into the kitchen.

'You a flatmate? Boyfriend?' Ben asked.

'Flatmate.'

'Yeah? Excellent.'

'Does Steve know you're coming?'

'Know?'

Ward nodded slowly Without fully intending to, he had reverted to an expression of glazed hostility, what Marina called his you-want-this-in-your-face-pal look.

'Does he know? I don't know,' Ben said

'You haven't arranged it with him?'

'Arranged?

Ward sighed 'Look, maybe you'd be better ringing up later and talking to him,' he said. 'I don't know when he's back '

'No, really. That's OK. Excuse me.'

Ben left the kitchen, and Ward heard the bathroom door lock. He was back in less than a minute.

'No, see, thing is, it's a surprise.'

'But he does know you?'

'He knows of me.'

'Now, you see, that's not quite the same thing, is it?' Ward replied gravely

'He knows someone I know, really, really well Really well,' Ben added, giving Ward a meaningful look

9

Ward retreated back to the couch in the front room He didn't want this Ben in the house, but he wasn't finding the right words to get rid of him.

Ben ambled into the front room.

'Nice,' he said, smiling at everything· Ward, the ceiling, the television 'Really nice.'

Ward noticed that he was still holding the sports bag. Ben sat down on one of the armchairs and cradled the bag on his lap.

Kelvin and Marina came in three-quarters of an hour later, and Ward was more than happy to hear their key and their voices.

' . not just right now, OK?' Marina was saying, and Kelvin uttered one of his high, short sounds. Fine by me, it said.

'Oh,' Marina said, and stopped short in the doorway.

'This is Ben,' Ward said, obscurely guilty and embarrassed, a not unusual state for him to be in. 'He's someone Steve knows '

Marina smiled hugely at this Ben person and tried to calculate just how difficult he was going to be to get rid of. He looked manageable, she thought. 'Someone Steve knows' could cover the ground from toilet trash through silky confidence tricksters to cocky youths in military surplus. And music teachers, for some reason

'Have you booked?' she asked brightly, and looked sympathetic. 'I just mean, if this is something you cooked up with him months ago, he'll have just forgotten and everyone will be embarrassed.'

You're fantastic, Ward said to himself, as he watched her bright, cheerful, determined face and body. Kelvin slunk in behind her, with a miscellany of deceitful and disloyal expressions accompanying him like a small pack of well-behaved dogs

'He hasn't mentioned anything to me,' she went on, 'and usually he tells me everything Well, everything that's fit to tell ' She was like a peak-time television presenter, Ward thought, one of the really good ones Carol Vordeman perhaps He felt a stiffening in his crotch and watched derisively as Kelvin tried to look fierce.

'Tell you what, come back later and we'll all see the look on his face!'

Ben looked completely blank. His smile was slow coming, not convincing when it came.

'No, really,' he said, and opened his hands to show helplessness. 'It's cool Really.'

Marina sat on the edge of a chair and regarded him steadily

'Listen, Ben, is it? Listen, you can stay and wait for him, OK? But you musn't steal anything, OK? Not damage anything? OK?'

Fuck, Ward thought, you're good at this

'All right? Do you promise, darlin'?'

Ben smiled his odd smile and nodded.

'Promise.'

'Well, that's fine, then. Problem solved.'

She went out into the kitchen, and Kelvin came and sat down.

'So what brings you down here, then?' he asked, his manner bigger and brasher than usual

'Oh, you know,' Ben said, and Ward tried to place the accent. Bristol? Just a little bit of West Country anyway.

'Yeah?' Kelvin said.

Ward, relieved from his watch by Kelvin, took the opportunity to leave, and went to read *Ecce Homo*, which wasn't quite what he thought it was going to be, but by Christ it was Germanic. He liked it. He was making it last, because he'd stupidly promised Marina he'd read *The Satanic Verses*, which she raved about, after he'd finished it, and he was in no hurry There was something about the look of it he just didn't like.

Kelvin sat and made conversation with the stranger They laughed a few times, and after a few minutes Kelvin found Marina's all too obvious suspicion embarrassing. She went back and forth from the kitchen She was making something for tonight, the first anniversary of Steve moving in She remembered things like that It was going to be a surprise. It was also, incidentally, another year of her and Kelvin being together (three in all now), another year on the dole and avoiding any decision on retaking his first year at university for Ward, another year of drift for Kelvin. Two years now since his Fine Art degree show had attracted no controversy whatsoever, two years of thwarted ambition and absurd schemes and seemingly irreversible failure. Being an artist. Marina wished, often, that he would be something else. Not that she cared about money, it was the futility of it that got to her And he wasn't happy She wished he could be happy. Was that so much to ask?

She had made a cake in the shape of the female genitals, and it needed a lot of attention. She was using six different food dyes Kelvin tried not to think about it

Marina just knew that this Ben person would take the video. She was certain and that was that. There was nothing else to take Nothing expensive-looking anywhere Crap, in fact. She felt a twinge of embarrassment at the paucity of burglarable items Hardly worth your while, she wanted to say, sorry

Time passed. Steve was nowhere in sight Ben sat on the sofa, not relinquishing the bag, being perfectly polite and tractable, but giving nothing away He even took it with him to the toilet, on his many very short trips there. Marina brought him cups of tea, even made him a boiled egg and toast She believed that if you treated people well then they'd feel too guilty to steal the video when the time came. She explained to him, in bright middle-class tones that set Kelvin cringing, that the video was rented and that they had no insurance

'You won't steal it, now will you? Please?' she wheedled, and Ben smiled and said of course not He didn't seem remotely offended by this treatment.

'And if you really must steal it, then you have to wait until I've seen *Even Cowgirls Get the Blues* OK? Then make sure you rewind the tape before you take it out. I couldn't stand being fined for that as well as losing the video '

Ben took all this without complaint Apart from his frequent dashes to the bathroom, he seemed nailed to the chair, responding when spoken to, but perfectly content to sit silently as well. Kelvin meditated briefly on an experiment to see just how much inconvenience this guest would put up with He considered putting the central heating on, letting the sun in full blast, closing the windows. He thought about putting Marina's anti-party tape on, the one she used to clear people out. Madonna B-sides, an interminable remix of 'I'm Every Woman' and, the ultimate secret weapon, the longest-known mix of Jimmy Somerville's 'You are My World' Rare was the guest who stayed to the end of even the first verse of that. But, Kelvin thought appraisingly, Ben looked quite capable of remaining, through well-crafted verse and bridge and chorus and middle eight, even through horrible unbearable screeching finale Someone had played David Bowie, 'Let's Dance', at sickeningly high volume to try to end a siege somewhere, he remembered Maybe that meant that it was, in a sort of official sense, the most irritating record ever made. He might just nip out and see if he could find a tape of it.

He joined Marina in the kitchen, where she was adding dye to some icing mixture, red dye, one drop at a time.

'Man of Mystery,' he said, and Marina nodded.

'Do you think he's all right?'

'Oh, no '

'No, I don't either. Maybe we should hack him to pieces and arrange the parts in our shrine '

'Shrine's a bit full, I think, sweetheart '

Another drop went in, and Kelvin noted the way her breasts swung as she mixed. She was mixing vigorously.

'Well, we'll just have to get a bigger shrine.'

She examined the mixture 'Kel? Is that about right for labia minora?'

'Whose labia minora?'

'How many do you know?'

'Listen, do you mind if I don't think about labia just now? Close to your heart as I know they are '

'You're like one of those sad men in sex surveys who don't know where things are Aren't you?'

'I know where things are, I just don't want to think about

where things are right at this moment. I haven't eaten.'

Marina pulled the fork out of the icing mixture.

'Here, darlin', have some loverly labia.'

Kelvin went back to the front room and turned the tape over Jamiroquai, whom Kelvin strongly suspected of being very irritating indeed. Let's see you sit this one out, tough guy, he thought. Ben, however, barely flinched. He had inner reserves of tranquillity clearly, a quiet place to go to when bad things (like Jamiroquai records, for instance) happened. Kelvin envied him

Ben slept for an hour between six and seven. When he awoke he seemed nervous and jumpy and went to the bathroom, where he stayed for almost fifteen minutes It was still full daylight outside.

'No sign of our Stevie,' Marina said 'Where can that naughty boy be? He finishes at seven tonight, he said '

'Listen,' Ben said, 'I have to make a phone call. Is it all right if I use your phone?'

'You can try, darlin', but I think you'll find it's incoming calls only. We're cheap like that.'

'Bummer '

'Yes, isn't it?'

Ben sat and thought for a moment 'Listen,' he said again, 'I have to go out for a moment.'

'Phone call, is it?' Marina asked brightly

'Yeah yeah yeah But, you see, thing is I don't want to lug this bag around with me.'

'Leave it here darlin'. We won't steal it.'

'Thing is, can I put it in Steve's room? He has got a room here, yeah?'

'He has indeed '

'How'd that be, then? If I just left it in his room.'

'OK ' Marina stood and showed him the way Ben followed her, the bag snuggled to his chest, cradled in both hands

Steve's room was small, dark, at the back.

'Just dump it down here '

'Yeah '

14

Ben stood by the bed and looked at everything. Marina watched him. She knew perfectly well what he wanted. He wanted her to go so he could hide his bag. You're a little rascal, she thought.

She stood in the doorway

Ben was sniffing. She sniffed too Fuck. Burning. From the kitchen.

'Nob!' She ran for the cake

Ben swiftly and expertly checked over the room, found no obvious place, thought for a second. Then he stripped a pillow-case off one of the pillows, stuffed the sports bag into it, smoothed it out as best he could, replaced it where the pillow had been, stuffed the denuded pillow under the bed. He gave the phoney pillow a final adjustment and straightened the duvet over it, then quickly left the room.

Marina was fucking and buggering in the kitchen, swearing like a convent girl, but it wasn't as bad as she'd thought, she could scrape bits off.

Ben called out as he passed the kitchen, 'Right, I'll just be a minute, then I'll be right back.'

Marina gave him a hurried glance and sucked a finger she'd burnt on the cake tin

'Ben,' she called out, 'you wouldn't bring a pint of milk back, would you?'

'Sure.'

He pulled the front door to and walked as fast as he could without looking suspicious down the stairs and out into the brilliant, warm evening The smell of burning followed him out.

Marina sat with Ward for a moment, enjoying as always his massive immobility She patted his leg

'All right there?'

'Glad that joker's gone.'

He had the same dark cloud round him that he'd had all day yesterday.

'Had a good day there, darlin'?'

'Actually, no '

15

'Ah, well,' she said absently. 'Ah, well. Soon be dead ' Much of her time was taken up managing Ward and Kelvin, keeping them sweet They were both pretty hard work in their own ways Steve, thank God, was perfectly straightforward, up or down

'Well, I've got a lovely big thing to type tonight It's all about society and interesting things like that. I'll read it out to you if you like.'

Ward grunted and she pushed against him.

'Give us a smile, slugger,' she said. 'Might never happen.' And he grunted and said he was bloody sure it wouldn't. Not today anyway

'What we going to do with you, eh?' she said

'If you're wanting to cheer me up,' he said, 'there is one thing you could do for us actually.' He gave her his trying-it-on-with-the-lassies-dark-horse smile and she stood up abruptly

'Now,' she said, 'we have been over this, haven't we?'

'Could go over it again if you like,' he said, and made a face. 'Entirely up to you. All the same to me, like.'

'What we going to do with you, eh?'

He shrugged and returned to the *Guardian*, reduced now to reading the peculiar little ads at the back for interesting underwear None of it appealed much He started in on the cable and satellite listings for the week ahead.

He looked up again to see Marina staring down at him

'What?'

'Ward, have we got cable? Have we got satellite?'

'So?'

'Well, I worry that you're perhaps not really seizing the day terribly, do you think?'

'I just want to know what's on I'm interested in the world '

Marina gazed down, incredulous at such a comment, such transparent and futile self-deception

'Anyway, they've got cable at Bazza's now '

'Ah, the lovely Bazza I suppose he's "interested" in "the world" as well?'

'Yeah Right '

'Oh, good Well, no need to worry about the world, then, what with you and Baz working on it round the clock.'

He jumped up and shouted and started to swat at her with the paper, then tried to wrap her head in it, but Kelvin came in and they had to stop

stoned

Ben nearly got run over crossing the road to the phone box and aimed a good hard kick at the passing bodywork He was having a difficult enough day as it was without attempts being made on his life by bloody Volvos.

The car slid to a halt a few feet away and the driver's door opened. The man emerging from it, Ben estimated, was six foot seven, and looked as if he was feeling every inch of it Ben glanced over and tried again to cross, but he was prevented by a stream of traffic newly liberated by a changing light. Bollocks He started to walk away, big Volvo man started to follow No matter that his car was now parked on a double yellow near a corner, at something of an angle. Had he even locked it? Ben hadn't seen him doing so

'Hey,' Volvo man was calling, not shouting exactly, but none the less demanding Ben's attention

Ben had no intention of running, and in any case his right foot was feeling bruised from its unauthorized contact with the legendary build-quality of the Volvo He was only wearing old green Converse canvas boots Now, if he'd had his steel-tipped Docs on, that would have been a different matter altogether As it was, he couldn't see what damage he could possibly have done to the sleek maroon steel of the Volvo It had hurt him more than the other way round Bollocks He walked faster

'Hey!' Volvo man called again, and, damn it, he was now only a few paces behind. Ben turned and put a knee to Volvo man's groin, then cleverly took advantage of his confusion by taking hold of his head and banging it against the wall.

Volvo man slumped, trying to hold on to various bits of his body simultaneously, and Ben decided to capitalize on this by getting as much kicking in as he could manage. He had to use his left foot, which was much less efficient than his right, and he had to balance on his right, which was complaining mightily His toe got caught somehow for a second in the man's belt, and Ben cursed and fought like a rat in a trap. There were a few people about, but no one seemed to be taking any interest. The building against which he had just concussed the driver was a pub. Ben forgot himself for a moment and kicked with his right.

His foot immediately flared up in agony. Shit. Volvo man was as solid as his fucking Volvo He must have broken his fucking toe or something. Ben was panting and there were spots in front of his eyes. He was not used to this level of exertion or annoyance. Volvo man was struggling to his feet, saying something, and Ben decided enough was enough. He started to hobble away, but his right foot was now almost completely out of action. He hopped and stumbled, holding on to the side of the building, but progress was slow and the foot was now sending flares up into his leg and groin. He saw a taxi and flagged it down, jumped in and gave the only address he knew in Brighton· the pier

Volvo man watched him disappear with a look of numbed astonishment. He'd only wanted directions to a car park. Hell of a town this, he thought, and struggled back to his car. There was a vague greenish smear on the rear nearside

'Stop here a minute,' Ben said. 'I just have to make a phone call.'

'Can't stop here I'll have to pull in round the corner.'

'Whatever.'

He slapped his pockets for money for the phone and came up with a meagre handful of change. All his real money was in his other trousers, which were in his bag, which was stuffed inside someone's pillow at that weird house with that woman in it. He had to get back to it; he couldn't just leave it there. Anything might happen. Meanwhile he had no way of paying for this taxi. He was gnawing his knuckles with impatience.

He jumped out of the taxi and ran for the phone box. No answer at Trevor's. The machine came on and Ben started to leave a message – he'd missed his contact, he didn't have a number to ring, he'd call again – but before he got anywhere his foot sent up a great flare of pain into his leg and hip and he said, 'Ah, Christ,' and dropped the phone, grabbing for the injured member. The receiver swung in the air as he danced about in the phone box, trying to stand on one leg and brace himself against the walls. By the time he got the receiver back, the line had gone dead. He had no more change This was all getting much too annoying. He jumped back into the taxi and gave Steve's address

'That's back the way we just came, isn't it?' the taxi driver asked, creasing his face into a peculiar kind of a smile. The little plaque on the dash said he was called Brian. Figured

'Yeah,' Ben said, and smiled. 'Yeah. Back where we come from '

'Hold on now,' Brian said, and took the keys out of the ignition 'Now let's just back up a second '

Oh, fuck, he's one of those, Ben thought There were taxi drivers who didn't bother to use their brains, just shut them off and drove about, and there were others who were philosopher-princes This was a philosopher-prince. 'Brian' is an anagram of 'brain', Ben thought.

'Now, when I picked you up you wanted to go to the pier . . . '

'Change of plan,' Ben said quickly

'Yeah, and then you need to make a phone call, and then . '

'Yeah, I know,' Ben said, and tried to smile engagingly. What a crazy guy! Brain was having none of it

'Tell you what, son How about you pay me for the trip so far and then I'll be happy to take you anywhere you want to go What do you say?'

'Yeah, that's the point, see, I've just realized, all my money's back at the house . . '

Brain looked pained

'Now you do know, don't you,' he announced portentously, 'that it constitutes an offence in law to commission a public hire vehicle, such as myself . . '

Oh, Christ, Ben thought, he's not just a brain, he's Mastermind Brian of Britain His specialist subject was probably 'The law as it relates to the commissioning of public hire vehicles' He was going to start talking about contracts and torts any minute.

'Now technically,' Brian began, screwing his face up into that how-can-I-put-this-so-you'll-understand smile, 'what you've done constitutes a tort in common law .   '

'Bollocks,' Ben said, and scrambled out His foot was swollen up now, pressing against the canvas He ran anyway and ducked down a one-way where Brian Einstein couldn't follow

He had no idea where he was. Everything was hot and bright and unfamiliar. He hobbled to the end of the street and turned the corner. The sea stretched out in front, glittering exuberantly He desperately needed to rest his foot.

Daggers of light flew into his eyes off the sea There were few people about, it being early in the season and rather late in the day. He went down some steps and through a low ornamental garden and a curious sort of cement maze, and on to the beach. He wanted to lie down for half an hour. Think

He positioned himself in the shade of an outfall, where the heat and aggravation lulled him to sleep, despite the stones digging into him and the throbbing of his foot

Twelve feet or so above his head, on the ridge of the outfall where anglers exercised their grim, grisly compulsions, three boys, aged about eight, were fooling about with big plastic water-guns

'Let's drop a big stone on his head,' one of them said

They found a stone they thought a suitable size, about as

big as a baby's head, and one of them aimed carefully, holding the thing in position above Ben for a few seconds before releasing it. Ben was concussed immediately, felt nothing, had just time to look up to the sky and utter one word – 'Stoned!' – before curling into a foetal ball and succumbing to blackness Money and taxi drivers and phone boxes all crept away

He was discovered a few hours later by a wiry man with a metal-detector who called for an ambulance and, when it arrived, told the paramedic about a Saxon sword-hilt he'd found twelve years ago. Ben knew nothing of any of this and was still unconscious when he arrived at Accident and Emergency He lay perfectly still as the professionals surrounded him, with a look of gentle surprise on his motionless face. Dribble gathered under his chin, he smiled, and died dreaming of mountains on a trolley half-way down a long, low passage.

cake

Marina waited till nine. No sign of bloody Steve. The wanker in the upstairs flat was thumping about, getting ready to go out. He was heavy-footed and everything he did transmitted itself to the flat downstairs You could even hear him talking sometimes, an interminable baritone drone. Marina frowned up at the ceiling as his routine got under way. the music, the running of taps, the banging about

Ben seemed to have disappeared as well as Steve Maybe he'd forgotten the house number or something She imagined him wandering about outside, ringing doorbells at random She peered out of the window a few times, but there was no one about

'Right,' she said grimly as the clock on the video flipped over 'Right, then We'll just have it without him '

They drank most of a litre and a half of something bracing if unremarkable and she went away into the kitchen.

When she came back in, her lovely face was lit from below by a single birthday candle positioned approximately where the clitoris would be

They straightened up and cut the cake Ward kept saying, 'What bit's this, then?' in a voice that suggested this was just about the funniest thing he or anyone else had ever thought of They started another of the big bottles and lay about all over the place and talked nonsense. Marina kept wanting a

23

toast, but couldn't think of anything new to make it to.

'To cake,' Kelvin said, and they all clinked glasses and drank to that.

'To cake '

'So where's bloody Steve, then?' she said for the millionth time.

interpretative dancing

Steve was getting the eye

He hadn't intended to come out really, he'd meant to just head home after his shift, but out he was. He was in an early-evening pub and there was someone by the fruit machine, glancing over. Steve ignored him. It was his practice to ignore anyone who fancied him, preferring instead to concentrate solely on the men he fancied, men he would never, ever get anywhere near and who would never look back at him. This perfectly self-defeating strategy, refined over hundreds of long, tense, beery nights, was now so ingrained that he was barely conscious of it. He could easily spend all night just looking at someone, edging round them, nerving himself up to speak, backing away, getting pissed, getting nowhere. Going home

He'd been in Brighton for three years, signing on for two of them, low-grade clerical drudgery for six months, then back on the dole His claim was supervised with ever-increasing fanaticism by a scowling zealot called Claire, who now needed to see him every month. He worked five or six sessions a week behind the bar of what Kelvin referred to as the Legover Arms, a steadfastly down-at-heel gay pub where the landlord spun out repetitive garrulous routines over the mike during the pub quizzes and mispronounced things, while the carpet grew ever stickier underfoot and a solitary game machine played with itself in the corner. A quiet kind of a place for the most part. Occasionally a fat man in a dress was booked to sing and deliver leering single-entendres, the dress somehow conferring a talent where none had been before and which would not survive the taking off of it. Steve just blanked it out.

Most of the people he knew from Maidstone had gone to live in Hastings or Eastbourne, where the drugs were plentiful and the Benefits Agency staff less well motivated But Brighton was where the sex was. In theory anyway He'd hung around hopefully in enough gay places to know that it was entirely possible to go for months without any decent sex at all, even while you were surrounded on all sides by men who were perfectly willing. It was just like that. It wasn't that he was unattractive, exactly. He caught a glimpse of himself in the reflective glass of a picture of a man in gleaming white 1970s underpants on a kind of trapeze. Steve was hugely attractive, seemingly irresistibly so, to a particular kind of man.

The person giving him the eye now, for instance. He was tallish and reasonably well-made, but looked as if he would at some stage want to talk, at length, about iconic representations and positive images in the media Barbara Stanwyck, Doris Day, follow the sodding yellow brick road. Irredeemably soppy in looks and with an irritating air of being amused by everything There was nothing here, Steve scolded, that could in any sense be regarded as amusing Absolutely not The barman had the right idea A big fat-bellied, fat-arsed man, he was dressed in combats and a vest, and carried himself as if his back was killing him and he didn't care what you wanted to drink Just didn't care. Giving change was a kind of martyrdom for him. He would press the coins into your palm while simultaneously squinting wearily at the next one, trying to look as if he cared at all about whatever it was he wanted. He looked like the kind of man who would turn up to the AGM of some blameless AIDS charity and furiously challenge the accounts At slack periods he would be found conspiring morosely with a thin man who had been coming here, every day, for seven years He was called Graham. Steve knew him slightly from having worked a bar with him when he'd first arrived in Brighton, but Graham would never acknowledge that they'd so much as set eyes on each other, ever; he'd die first. It was some kind of code he had

It would be busy later, but Steve wasn't sure he had the patience to hang on. He really wanted to get home and have something to eat. He decided to give it another half an hour

The barman squeezed the change into his hand and Steve went back to his place. The soppy-looking man by the fruit machine had stopped glancing over. Steve recklessly left his pint unattended and headed for the toilet. Soppy man came in shortly after and some kind of rudimentary conversation took place. Yup. He was exactly the kind of man who would be attracted to Steve, the kind Steve always wanted to knee in the bulgy little bollocks and say Judy-fucking-Garland that, Toto. The rudimentary conversation rolled on, though, a lumbering, ugly, stupid thing, and somehow or other this seemed to go on for hours. Before he knew it, Steve was far enough into his third pint to have forgotten all about eating and going home, and was calculating how to make his money last. The pub started to fill up, he got talking to someone, suddenly it was last orders and time to say, you going on?

An hour later he was sitting on a high stool in the upstairs bar of the only viable club A scattering of depressed solitary men and a few groups of three and four noisily deconstructing their masculinity in the approved manner at the bar. A scaffolding crew possessed by the spirits of parrots.

Someone passed his field of vision, smoothly anonymous in old-style moleskin combats and white T-shirt. Age indeterminate, somewhere between thirty and fifty-five. The faces sometimes froze permanently at a particular point, a result perhaps of too much expressivity at an early age You could only get an accurate reading sometimes by checking skin elasticity, brittleness of fingernails, dental work, etc. Later, of course, you could do direct assays of things like CD collections, cultural references, sagginess of the balls, vileness of breath, degree of domestic fussiness, lung capacity and general vitality and stamina levels.

This one, this basking shark, moved on and Steve contemplated the upstairs dance floor, where it would be forever 1986. The men here were older, habitual, professionally friendly, with a vast repertoire of smiles and winks and small utterances. None of it meant anything at all.

There was one other who interested Steve, apart from the basking shark he was no more than twenty, thin, short and with a loose-limbed swagger He was clearly trying to be hard as fuck, and was almost making it: he looked ill at ease and stroppy and slightly indignant, as if he'd just been short-changed. He nodded almost imperceptibly as Steve passed him. He didn't seem to be with anyone. Steve noted him for future reference.

He stood and watched the dance floor. There was a vast amount of enthusiasm for even the most negligible of records, much movement, little skill. Tight knots of skinny men, and occasional older women with big blonde hair and expensive leather jackets. He moulded himself into the wall and after a few minutes had fallen into something of a trance

Suddenly there were people all around him, thin young men in skinny T-shirts and tight jeans, cropped bleached hair, animated voices, bottles of mineral water Every detail branded and remorselessly current They all had compulsive grooming disorder. They all seemed intent on kissing him, touching him.

They were his previous flatmates, the people he had fled from to the relative calm of Aqueduct Road: the vacuous fags from hell. They had erased all cognitive processes and neatly replaced them with catchphrases They spoke, thought and, for all Steve knew, dreamed in catchphrases They were very, very busy, all the time In the summer they piled into a Daihatsu 4×4 and cranked up the idiot music, driving fast and shouting out to anyone who caught their eye 'Good legs!', 'Work it!' and 'Faaaat!' were the most frequently used They pounded and throbbed at traffic lights, needling the drivers around them, grinning, leering, calling people 'girl' when this was clearly incorrect.

They and Steve misunderstood each other perfectly from the start, and Steve began to find that his face was hurting from enforced, effortful smiling and that his jaw often ached from grinding his teeth. He felt himself being eroded by wave after wave of relentless triviality Who knew what might happen if he stayed? He might have to talk fatuous nonsense for the rest of his life to people who knew just a little bit too much about *Prisoner Cell Block H*. He'd replied to an ad for a room going in Aqueduct Road and the minute he met Marina he knew he would stay.

His departure from the House of Homos had been a relief for everybody. There had been no pretence of intending to stay in touch. They would see him around.

And now here they were, in this half-empty mid-week pick-up club. They were all on a pill naturally They poured out effort and energy and enthusiasm, just leaked it, haemor-rhaged it. Steve felt like a depleted battery standing next to them They seemed to leach the very juice out of him Their hands were in ceaseless motion, their faces registered ceaselessly replenished wells of precarious optimism They were a little like the kind of life form that would materialize in *Star Trek* from time to time, a glittery, sparkly, insubstantial thing that enveloped the ship and spoke no known language We are Borg, you will be assimilated

They were inordinately delighted to see him, and then were off again almost at once, except one of them who hung around for a moment, jiggling, to what purpose Steve couldn't discern. It was perhaps some kind of advance. Then the distance from the others suddenly went critical and he too was off, off on the unending E-head trail Over there! Over there!

Twelve-thirty The place was as busy as it was going to get on a Wednesday. There was a strenuous though enervated quality to everything, dancing, talking, even just standing. Steve wandered away in search of basking shark and, when he found him, stood a few feet behind and watched.

There really wasn't anything much wrong with him, as far

as Steve could see. The neck was good, thick and just slightly rippled; the shaved hair followed the contours of skin up into the scalp, forming little bristly valleys and ridges. A good, big, mean, meaty kind of head. Solid upper body, not narcissistically defined but strong and hard. The combats swelled and bulged in all the appropriate ways; the arse was full and lent itself to the right kind of speculation. Beefy forearms, big hands.

Steve stood behind him and watched. The man was standing more or less at ease, in the military sense, legs slightly spread and hands cupped behind the back He was completely motionless: he hardly seemed to be breathing. Steve moved round a few paces so he could see the front.

Everything in order. Hard face, slightly snub nose; he looked, somehow, like a dog. Big chest, and lots to see and do between the legs. Expressionless, except perhaps for a slight trace of petty sadism round the eyes.

Oh, yes Steve satisfied himself that the man was indeed exactly the kind he liked. Miles out of his league. Need not, therefore, be approached or even smiled at In any case, he was now within his field of vision and there was not as much as a flicker of interest Perfect

He watched covertly, partly screened by a pillar In between, he surveyed the dance floor.

A record came on, 'Sunshine after the Rain', and immediately several dozen pairs of arms came up and fingers fluttered. They were being 'rain', or 'sunshine' – it could have been either. Maybe they were being 'after'. The gestures continued well into the song, with hands spread for 'blue-birds', fingers pointed at eyes for 'I', arms spread for 'rainbow' It wasn't like the mass Nazi-style stiff-arm saluting that unaccountably broke out at raves sometimes this was Interpretative Dancing When Steve was at infant school they had called it 'music and movement' He'd never thought he might need it later in life. Now he wished he'd paid more attention Basking shark wasn't doing interpretative dancing. He looked like he knew maybe three gestures, all grossly inflammatory and intended for use with police at away matches. Steve approved of him more and more. He wandered off to get a drink and also for the pleasure of coming back, and the man was still in place, motionless, stern

And then it happened. Another record came on, the burden of which was that you had ooh aah, just a little bit, and then you had ooh aah, a little bit more The ooh aahs were flagrantly, even shamelessly calculated to appeal to a particular kind of person, many of whom, regrettably, were present The appropriate gesture seemed to be pointing with both hands to the ceiling. Steve watched them in dismay Human dignity was here being willingly forfeited.

But worse, much worse: the record was starting to have its insidious way with the basking shark It was eating away at him, eroding his superb military bearing, nibbling at his magnificent indifference, his ferociously maintained discipline. He held out manfully for the first full assault of the ooh aahs, his face a grim motionless mask, jaw clenched It went away and he relaxed fractionally. Steve watched him with held breath But then it came round again, and it was too much even for him. Something just started to give at the waist: it was no longer motionless, it was starting to sway The hips were gyrating, ooh aah, just a little bit, barely visible to a casual observer, but Steve was hardly that It was less than a quarter of an inch in amplitude this gyration, but it was enough. Steve glared in disapproval and wandered away. He'd seen all he needed to see.

There was nothing else worth looking at. His fallback from earlier on had vanished, and Steve was out of money and feeling sober He headed home alone for a joint and a wank, not for the first time, not for the last. He'd spent far too much He still hadn't eaten. Darren the coat-check man smiled at him, but Steve hardly noticed He tried to improve his posture and smile as he nodded good night to the bouncer, tried not to look as low as he felt Not really going home alone to a cold bed in ignominious defeat, he tried to imply, just going on to the next exciting chapter of my exciting life The bouncer looked fastidiously away He knew defeat when he saw it.

31

His route home took him past the Royal Pavilion, recently repainted and now all-over magnolia, as if to negate the florid, gleeful absurdity of the building. Floodlit also, presumably in order to highlight the drab, obsessive uniformity of the magnolia paint. Look! it screamed, the same boring colour! All over! It looked good and ready for another bomb outrage, he thought

Steve brooded darkly as he walked, the same thought over and over again Going home on your own. Again. He really had to sort this out Something had to change.

puppies

It was some time after four a.m. when Steve finally got in. He had someone with him, someone he'd picked up on the seafront on the way home from the club He couldn't remember this person's name, though he had certainly been told it a number of times He had picked him up almost accidentally. The person was there, standing about in combat gear, Steve had smiled as he passed, held his eye for a second and that was that. He had no recollection of speaking to him for the first time.

He parked him in his bedroom and swayed out to the kitchen to make coffee Things fell down and spilled, and he managed to put his hand down flat on something bright and sticky, the remains of some kind of cake The person, his inamorato, was sprawled out on the bed when he returned, and Steve looked at him closely for the first time and was not pleased He was younger than he'd looked, and notwithstanding a mostly good upper half, the lower half was somewhat less solidly made than Steve had thought Also he was passed out, which meant that any sex that was going to happen would be of the necrophilic kind. Steve had had such sex before, of course, and had also been the recipient of it. But he was close to passing out himself, just ticking over, with the embers of rationality and good sense dying down to a dull smoulder inside him. The man now snoring faintly on his bed

33

had had a joint on him, some kind of killer skunk, and Steve was now off his head Completely. There had also been a quarter of a gram of speed somewhere along the way, but it stood no chance in the tidal wave of beer and joints that Steve had flooded his alluvial plains with; it was just washed away, leaving only a faint stirring in his stomach.

Steve wanted to pass out as well but this person had got there before him. Also he wasn't going to be able to afford to go out again for at least a fortnight, so he had to get value for money from this one, dammit And anyway, he was just curious Steve pawed at him half-heartedly, even getting as far as unbuttoning his combats, just to have a look, when he found that his head was too heavy to move any more and he had to lie down, at once His head hit the pillow.

Fuck! He sat up again and dragged the pillow round to where he could look at it properly. It was stiff and lumpy and horrible, not his pillow at all. Someone had done some kind of practical joke and swapped his pillow for some nasty lumpy thing He chucked it on the floor and tried to drag a few inches of pillow from beneath the comatose head of his guest, his betrothed, but with little success. He managed to grab a corner of the duvet and bunched it under his head, then found that he was too hot and couldn't settle. He gave the annoying figure beside him a few prods and pushes, but he was rewarded with nothing except a low droning sound. He opened the window, then got undressed and wrestled some more of the duvet out from under him Still couldn't settle He started looking about for his secret stash of emergency dope, which was ridiculously tiny now, too tiny to melt without burning his fingers, couldn't find any sodding papers, found the sodding papers, made something that would have been a joint if he could only have got the bit of cardboard shoved down the end of it, lit it, burnt his arm, singed an eyebrow, took a few drags, dropped it on to the unknown soldier (who grunted), let it go out, chucked it on to the floor, collapsed

As always after a binge he woke ridiculously early, well before ten. His comrade-in-arms had already gone, and Steve luxuriated in having the whole bed and duvet and everything to himself There was a faint smell of unfamiliar sweat and a general beeriness overall. He saw the aberrant pillow lying on the floor where he'd thrown it and decided to investigate. He reached for it and dragged it back into bed with him, then sat up, naked, with the duvet tangled round him The room was in half-darkness, the curtains showing patches of mottled daylight It was hot already

He rummaged about inside the pillow case and pulled out a sports bag, Asics, three-quarters full and heavy at one end, which was where all the lumpiness was.

He unzipped it. There were a few items of clothing, T-shirts, a small towel, an address book, an alarm clock, a passport He removed these things and reached deep inside the bag. His hand found something smooth, shiny, cool to the touch. It gave slighty under his fingers, it was dense, springy. A package of some kind. He pulled it out into the light.

About the size and shape of a bag of sugar. A clear poly-thene bag full of a white substance, powder. It was fastened round with brown sealing tape and smelt strongly of linseed oil He held it under his nose for a moment. There was a little sticker on the back with a scrawled pen mark, an initial. Some sort of quality control or batch number The bag was like a bag of sugar but heftier Steve held it in one hand It was like a big fine puppy, glossy, with the feel of muscle under the coat, smoothly contoured And something else, though this was certainly a delusion, but a feeling as if there were something living about it It seemed to breathe or pulse. A warm, heavy, snoozing puppy, held securely in one hand, a lovely bundle of something.

Steve felt a kick in his stomach He laid the package out on the duvet and rummaged about again He pulled out four more of the bags, laid them all out, regarded them. Five fine strong little puppies. He did an instant, involuntary calcula-tion; it was almost a spasm If it's speed, then this is five kilograms, which is £25,000 If it's cocaine, then it's ten times that – £250,000. Quarter of a million If it's anything else, then I don't know what it is. He held the bag and felt his heart galloping in his chest.

He decided to keep this strictly to himself, until he'd had a chance to figure out what it was. He pushed the packages back into the sports bag along with everything else and hid it under the bed

Marina and Kelvin were up and about and doing something in the kitchen. She gave him a disparaging look.

'Busy night, was it?'

Keep it strictly to himself.

'My ROOM'S full of DRUGS!' he burst out. Bugger!

Marina turned to face him.

'What drugs?'

'I don't know what drugs White drugs Drugs drugs drugs!'

Kelvin looked at him. 'There's always drugs in your room,' he said, all good sense and solid reasoning.

Ward came in, sleepy and cross

'Who's making the noise?' he demanded, and Steve yelled at him that there were DRUGS! IN HIS ROOM! He started back to his bedroom.

'Steve . ' Marina followed him, with Kelvin and Ward taking up the rear She watched him as he reached under the bed and pulled out the Asics bag.

'In here.'

He unzipped and unpacked the other things from it, then pulled out one of the five plastic bags

'Fuck me with big things ' Marina looked at it, and Steve held it out for her to take, but she didn't. She just said 'Fuck' again, softly. Kelvin took it and sniffed at it suspiciously He passed it on to Ward, who did the same

'What is it?' she asked, and Steve brought out the other four

'I don't know,' he said.

Marina looked at the bags, then looked back at Steve, who was following her eye. 'Hide them again,' she said, and went back to the kitchen.

*

36

They held an emergency house meeting.

'Steve, have you ever known someone called Ben?' Marina demanded.

'Not lately. Ages ago.'

'Who was he?'

'He was just this lad I kicked round with in Maidstone He was with some squatters' rights group He was a mate of someone else's really '

'When did you see him last?'

'Marina, you seem to have become the police.'

Marina gave him a withering look

'Steven, he was here yesterday As you would have known if you'd shown your face like you were supposed to and had your nice cake that I made for you specially instead of pissing it up all day and night and leaving us alone with him He was horrible. He was really slimy '

'That sounds about right That's his bag, isn't it?'

Marina nodded She got up to make tea. Her hands were shaking

'Where is he now?'

'Fuck knows He went out to make a phone call about seven yesterday and never came back He was supposed to bring a pint of milk back with him.'

'You know what this is like, don't you?' Ward said darkly

No one did

'Yeah, you know. That fillum With all those Scottish cunts in it. Whatever it was You know.'

They watched him as he struggled with this weighty recollection Kelvin twitched, scraping his fingers against his palms It was rarely quick with Ward It was rarely profitable either

'*Dr Zhivago*,' Kelvin said at last.

'*Dr No*,' Marina said

'*The Poseidon Adventure*.'

'The what? No, look, that fillum You know '

'Oh, right. That one, right '

'*Battleship Potemkin, Whisky Galore, Sheep Lover 2*

'There's no *Sheep Lover 2* '

'Oh, really?'

'Look,' Kelvin said abruptly, 'does anyone care about what fillum it is or can we just move on? Can we vote on it, please? Anyone interested in what fillum it is say aye All against, carried Now can we get on?'

'OK Listen,' Steve said. 'Until we know what this is about we'll have to hide it '

'Hide it where?' Kelvin asked.

'I don't know. Just go and hide it somewhere. Bury it somewhere maybe.'

'Kind of like in a shallow grave?' Ward said, and everyone looked at him

'Just hide it anyway '

Marina nodded slowly. Then she said, 'Look, let's just hand it in.'

Kelvin snorted.

'Oh, right Absolutely. Here you are, officer, here's five bags of something which we think might not be sugar. Thank you, sir, thank you, ma'am, good to know there are still public-spirited citizens about, here, have a commendation.'

'Kel '

'They'll kill us Ben will just deny everything, and then there we are, found in possession of five lovely big juicy bags of illicitness '

'Kel, we could do it anonymously, just dump it somewhere and ring them up ' She shivered suddenly 'I really don't think we should touch it It's bad news.'

'Marina. If this is bad news . . I mean, if this is not your definition of a gift from the gods . . ' Kelvin shrugged 'Tell me something that would be good news, then. Marina, this stuff has got to be worth a fortune, whatever it is '

'It's not ours, Kel It must belong to someone '

'Not Ben, presumably '

'No, no, he'd just be carrying it.'

'It's not ours,' she insisted Her voice had the evangelical intensity of someone trying to convince themselves of something

'Oh, so we should hand it in to the bastard police, because

we haven't got a receipt for it?'

'Kelvin, it would be wrong to keep it.'

'And that's why you want to hand it in?'

'Yes.'

'Because it would be wrong?'

'Yes.'

'And it wouldn't have anything to do with being scared shitless of someone coming after it?'

'Yes, that as well.'

'Mostly that '

'Partly that.'

He was wearing her down, he knew just how to do it.

'Nearly all that, if you ask me.'

'What if it is anyway? I think it makes sense to be scared of it.'

'All I'm saying,' he said, leaning back and giving her a narrow-eyed look, 'is that you being scared of it isn't the same as you wanting to do the right thing.'

She glared helplessly at him

'Is it?'

'I'm not handing it in,' Steve said. He was gripped by the strength of feeling behind this. 'No way. At least not until we know what it is. What it might be worth '

Marina came up to him and grabbed hold of his hand, her eyes sparkling.

'I knew he was a funny fish. I could just tell.'

'Your instincts are unerring.'

'What are we going to do?'

It was just between the two of them now Kel and Ward watched quietly.

'Hide it Now, today The police could be round any time,' Steve said

'Right now?'

'Yeah. Don't you think?'

Marina thought.

'And not hand it in?'

'Not.'

'Give it a week, say See if Ben shows up See if anyone comes looking for it ' She was talking herself into it Kelvin and Ward stood about nodding sagely She let go of Steve's hand and sat back Everyone watched her.

'I was hoping you'd say that,' she said finally.

'And I know just where to hide it,' Steve said.

The zealot Claire, who was in charge of Steve's benefit claim, had earlier in the year bullied him into what she, with fundamentalist vigour, called a 'placement'. Essentially, unless he wanted his money docked, he would have to spend four afternoons a week for three months being an assistant at a place called the Brighton Fishing Museum. This was a large cavity, an arch, under the seafront which had been filled with a random assortment of old things loosely connected with fishing, some photographs of stern men in stern moustaches looking appropriately wet, and the hull of a fishing boat which contained a dummy of a sailor in a life-jacket. Most of the exhibits were cast-offs from the official museum, brought together by a councillor trying to make a name for himself who had subsequently lost interest

It was every bit as pointless as it sounded Steve sat, freezing in front of a little electric heater, and breathed in the damp, musty air and the faint smell of tar coming from the boat as gales and icy mists blew in from the sea and scoured the deserted promenade. No one came, naturally The councillor bustled in and out to start with, then left him mostly alone The days passed. An American couple wandered in one day and asked him questions about currents in the English Channel and Steve sold them a poster Drunks staggered in, stood swaying and looking at the boat and saying 'Eh?', and Steve would gently usher them out again. It hadn't reopened up after his period had finished

He still had a key There had been a mix-up early on and he'd been given two, only one of which had he returned at the end of his placement

'Listen,' he said 'I know the perfect place, but we'll have to wait till late Six o'clock, say – a m , I mean. Wait till everyone's in bed '

*

It seemed to take an eternity to get dark. Daylight lingered in the rooms, poking about in odd corners as it slid up the walls of the houses outside, brilliant warm buttery yellows and sugary pinks and gleaming bone and ivory. It flashed off the upper windows and lit up the terracotta of the chimneypots, finally staining the whole sky a quite absurd shade of magenta.

They waited in the house, walking quietly and whispering

The five bags lay quietly side by side on top of the television, a neat row. Marina, Kelvin, Steve and Ward sat quietly looking at them.

Nine o'clock and it was fully dark.

'If Ben hasn't come back by now,' Kelvin said, 'then he isn't going to He has quite obviously been abducted by aliens.'

'Yeah, that keeps on happening to me too,' Marina said. 'And that bloody implanting business.'

'Two million American citizens go missing every year,' Ward said darkly

'The spaceships must be getting a wee bit overcrowded by now.'

'And full of bloody Americans,' Kelvin said 'What would they want Americans for? Do you think they charge them admission?'

'Look, we're supposed to be talking about Ben Why hasn't he come back? Why has he left this stuff here?'

'Three possibilities,' Kelvin said officiously, and ticked off the fingers on one hand. 'One: he's been taken away and shot somewhere by drug criminal types. Two. he's been arrested. Three: he's been involved in an accident.'

'If he'd been shot it would have been in today's paper So I say an accident '

'If he'd had an accident he would have rung to tell us, and want his gear back He wouldn't just leave it here.'

'Not if it was a fatal accident.'

'No, Ward, obviously not if it was a fatal accident '

'Wouldn't the hospital have rung us, though?'

'How could they? He's hardly likely to tell them this address, is he? Only way they could connect him with here is

41

if he tells them, and I don't think he's particularly likely to want to lead them back to find this here. Same with the police.'

'He's dead, got to be,' Ward said. 'Nothing else makes sense '

'Anyway, he was only carrying it for someone else He couldn't possibly have owned it himself.'

'So whoever it belongs to is going to start noticing any minute now that it hasn't got to where it was supposed to go, and he's going to want to know where it has gone instead.'

'So why hasn't he shown up, then?'

'Ward, no one knows Ben was ever here. It was obviously an unscheduled thing. Say whatever it is got here from Amsterdam, say it was on a little yacht or something. Arrives at the marina. Ben goes there, picks it up, is supposed to take it somewhere, Birmingham or Bristol or whatever. If it's what I think it is, then it'll probably get turned into crack He's getting paid maybe 300 quid or so Stupid cunt, though, he gets it all wrong somehow, doesn't know what to do, so he shows up here to give himself time to think and maybe make new arrangements Doesn't want to be lugging it around out there, so dumps it here. Wanders off, gets into some kind of stupid trouble, end of story '

'How did he get this address anyway? You said you hadn't seen him for years '

'Well, we both knew this lad Lee in Maidstone It's possible that I may have given Lee the address here '

'So this Lee might know he'd been here?'

'Listen, to be candid about it, Lee doesn't know what day it is any more. His head, as they say, is fucked. Last time I spoke to him all he wanted to talk about was this thing he was doing, painting "Xanadu" over road signs so every road would be the road to Xanadu. You know? Except he thought you spelled it with a Z. He's not with us any more. He's not going to remember something like Ben getting my address off him Anyway, I'm willing to bet money Ben's going to come crashing back here any time If he doesn't get this back to where it's supposed to go, he's going to suffer potentially adverse consequences. Just a little bit. He'll be back '

'Unless he's dead,' Ward said stubbornly, and Steve agreed: yes, Ward, unless he's dead, obviously, if he's dead then probably he won't be back, no.

Ward wanted the news on Interested, he said, in the world, though he hardly listened to a word

'Dead, got to be,' Ward said as the ingenious and brightly coloured horrors unfolded.

By the time the local news came on, all apocalyptic title sequence and presenters who looked like they spent their leisure time grinning in the foyers of provincial arts centres, Ward was alone

Dead, he was thinking, and suddenly there was a police inspector being interviewed. He was saying that a body had been found on the beach yesterday evening and had died in hospital No identification was possible yet There was a picture of one of the groynes on the beach in between the piers, and yellow and black 'Police Line: Do Not Cross' tape flapping about between metal posts stuck into the pebbles. Nothing had been found at the scene, no weapon, no traces of a second person, no sign of any struggle. Post-mortem examination had shown traces of cocaine, cannabis and ketamine in the blood and urine, and a small amount of cocaine had been found in a pocket of his jacket

'Cocaine,' Ward said, and yelled to the others

'He just said cocaine on the telly! Oi!'

Kelvin came in and said, 'Did he just say cocaine?'

Police were not seeking anyone else in connection with the death They were assuming that the person had been intoxicated, had stumbled and fallen, cracking his head on the groyne. Time of death was estimated between eight and nine-fifteen p m Witnesses were asked to come forward There was no picture, they wouldn't broadcast a picture of a dead man until they'd found his next of kin, though there was a description: male, twenty to twenty-five, dressed in loose casual clothes, with a goatee beard and long plaited hair

'Not plaits,' Marina said, from the doorway, 'locks '

There was a distinctive 'Fluffy' logo on the sweatshirt .

'It's him,' Ward was saying, 'it's him, it's him . .'

'Dead,' Steve said, from behind Marina's shoulder. 'Christ'

'Could it be someone else?' Kelvin asked

'Oh, yeah,' Ward said, 'it could be his identical twin. Right size, right shape, right hair, right clothes, right fucking facial hair, with all the right drugs in his system at the right time. Didn't I say he was dead? It's him, it's him, it's . .'

'Stay calm, Ward,' Marina was saying, 'just breathe deeply now, in, out . .'

'No one knew he was ever here, no one saw him come in or go out, no one knows we knew him.'

'Poor little bastard, what happened to him?' Marina said

'So what you're saying really is that no one knows there are five kilograms of something here, that the only person who did know is dead . .'

'Except possibly Lee.'

'Who, as we agreed earlier, is as likely to remember anything about this as my dad's dog.'

' . . and that therefore . . .'

'Therefore . '

'We just made a quarter of a million pounds'

'Let's all just be calm now, breathe in, breathe out, breathe in, breathe ' Marina kept saying, until Kelvin put his hand over her mouth.

'It's ours,' he said. 'It's all ours.'

'We still better hide it. Just for a day or two. And incidentally we'd better burn his bag too'

'Wait,' Steve said 'Hold on Think for a minute. Ben was carrying it for someone. They're going to want to know what's happened to it. Now, they'll find out that Ben's dead, but they won't know where the stuff is. Yes? He had nothing on him, remember'

'Thank God.'

'No, listen. They're not going to just give it up But if the police should find his bag . '

'With his passport in it, incidentally'

'They find his bag, and more importantly they report that they've found his bag, and whoever is looking for the stuff will think, shit, that's the end of it, the police have got it. They're not going to guess that it isn't still in the bag, are they? And they can't exactly go and ask the police about it, can they? Excuse me, officer, about the bag belonging to that mysteriously dead man on the beach, well, me and my friend were just wondering . . . They'll just have to write it off. In fact, they'll probably think that's why he died, cos someone robbed him of it.'

'Makes sense, that does,' Ward said

'Dump his bag, somewhere near where they found him. Hide the stuff. Leave it a few days, give them time to find out what's happened And then it's ours. Not till then, though. We've got to get the bag on to the beach '

'And not be seen doing it,' Marina said

'Correct '

'Won't the police think it's a bit funny, his bag suddenly turning up like that?'

'They can think what they want Tell you what, we'll wet it, then they can think the tide took it and it just washed back up again Anyway, there's no way to trace it here, that's the point.'

The hours crawled by They kept the television on in case there was any more news, but the same report just came up again, nothing new

'Poor sod,' Marina said from time to time 'I gave him a boiled egg. It was the last thing he ever ate ' Her voice was hushed, awed

'Shit, you don't think they can trace it back here from his stomach contents or something do you?' Kelvin said, and Marina sighed and cast her eyes aloft

'Poor little sod,' she said again. 'I quite liked him. I mean, he didn't steal the video, did he?'

Six a m finally The last of the late clubbers had staggered home; the town was quiet. They left the flat as normally as they could contrive Steve carried the powder, which he'd put inside a Waitrose bag, and Marina carried the Asics sports bag. The short walk from the front door to Marina's Fiesta almost crippled him with fear He flung the bag inside the car and locked himself in, sweating. Ward and Kelvin sat in the back.

They drove down to the seafront and then, illegally, on to the pedestrian lower level, much to Marina's disapproval. No one about. They parked outside the locked-up Fishing Museum and Steve held the bag between his feet as he found the key and jiggled the lock, which was sluggish with disuse and salty air. The others followed him in and he banged the door shut behind them and locked it again and disabled the burglar alarm. He switched on his torch and huge shadows floundered over the walls and ceiling, the beams dark and dusty and dead-looking.

Steve led the way to the fishing boat and stepped over the rope the councillor had put there to keep the surging hordes of heritage-seekers out. The dummy sailor was sitting in the back curiously bent over and hunched, sinister in the torchlight.

'Sorry about this, shipmate,' Steve said, and lifted the life-jacket up while Marina held the torch in place. The dummy had on a fetching grey woollen item underneath and Steve lifted this too, revealing the smooth coffee-coloured plastic. He shoved the Waitrose bag down the loose white trousers and covered the resulting bulge with the shirt and then the life-jacket.

'How is he?'

Everyone scrutinized him for a moment, but he looked fine, or at least no odder than before.

'I think it may even have straightened him up a bit,' Marina said 'He's a bit more luscious in the arse now, though '

'Do him no harm,' Steve said 'He could do with a bit of meat on him Skin and bone.' He made a few small adjustments, then stepped back and took a last look. The sailor gazed at him, slumped and groggy and lumpy.

Oddly enough, no one wanted to hang around and look at the pictures of the stern wet men. Steve locked up again and they bundled back into the car. They stopped near the groyne and Steve got out and dunked the Asics bag into the sea, then flung it on to the beach near the police 'Do Not Cross' tape It was the last identifiable trace of Ben The police would find

46

it tomorrow when they came to take their tape away. They might wonder why they hadn't found it before, but it wasn't traceable to anyone No one had seen them.

'Christ, we're safe,' Kelvin said. 'We're actually safe.'

'Not yet,' Steve said. 'We need to give the police time to find the bag, put out the report Couple of days If no one comes in seven days, say, then we're safe.'

'Poor Ben,' Marina said suddenly, and everyone looked at her. 'Well, he didn't deserve to die, did he? He was just doing a job for someone. I bet they weren't even paying him that much. Poor little sod '

'Well,' Kelvin said after a minute, 'yes, poor Ben, I suppose '

'He wasn't that bad,' Steve said

'At least they can identify him now,' Marina said. 'They probably can't bury him until they identify him. His mum and dad probably don't even know yet . . . '

Her voice cracked and she started to cry silently, guiltily, in front of everyone, and Kelvin reached awkwardly over the steering wheel to stroke her shoulder while she blubbed something or other about a pint of milk

'Right, come on, then,' she said after a few noisy damp minutes, and drove on, sniffing.

'Stop!'

Marina trod on the brake and they shuddered to a halt and stalled.

'What! What is it?' she demanded.

Steve said, 'We've got to go back '

'What for?'

'We need a sample For testing For testing what it is '

'Nob,' Marina said, and thumped the wheel 'Nobholes ' She started the engine up again and executed a spirited if technically flawed five-point turn They drove back to the museum in a tense, ferocious silence.

'Marina,' Kelvin said from the back of the car after a few minutes, 'what exactly is a "Nobhole"?'

'You know,' she said through gritted teeth 'Hole at the end of your nob '

'You refer to the meatus?'

'Yeah, well, one man's meatus . . . '

Kelvin and Ward lurked in the car while Steve and Marina, with much trepidation, went back into the museum. Marina held the torch.

'I just thought,' he said, with his arm half-way down the seaman's trousers, 'we haven't got a bag. We need a little bag to put the sample in.'

Marina put the torch down and fumbled her way out, cursing and tripping over things, back to the car.

'Nob nob nob,' she said, 'we need a nobbing bag.'

Everyone ferreted about for one, until she found an empty Opal Fruits bag in the squalid area under the ashtray and radio

'Marina,' Kelvin said, 'I've got an idea.'

'What idea?'

'Why don't you try constructing a sentence that hasn't got the word "nob" in it? Just as an experiment?' She ignored him and dashed back with the Opal Fruits bag Steve was sitting beside the sailor, and they looked curiously similar in the torchlight. Steve, trying simultaneously to be incredibly careful and incredibly fast, slipped a little of the powder into the Opal Fruits bag Much, inevitably, ended up on the floor. He wrapped everything up again and replaced the bag

'OK.'

They scurried back to the car and drove away, sweating. Kelvin was keeping a lookout, but there was no one around

'I think we got away with it,' Marina said after a minute. 'Do you think?'

No one answered her.

'Steve,' she said after another long pause, 'are you absolutely certain no one ever goes in there?'

'No one. Ever.'

He played with the Opal Fruits bag.

'Well Hardly ever '

'Oh, hardly ever. Brilliant,' Kelvin said, and Steve gave him a wounded look. 'I mean, what if they decide to open the bloody place up again?'

'They won't.'

'Yes, but what if they do?'

Steve said nothing for a moment.

'Anyway, even if they did, why would anyone want to go poking round in old Seaman Staines's trousers?' he said.

'Tourists,' Ward said. 'You know what they're like. They always want to touch everything '

They drove on in silence.

'I've got it,' Ward said abruptly, making everyone jump as they sat at lights. 'That fillum . . '

'Fuck, what's that?' Marina screamed as something shot out in front of the car, something low and lithe with brilliantly reflective eyes that caught the headlights full on for a moment as it looked at them

'Cat,' Kelvin said.

'Fox,' Steve said, craning round to try to follow it

'Oh, nice one,' Ward said. 'Brilliant. I had it then '

Kelvin patted his leg and they drove on. Marina breathed deeply and drove with the exaggerated caution she used when she'd had a smoke It took her some time to park.

trevor

Trevor parked the dirty bottle-green Saab and walked up the raked gravel path to the big canopied door There were pillars and steps, a real Solihull palace The motion sensor came on and he saw a figure standing by the potted bay trees His daughter Naomi, wearing a sleek black dress with very narrow straps. She watched him as he rushed past and fumbled for his keys.

'It's open,' she said, and he stood for a second taking in the sight of her She seemed to have new breasts and collarbones and a new way of making him feel sweaty and ill-dressed, a new derisive smirk. He couldn't think of anything to say, and she simply ignored him.

He ran up the stairs and into the poky spare room, his office He started in on his messages Just as he feared, it had all gone stupid Calls had started coming in last night, Wednesday.

'Yeah, Trev, it's six now, Wednesday evening, I'm at Waterloo, no sign of your man yet, I'll call again ' This was Martin Whatever his name was was supposed to bring the consignment up from Brighton and meet Martin

Martin again· 'Yeah, half-six, mate, anything your end? No sign of your man I'll hang on here, but give me a call when you get in, yeah? Cheers, bye '

A new voice: 'Hello? Hello? Er, listen, yeah   ' The sound

50

of fumbling and then a sudden sharp uuuh sound

'*Ah Christ* ' Then the sound of hissing air and a few confused bumping sounds, a body writhing in a phone box, some moaning.

Trevor looked at the number display: a Brighton number. This was whatever his name was who was supposed to have got the gear up to Martin at Waterloo. Dammit. God knew what this dickhead was playing at

A new voice, singing sweetly: '*Midnight at the oasis I ain't had no satisfaction, knowwhatIsaying, I got my people, they all ready to rock here and they saying what The Fuck, KnowwhatIsaying? So yeah we be talking real soon now*'

This was a local number, Birmingham. The buyer. Not happy.

'*Yeah, half-past midnight, and you making me look bad, man, I got people jumping all over me, you know how they get, so I maybe have to come jumping all over you, youknowit? So yeah Call me* '

There were more of these throughout the night. Trevor knew better than to worry about such calls, but it was all bad PR none the less He was looking unreliable again

'*Hello, Trevor, it's your mum, it's about ten o'clock Thursday morning, it's Naomi I want really, just to wish her all the luck in the world for tonight and not to get too nervous, I hate talking to these things, that's about all really, so I hope you get this message and Bye* '

'*Woh-oh-oh, ooooh baby, yeah. It's Thursday and the sun is shining, so I thought maybe I take a drive out to that nice place you be living at, with all those nice big trees, and people to mow your grass and all that, maybe just swing on over and we be having a real nice talk Real soon* '

Shit Whatever his name was, the lad who was collecting it at Brighton, Ben, that was it, had messed it up. He, and presumably it, were still in bloody Brighton, and it was now more than twenty-four hours late Trevor scraped his fingers against his cheek for a moment, then came flying down the stairs again and out.

Naomi was still there, just standing about He had no idea why.

'Fancy a trip to Brighton? I'll get you a stick of rock.'

She did her new fuck-you look.

'Oh, right So I'll just cancel the concert and piss about with you in Brighton, then, eh?'

'Concert tonight, is it?'

'No, I'm just dressed up like a call girl for the hell of it, like I do every night. Didn't you know?'

'Baby, I just didn't think it was tonight, that's all,' he said, woefully conscious of his flop sweat and slept-in hair and man-from-the-wheelie-bin suit Where did those breasts come from anyway, he wanted to ask her He was sure he'd never seen them before He tried not to stare 'If I'd known .   . I mean, I knew it was soon, I just didn't . . . '

'Yeah, well, it is Tonight.'

He stood helplessly for a moment. Then he ducked his head down to kiss her and she pulled away

'I'll bring you a stick of rock back, then,' he called from the car door, and she gave him a tight, dismissive smile. Her mum came out on to the porch and glanced at the Saab as it chewed up the gravel.

'Was that your dad, then, love?' she said, and started fastening a slim silver brooch to the front of Naomi's dress, biting her lip as she did so.

'He said did I want to come away to Brighton '

'He said what, love?'

'Brighton, he said He said did I want a stick of rock.'

Her mum looked at her for a moment.

'Take no notice, love I never do. It's his time of life.'

'And he smells '

Her mum stepped back to take in the effect of the brooch and then gave her a hug. 'Right That's you ready.'

raver

No one was willing to try it out themselves, except for Steve, who was all for it but was held back by Marina What if it was really pure, so pure that it just killed you immediately or left you in a persistent vegetative state? Kelvin suggested that in that case Ward should try it, since it wouldn't matter. Or what if it was all mixed up with something else, rinderpest tablets or worming tablets or just poison of some kind? Or what if it was some unknown new thing, not speed or cocaine or MDMA powder, something so addictive that you would just turn into a junkie immediately and spend your whole life in a council block in Edinburgh talking bollocks about Iggy Pop?

'Look,' Steve said, 'either it's speed or it's cocaine Probably Either way you just stick it up your nose and start to have good times '

'Could be that other stuff,' Ward said

'What other stuff?'

'Can't think of the name of it '

'Fantastic Ward saves the day again . . '

'K Vitamin K. Whatever it's called.'

'Ketamine,' Steve said, and looked thoughtful

'It's a funny thing, but no one seems to have much good to report about ketamine,' Kelvin said 'You know, nightmare hallucinations, paralysis, panic attacks, severe paranoia I

53

don't think I'm all that keen on it if it's ketamine '

'Well, I'm not finding out,' Ward said.

'We are hampered,' Kelvin summed up magisterially, 'by a paucity of information '

'Let's ring up one of those drug advisory agencies,' Steve said, but Marina was sure they wouldn't tell you anything worth knowing

'I knew this girl, Ruby, who worked for one of them She had to go to raves and give out these ridiculous jazzy leaflets and tell people to drink water Everyone laughed at her. They called her Leaflet Woman. She had this arsehole boyfriend who was a web-site designer or something ghastly like that Nightmare, frankly.'

'I could ask John,' Steve said hesitantly, and everyone lifted eyebrows and groaned.

'I know, I know, but he has got track marks and everything '

' . and he's read *Trainspotting* all the way through,' Kelvin completed the sentence for him.

'Well, so he says,' Marina said. 'But can he prove it?'

'Can anyone think of anyone else?' Ward asked, and no one could.

'I'll ring him, shall I?' Steve said, and Marina shrugged Bloody John. At least if it was toxic or nasty or just crap, it would only be John on the other end of it Little further harm, it was thought, could realistically come to John now

John had raved long and hard for many years, had devoted untold resources to it, and still could find nothing interesting to say about it. Characteristically he was restricted to 'whatever', 'nice one' and ''ard', which he mixed up to convey whatever dull thing he was trying to communicate. No one could stand him for long Steve kept in touch with him purely for the purpose of buying pills on the half-dozen or so occasions a year that anyone wanted any He lived with a gorgeous woman who smiled unceasingly and was widely rumoured to be brain dead

He couldn't be invited to the flat, or at least he never had

54

been before and Steve thought it would sound odd and spark off some latent paranoia. He arranged to meet him in a big ravers' pub at the far end of town

John was sitting with a large fidgety group of people near the bar. The pub was fitted out with big squashy sofas and exuberant chalk boards advertising 76,000 different flavours of vodka. There was a DJ; there was even a bouncer, a mean vindictive-looking swine. Steve met his eye and noted him down for future reference as they went in

John had a splendid face, a noble face even. He looked something like a late Roman bust, his cheeks deeply creviced and hollowed-out, the eyes deep-set and glittery, and the whole thing so burnt away and refined that he now only really had two expressions 'waiting' and 'surprised' He was surprised to see the four of them as they trooped over to his group

'All right!' he said, a look of immense eagerness flashing momentarily over him before it was submerged into 'waiting'

Steve said hello, and chairs were found and dragged round to accommodate everyone Steve's people nodded and smiled at John's people, who were smiling and nodding anyway and would continue to do so for several hours

'What can I do for you?' John asked, and Steve explained

'We want you to try something out for us. It's white powder of some kind ' Steve was trying to be heard over the music, but trying simultaneously to whisper

'Speed?'

'Well, we don't know We haven't tried it '

John looked surprised for a moment Not tried it?

'Sorry Say all that again,' he said, and bent his head towards Steve He listened carefully, his eyes flickering over the walls and ceiling

'Right,' he said, and nodded 'Right.'

Steve was still uncertain that he'd been understood He'd never tried to explain anything of such complexity to John before

'You got it on you?'

Steve nodded and patted his pocket where the Opal Fruits bag lay.

'OK. Listen, come out with me.' He stood and smiled at everyone, and he and Steve left. He saw Marina nod at one of the girls on the sofa. The girl nodded back and did something with her hands. One of the other girls waved back and they were off again.

John lived in a small one-bed flat a few hundred yards away. It was dark and cramped, and the hallways were full of bicycles and bits of fridge. The gorgeous girlfriend was asleep, so they had to be quiet They went into the kitchen.

'Right, then. Let's have a look at it.'

Steve produced the Opal Fruits bag and handed it over He guessed there was about a gram or so in there, but it was hard to tell exactly. Could have been a gram and a half, could have been two John held it to the light, saw the shiny little flakes, not just on the surface, not just dressing, but all through it Oh oh oh, he thought. I've not seen Charlie looking so well for a long time. Welcome home, fella.

John poked a finger in and had a little dab. His face registered nothing.

'Hm,' he said, and looked hammily quizzical. 'Golly What can this be, now? Eh? I wonder Hm.'

He took down a cookery book and gently tipped a little pile out on to it A tiny pyramid of white powder He chopped it up with what looked like a video library membership card, then spread it into a line, divided the line into two, moved one half away from the other His movements were sure and casual He winked up at Steve, who was hovering anxiously over his shoulder.

'What do you think? Speed?'

John nodded 'Oh, yeah Speed, yeah Probably Yeah Uncut though, which would be unusual. Or cut with something bitter, paracetamol maybe Usually you'd just cut it straight up with glucose Sherbert, basically No, I'm afraid I'm going to have to have a bit more To be certain like '

Steve watched him suspiciously John knew drugs There was

no way he didn't know about this stuff. Steve watched his sample being made ready for absorption into John's raddled system. John rolled up a £5 note and applied it to a nostril, blocked the other one, lowered his face to the smiling photograph of Delia Smith and hoovered up one of the lines, changed nostril and took the other. He stood and shook his head. He sniffed and cleared little traces of powder from his nostrils and rubbed the finger against his gums and under his tongue

'Pwoor,' he said, and grinned briefly.

Steve watched him closely.

John stood smoothing out the fiver and licking up tiny traces of powder from inside it.

'What do you think?' Steve said, and John held up a hand He was playing with the Opal Fruits bag now, his eyes moving restlessly over the table, as if he was looking for something His eyebrows lifted up and down a few times. 'Yeah,' he said after a few minutes, and glanced up at Steve 'Yeah.'

'Yeah what?' Steve asked, trying to be gentle 'What is it? Speed?'

'Yeah,' John said. 'Yeah. Speed I think.'

'John, I haven't got any more, if that's what you're holding out for Just tell me what it is '

John frowned for a moment. 'Give us a minute.' Absently he tipped out another pyramid, emptying the bag completely. He ran his finger round the inside of it. The new pyramid was formed into one thick line. John rewound the fiver and performed a herculean inhalation, the line of powder disappearing beneath the tip of the fiver with mesmerizing precision He left only the barest of traces behind, and the finger was soon back mopping them up.

'Is it good? Is it OK?'

John shook his head, a quick compulsive tremor 'Fuck,' he said He looked back at Steve 'This is first cut and mix,' he said. 'You know Fuck.'

'Can you be any more specific?'

''Ard '

''Ard?'

'Oh, yeah.'

John took a half-step back and wedged himself into the doorway 'Fuck '

Steve guessed he should act quickly. 'Look, John, I don't want to press you on this, but . . '

'It's not speed.'

'Not '

'Fuck no.'

'So therefore . . ' Steve waved his hands suggestively and made an inquisitive face.

'Lemon.'

'Lemon '

'Oh, yeah.'

'What's lemon?'

'What is it?'

'John, what is it?'

'Lemon barley Charlie '

'Charlie? It's cocaine?'

John looked as if a train was going through him. He looked very surprised indeed.

'Devil's dandruff. It is '

'Good cocaine?'

'Fucking . '

'Fucking good?'

'Jesus . ' A big happy smile passed over his face, and went away again

'Can you make a guess about the purity?' Steve felt like a Hereford restaurateur on *Antiques Roadshow* with a disputed nineteenth-century watercolour and a drunk expert

'Pure '

'How pure?'

'Fucking '

'Fucking pure? Give me a percentage.'

'Fuck I'll give you a percentage if you give me a snog.'

'You're straight, John '

'That's your percentage '

'Good, huh?'

'Good.'

John sat down for a bit, then they went back to the pub, where Ward and Kel were glaring at a woman in shiny silver trousers and high heels.

Marina was itching to go.

'Let's get home,' Steve said, and everyone smiled and waved at everyone else, and they went home.

'So at fifty a gram,' Kelvin was saying, 'that comes to, comes to . . . '

'Quarter million,' Steve said instantly

'Can't be,' Ward said.

'We've got five kilograms,' Kelvin said. 'Five thousand grams, yes? It's fifty a gram, yes? That's £250,000 Quarter million He's right Divide by four, that's, fuck, I don't know . '

Marina was doing it in her head

'It's about £60,000 each. Bit more.'

'Er, just one little problem,' Steve said. 'Who are all these thousands of people we're going to sell it to at £50 a gram?'

No one spoke for a minute.

'Or do we sell it all to just one person?'

'Yeah. Some big dealer or something '

'Right, yeah. I'll have a look in *Yellow Pages*, shall I? Do you think it'll be under "b" for "big" or "d" for "dealer"?'

'What you mean, you don't know anyone?' Marina said 'You must do '

'Listen, the people I know, they buy a hundred pills and a couple of ounces of speed and they think they're the God-father or something You think some dickhead like John's got money like this? Or the distribution? This is a big deal we're talking about here This is getting found with fatal shotgun wounds in a Range Rover in a lane somewhere This is paying the police off, this is . . ' He stopped, spread his hands out to indicate the size of the problem 'You know?'

'And I would imagine,' Kelvin said, 'and I'm really just speculating here, that there are existing channels for this stuff all set up and the people who run them might get a little bit cross if we suddenly pop up.'

'Anyway, you need a mobile phone to be a drug dealer,' Steve said. 'And we haven't got one. We haven't even got outgoing calls '

They sat, deflated.

'Anyway, if we sold it all at once we'd only get about half the amount – £25,000 a kilogram, something like that.'

'So, £30,000 each, then,' Marina said 'I'm not complaining.'

'Cocaine,' Kelvin said after a few moments. 'That's addictive, right?'

'Kelvin, you're not thinking what I think you're thinking, are you?'

'It's just a question.'

'No, it isn't just a question. You want to have some, don't you?'

'I'm just asking,' he said stubbornly. 'I just want to know.'

'Obviously it's addictive,' Marina said. 'Though probably only if you have a lot of it.'

'But you'd only have a lot of it if it was addictive, wouldn't you?'

'Maybe it's just really, really nice,' Steve said

'Is there a difference between "really, really nice" and "addictive"?'

'Addictive is a medical term. Really, really nice is more of a layman's term '

'I say we send someone to find out,' Kelvin said.

'Who?'

'Who's the cleverest?'

'Me,' Kelvin said. 'Me. I am.'

'OK Find out. Report back '

'Yeah?'

'Yeah '

Kelvin looked round at everyone and got approval

'OK, house meeting here one week from today And until then we leave it where it is Yes?'

Everyone nodded Steve looked pained, though. Marina stared at him

'Steve?'

'OK. OK.'

'Oh, just one last thing,' Kelvin said 'Whatever we're going to do with it, it might be an idea not to go round telling everyone about it. Do you think?'

Trevor, meanwhile was in his room at the Metropole in Brighton, watching QVC He'd rung the number Ben had called from, with the 'Ah, Christ' message; no reply. A woman was putting up cards for prostitutes in the phone box and ignored it as it rang. He'd also rung up the two dealers he knew in Brighton, Alex and Paul. Neither had heard anything. No one knew anything; no one ever did He described the bags, the initialled sticker on the back, and indicated that it was in no one's interests to buy them should they be offered, but that he would like to hear about it He didn't want any trouble about this, as he kept on saying, not after last time. It was all probably a misunderstanding. It was just business He just wanted it back.

He left messages with anyone that Ben was likely to get in touch with and had his calls diverted to his Metropole number Now he was waiting for the phone to ring, there really wasn't anything else he could do QVC Minibar Look out the window

He sighed Everything was so much trouble lately He wandered to the bathroom and fiddled with things, ran the taps, sighed. He'd already brushed his teeth twice Bloody Brighton, he thought, gazing blankly out at the sea and the sky and the traffic. He considered briefly the possibility of going out for a walk, buying a stick of rock for Naomi The whole idea depressed him unbearably, and he lay back down on the bed

Where is it, he thought, staring at the ceiling Where in fuck is it?

modal scottish cocaine-using man

'Modal Scottish Cocaine-Using Man,' Kelvin began, and flipped over the first page on the Nobo flip chart to reveal a matchstick man wearing a kilt and a woozy smile, 'is what we clever people, Ward, call a "statistical fiction". Modal means the thing that comes up most often in a sample If you take a class of children and get their shoe sizes, the most common is the modal one Our man is a kind of average of all sorts of people, all the people in the study. If you took them all, minced them up in a big mincer thing, and then made one person out of all the mince, this is what you'd get He's aged twenty-seven and has lived with his partner for more than a year. He completed his education at university, where he obtained a degree. That's "university", Ward, not "some jumped up further education college masquerading as a seat of learning". He is currently working as a sound and vision equipment operator, and earns between £10,001 and £15,000 a year. These are '92 prices incidentally.'

'What's a sound and vision equipment operator?' Steve asked.

'Look, I don't know. I'm just telling you what it says here,' Kelvin said, and started to draw something on the picture. He turned back. the matchstick man was now holding a long boom mike. 'He holds the boom on daytime TV shows. All right? Richard and Judy. That bloody supermarket thing '

'Just so I know,' Steve said

'He's used many illegal drugs in his time . . '

'Oooooohhhhh,' everyone said at once, like a well-trained studio audience.

'   amphetamines, SSRIs – Ecstasy, Ward – cannabis, opiates, hallucinogens and tranquillizers – but he has never used crack '

'Never?' Marina asked.

'Never ever ever,' Kelvin said, and shook his head firmly 'Crack is cocaine that's been cooked with baking powder. It forms into a crystalline solid, which you then break up and smoke If you're completely stupid, that is You get a ten- or fifteen-minute high, then you want it again It's lethally addictive like that. Our man doesn't do it that way And he's never injected anything.'

'That's what he says,' Steve said

'Crack is strictly for losers and dickheads only Jabbing is for scumbags and media types. The two groups may overlap Now Apart from cocaine, the only other drug he's used in the last three months is . . '

He flipped another page and Jock the kiltman now had a fat joint hanging from his lips and a smile that was woozier than ever

' . Can-na-bis!' everyone chanted, and Kelvin smiled

'That's right, children Cannabis, but he would use amphetamines, hallucinogens, et al , if offered them free.'

'Oh, well, there's a surprise,' Steve said 'Scottish people taking something for free. Never heard of anything like that before '

'Parasitical scum the whole ugly mob of 'em,' Marina said firmly 'Nightmare.'

'I wouldn't want one of them shagging my dog,' Steve added.

'He's never had a drug-related illness or been convicted of any offence related to his use of drugs,' Kelvin continued. 'He knows   ' another flamboyant flip '   five other people who use cocaine, three of whom are male '

There they were, five little stick people, two of them in ghastly knee-length A-line skirts and pigtails

'That's what women look like, is it, Kel?' Steve said, and Kelvin continued.

'Actually, he hasn't used cocaine more than five times in the last year, but would use some again if . . '

' . offered it free,' everyone chimed in in ragged unison

'He likes cocaine because it makes him . . ' flip '.   energetic, and better at communicating.'

His kilt was swinging wildly as he waved his arms about and one leg was up in the air. There was a little bubble from his mouth: 'Wa-hay the noo!!!' One of the A-line women was watching him admiringly

'I'm not certain I'd class that as communicating,' Steve said. 'That's more what I call making a big tit of yourself.'

'Whatever It increases his self-confidence and makes him feel both relaxed and more creative. For him, it prolongs   .' flip '   sex and makes it more pleasurable, and generally increases feelings of excitement.' Kiltman was lying awkwardly on top of A-line woman now, in an embrace that looked both nightmarishly painful and anatomically improbable They were both smiling hugely, vacantly.

'Why hasn't he got his kilt off?' Steve wanted to know, and before he could stop it Kelvin was hearing 'get your kiiilt off, get your kiiilt off, get your kilt off for the lads Geeeet your ki-ilt o-off for the lads.'

'However,' he continued doggedly, holding up one hand, 'however, he thinks cocaine is too expensive, and leads to sleeplessness and insomnia.'

'Kel, look, would you flip over please?' said Marina 'I don't like thinking about this horrible coming-together of kilt and A-line. It's just one of those things you don't want to think about too much, wouldn't you say?'

Kel nodded graciously to Marina and flipped over

Picture of kiltman with bags under his eyes and a big alarm clock, showing a quarter to four

'What's the difference between "sleeplessness" and "insomnia"?' Steve wanted to know.

'Don't know,' Kelvin replied briskly 'Now. He doesn't agree that cocaine creates either physical addiction or psychological dependence, or makes him irritated or depressed; nor does it have any unpleasant side effects.'

'Doesn't agree?' Marina said, and Kelvin nodded sagely.

'Doesn't Correct He says it's non-addictive and basically harmless '

'Oh, right,' said Steve, 'you'd go to a Scottish junkie for an unbiased picture right enough.'

Kelvin ignored him.

'OK Now, he has a past '

'He first snorted cocaine five years ago when he was twenty-two and visiting a friend in England, and was offered . . . '

' . offered it free . ' everyone said

'   in the friend's house, although he hadn't asked for it.'

'Well, you wouldn't, would you?' Steve said 'You don't go to someone's house and say, cup of tea would be nice and would you please offer me some free cocaine? Not even if you are Scottish.'

'In the year that followed, he used cocaine less than once a month, always snorting, and usually only a couple of "lines" when he did so However, when he was twenty-three he consumed rather more during what he now refers to as a four-month "heavy" period,' Kelvin continued, and flipped the page again, showing a jagged outline, like a mountain. Kiltman was skiing down the side, his kilt flying

'Kel, why is that a picture of a "heavy" period?' Steve asked, and Kelvin turned to look at it.

'Oh. I've got out of sequence, it should have been the one before ' He turned back, revealing a picture of the kiltman sitting in an armchair, with a small mountain of white powder on a little table beside him, and a long straw, which was fixed to his left nostril with a piece of Elastoplast There were £20 notes slipping out of his back pocket

'That's the "heavy" period,' Kelvin said.

'I really don't like this terminology,' Marina said wearily 'You people quite obviously have not the smallest notion of what a heavy period is '

'We'll talk about that later, shall we, sweetheart?' Kelvin said brightly, and went to his next picture, the mountain

'He has most recently gone back to taking cocaine less than once a month, and only about two lines on each occasion Looking back, he would say that his cocaine career was one where his use increased gradually until it reached a peak, from which it has since decreased. Here he is, see? He's skiing down the mountain, indicating his decreasing cocaine use.'

A new picture: one of the pigtail women, her A-line now transformed into a kilt by means of criss-crossing oblique strokes and a large safety pin.

'I had a skirt like that when I was twelve,' Marina said happily.

'Now this, surprise surprise, is Modal Scottish Cocaine-Using Woman. She is much like Jock, except that she is a year younger, knows ten other drug people to Jock's five, and has used more cocaine than him· eleven to thirty times, against his five.'

'She's a swinger,' Marina said approvingly.

'She agrees with him about everything, except this: she does think that cocaine makes her irritated and depressed.'

'Well, she would, frankly,' Steve said. 'I mean, the skirt tells you that ' He was duly glared at.

'And that's that,' Kelvin said, flipping over to his final picture, of Jock and Joanna, holding hands and walking into the sunset, with the words 'That's All Folks!' underneath. Everyone went 'Aaaaah', and there was a little applause.

'I'll now be happy to take any questions you might have. I'm sure there must be lots of things you want to ask. No? Fine   '

'Just one thing ' Ward's voice, the first thing he'd said 'You say kiltman's a statistical fiction?'

'He's an aggregate, yes A fiction '

'OK So what I want to know is, what does a statistical fiction wear under his kilt, like?'

Everyone groaned. Kelvin looked withering, and Steve patted Ward's hand and told him to keep taking the tablets

leaflet woman

Marina had decided that Kelvin was up his own arse as usual and sought further advice She found the number for the woman she used to know who was now some sort of drug adviser type. Ruby

When she came she had a man with her Ruby and Jeff were a short, dark-haired pair. he was prematurely receding, in mid-thigh leather coat and black polo neck; she was vivacious. She was fun at parties, as Marina well knew, fun all night long until she started to be sick and cry She never smoked anything, but drank much to compensate Jeff had been living with her for nearly a year, no one knew anything about him, none seemed to like him particularly. His face was vaguely pleasing but not enough to take your attention from his air of controlled desperation He had let it be known that he had 'a bit of a problem a few years ago', which was taken to mean a drugs problem, though it had uncharitably been suggested that what he really meant was that he'd had a joint once and it had gone out. They were both Christians No big deal, they'd say, smiling like crocodiles, it's just the way we are

Ruby had been a volunteer with 'RaveSafe' since just before Marina had lost touch with her, which was also round about the time she'd started talking about Jesus. She went to meetings in tight black jeans and a black vest and hand-made jewellery. She'd met Jeff at one of the training sessions and they were now engaged. She had a cheerful plastic ring to prove it. She had hinted drunkenly (just prior to a particularly spirited and athletic throw-up) that Jeff was a virgin. Marina had had difficuty meeting his eye ever since.

Marina had fully intended to ask Ruby specifically not to bring any leaflets when she came round. The words had been perfectly formed in her head when she dialled the number and heard first the over-excited ansaphone message ('Hi! Ruby and Jeff are having noisy sex in the shower right now . . ') and then Ruby's voice cutting in over the top, ragged and irritable The words, however, had not come out Marina's heart sank as she saw the little white cardboard envelope Ruby had clutched in her hand when she turned up on the doorstep. It was, she knew, full of leaflets.

They gathered in the front room and there was great awkwardness, awkwardness everywhere you looked. Marina matched vivacities with Ruby for a few minutes, then said, Let's go to the pub, which would be quiet at this time of the evening, and less, less . . . The words she wanted were 'desperately awkward' but she couldn't say them. Less . . .

Everyone agreed instantly, and they were in Rosie O'Grady's in a few minutes. Every single item in the place was either a reproduction of an old Guinness promotion, a current Guinness promotion or a decorative artefact with 'Guinness' written on it The music, while having no obvious relevance to Guinness, was Irish in the extreme: Cranberries and Sinead O'Connor and Pogues; odd records from years ago that were, apparently, by Irish people There was a merciful absence of U2, but many shouty, foot-stompy things with folky fiddles at the end.

Ruby was drinking pints of cider with bits of apple in the top She looked wearied and hung-over, her eyes sparkling but haggard. She was wearing an odd little scarf, which immediately made Marina think that Jeff must have tried to strangle her and she was hiding the marks. Virgin Christian Slays Vivacious Lush, Marina thought, and tried not to meet his eye He was sitting solidly next to Kelvin, who was grinning and twitching She tried not to meet his eye either.

Then she met Steve's and laughed and pretended it was a cough. Ward was gazing at Ruby. Perhaps inevitably, Marina thought, Ward fancied her. Oh, for God's sake, she thought. What are we going to do with you?

Marina split a round with Kelvin, and then Ruby and Jeff bought one. Marina noticed that Ruby had a little brandy chaser with her second pint. Go for it, she thought, and almost remembered why she had ever liked her.

Jeff smoked roll-ups, tiny little ones. There was more making than smoking. They went out after about ten seconds and left slimy wet little butts in the ashtray. He smiled at people and made everyone uneasy.

'OK, this is the situation,' Marina said at last and launched in. She didn't mention Ben or the five bags, she just said that they'd all been having a bit of cocaine lately and wanted to know if it was a problem

Ruby listened very intently, showing with every fibre of her body that she was listening Marina sensed professional training in the posture. She's trying so hard to look like she's listening, Marina thought, that she probably can't hear a word Marina was tempted to say something absurd to test her, but didn't

Ruby glanced up at Jeff when Marina had finished, as if to say, Jeff, OK if I handle this one? Jeff made some imperceptible sign, and Ruby sat back and fished the apple out of her glass

'You know,' she said, 'we don't see a lot of coke, do we, Jeff?' Jeff shook his head 'Mostly what we see is whizz and Es And acid. And spliff, of course ' She sucked the apple thoughtfully 'And horse.'

'Horse?' Marina said brightly.

'You know Smack '

'Oh, right, heroin,' Marina said

'Yeah. We like to use the words the users use, you know They call it horse '

'Are you certain?' Steve asked. He couldn't recall anyone saying 'horse' since Prince in 1988 The people he knew who had it called it heroin Ruby ignored him

'But coke, not really that much.'

'So you don't know about it?' Marina said.

'Oh, yes,' Ruby said quickly, and Jeff nodded his head simultaneously.

'It's just that we don't see that much of it,' he said, and Marina nodded politely

'Probably because it's so expensive,' she offered, and Ruby and Jeff both nodded at once

'That's really the problem with it,' Ruby said, and, looking at her ravaged, baggy eyes and her fidgety, distracted manner, Marina could almost believe that she might know what she was talking about.

'People will tell you that it's not actually technically addictive, and that may be so But you tell that to someone who's spent £500 last week and is going to spend £500 this week, and see what they tell you.'

'Five hundred a week?'

'Easily. Fifty a gram. That's only ten grams a week One a day and three for the weekend. For example.'

'Five hundred a week?' Kelvin said again, and Ruby matched his eye with her own

'Uh-huh ' She sat back to emphasize her point.

'But have you ever known anyone spending that much?' he said, and Ruby smiled.

'Have I personally? No '

'Nor me,' Jeff chipped in

'But it happens, believe me.'

'Oh, it happens,' Jeff said.

Marina was getting sick of him. 'OK, so it's very expensive But what if that wasn't really an issue? For whatever reason What else?'

'How do you mean?'

'Well, what harm does it do you?'

'You mean physically? Well, I'm not sure it actually does anything very much But of course you don't know what it's been cut with The problem with street drugs is that they get mixed up with all sorts of things.'

'What if it was unusually pure?' Marina said, and met Ruby's

70

eye Ruby was clearly trying to work out what this was about and Marina wasn't going to tell her.

'The main physical problem people get is with the septum. The bone in the nose. The cocaine can eat away at it. If you take a lot of it over a long period your nasal cavity can collapse Also you get a lot of nose bleeds '

'Oh, that doesn't sound so bad,' Marina said absently, and Ruby eyed her speculatively

'None of my business, but we're not talking hypothetically here, are we?'

Marina giggled and caught Ward looking at her scoldingly

'Sorry. Actually no, no, we're not '

'That's 26,000 a year,' Kelvin said.

'Right. Anyway, the real problems are psychological.'

'Irritability?'

'Yes.'

'Mood swings?'

'Yes . .'

'Insomnia? Depression? Loss of appetite?'

'Yes, look, you already know all this, clearly,' she said irritably, her mood abruptly swinging 'What is it that you're asking me?'

'Well, I'll tell you what I want to know,' Steve said, 'what's the difference between "sleeplessness" and "insomnia?"'

Ruby glared at him, and he raised his eyebrows 'Only asking,' he said.

'In ten years that would be quarter of a million. Give or take.'

'Look, I don't know what you guys have got yourselves into here, but if you're asking me if coke is dangerous, then the answer is yes It fucks people up '

Jeff flinched slightly at the word 'fuck' and Marina saw that he was blushing. Both of Ruby's glasses were empty and Marina stood to get another round. Ward intercepted her and made Steve share a round by rubbing fingers together under his nose

'So if you did that for forty years .. '

'Kel .   ' Marina said threateningly

'It'd be a million '

'What if you just have a little bit every now and again?' Marina said, pursuing the point, almost as if asking permission from Ruby.

'It doesn't work like that,' Ruby said 'It's one of those things You could have a little bit once a week for a year, and then you'd wake up one day and find that you'd had twice your usual amount the night before, and by that evening you'd have had as much again And so on until the money's gone It just gets in. Think of it as a guest. The first time he comes he's funny and sexy He stays for tea and it's fine. Next time he comes he stays overnight, and you notice that there's no milk in the fridge Then it's a weekend, and he's eaten everything in the house Soon you can't get him to go He just sits there, smiling and eating It's a greedy little bastard Very hard to get rid of it. Very, very hard. Better not to let it in in the first place, really '

'What if you've already started?' Marina said in a little quiet voice, and Ruby looked at her hard and long.

'Then the time to stop is now.'

Marina twisted her lips and Ruby gave her a little pat on the arm

It seemed to be taking Ward a long time to get the drinks and no one had anything to say Ruby started to fiddle with her cardboard envelope and Marina watched her with dread

'I've got something in here   ' Ruby was saying, and suddenly the table was tilting and lurching, beer was foaming about over everything. Ruby stood up fast but her skirt took quite a bit of the beer, and the leaflets soaked up quite a bit more She glared at Steve, who grabbed for his glass, swearing He used the cardboard envelope to swipe the beer away off the table and on to the floor

'And of course,' Ruby continued sitting carefully down again, not letting go of Steve's eye, 'depending of course on your point of view, there is a moral element here

The table trembled ominously.

addiction games

Seven days had elapsed since they'd buried it in the sailor dummy's trousers. There had been a tiny item on the news about the bag; the police had confirmed that the dead man on the beach was the owner of it

Trevor, holed up in his eyrie at the Metropole, watched it, swore softly, kicked a few things and went to brush his teeth again. Ben was dead, then, and the cocaine was God knew where It had gone Unless he just got stupid lucky, he'd never find it now Ben had presumably tried to be clever, sell it, got into bad company Amateur. Dickhead

Along with the story about the bag there had been a clip of a woman and a man coming down the steps of the Coroner's Court, Ben's parents, all the way from Bristol The verdict was misadventure, an accident caused, presumably, by Ben's drugged condition As far as anyone could tell, he had banged his head heavily against the groyne, knocked himself out and sustained further injuries as he fell. He had been unlucky. Death caused by unluckiness Yeah, right, Trevor thought Death caused by being a dickhead more like it The woman, his mother, had looked shocked into complete blankness as she came down the steps of the Coroner's Court, and her eyes burned into the camera for a moment as she and her husband got into a taxi. Nothing would ever be the same for either of them, you could see that in the way they walked slightly apart from each other.

Trevor watched the screen sombrely. It had happened before, it would happen again, but it was a pain in the arse anyway. He left the hotel and drove round the narrow, congested Brighton streets and along the seafront He passed by the place where Ben and later his bag had been found. Unless Alex or Paul came up with something, that was it. He tried to remember who had recommended Ben to him in the first place, but couldn't. Probably some other dickhead. They came and went these people. He drove back to the Metropole and installed himself in the main bar. Dammit. He got talking to a fattish man from Leicester who kept glancing round looking for prostitutes. He had very dry lips and seemed to take a particular interest in people's footwear

Trevor bought him a drink – Jack Daniel's – and they clinked glasses. 'To sodding Brighton,' the fat man said, and they drank to that 'To dickheads,' Trevor said, and the fat man said, 'I'll drink to that '

Steve and Marina had gone back to the Fishing Museum and retrieved the cocaine No one had come calling, looking for Ben No one had seen him. There had been no phone calls from menacing men with South American accents The police had failed completely to arrive stealthily at dawn with state-of-the-art door-breaking equipment and enthusiastic dogs. No gangs of hooded figures fronted by a psychopath with fancy trademark patter and stylish methods of violence. Nothing at all It was almost a disappointment.

Now it was theirs. It was certainly no one else's Next day was Saturday, and they had to go and watch Ward play football. Not real football, five-a-side on the grass by the beach But he pretended to take it seriously and demanded that they pretend to too

Steve, Marina and Kel stood stolidly behind the opposition's goalmouth and tried to concentrate on this dreary ritual, tried to act naturally, tried not to dance around and start yelling about cocaine Most of the action seemed to be at the other end It involved a great deal of shouting.

'Have you ever wondered,' Steve was saying during one of the many lulls, 'why it is that Ward plays in tracksuit bottoms and not shorts? Everyone else is in shorts '

'Bazza's in shorts,' Marina said. 'I wish he'd come down this end a bit more.'

'Maybe Ward's just got crap legs,' Steve said, and Kelvin looked wise and said, Actually, no, that's not the problem, but wouldn't be drawn any further There was a burst of shouting and the ball sailed past over their heads and bounced away towards the sea. Bazza pounded over to retrieve it, thick and stocky and sweating and, indeed, in shorts. Short shorts. Marina and Steve watched him go

'If you had as much as that woman was saying   ' Kelvin said

'Ruby. That woman was called Ruby '

'   . then we'd have enough for one person for . . . hold on now   Ten years '

'Can't be.'

'Ten years, right there at home on top of our telly '

'Can't be.'

'Steve, it's no good you saying can't be, it is. That's at ten grams a week, every week. One kilogram is a thousand grams. So one kilogram   . '

'Key,' Marina chipped in 'Don't they say "key" on *Miami Vice*?'

'Yeah, and they probably say "horse" as well,' Steve said

'Give us a "key" of "horse" chum, will you, and then I'll shoot you '

'And a pint of milk,' Marina said.

'One kilogram,' Kelvin continued, 'is enough for two years for one person at ten grams a week Thus five kilograms is enough for .   '

'Ten years,' Marina said

'Correct.'

'But there's four of us,' she added

'Thus, we divide ten by four and get two and a half.'

'Two and a half years each '

'That's if we want to have that much '

'So that means we have a little snort now, tonight, and we emerge, dazed and blinking, in October 2000?'

'That can't be right.'

'It is right.'

'But what about Modal Scottish Cocaine-Using Man?' Steve said 'He only had a heavy period for a while, then he started skiing down the slope and only had it after that when perfect strangers came up and stuffed it up his nose.'

'Forcibly '

'Against his will, apparently.'

'God knows, it happens.'

'Yes, but you have to ask yourself why he only had one heavy period,' Kelvin said

'OK, why?'

'Because it's very expensive.'

'If you have to buy it '

'So if you don't have to buy it   . '

'You could, probably, have one great big long two-and-a-half-year heavy period.'

'And then what?'

'Then you stop.'

'Just like that?'

'Just like that. Everyone in the study agreed that it was not, repeat not, addictive. Remember? I emphasize the word "not" '

'Yeah, but Ruby said . . '

'Oh, Ruby said. Look, if it's there you have it, if it isn't you go without As long as you know what you're doing with it you're all right Only wankers get addicted to things That's what the people in the study said, and they should know You feel low for a bit, but this is life we're talking about here after all. Ward's been feeling a bit low his whole miserable existence and it hasn't stopped him getting where he is today '

They watched as Ward executed a spectacularly late tackle, tripped himself up and fell swearing to the grass

Marina sighed.

'Two and a half years is a really long time. It's like from

76

twelve to fourteen and a half,' she said. 'A lifetime.'

'What if we have more than that?' Steve said. 'She wasn't saying that was the most you could have.'

'More than ten grams a week? That seems like a lot.'

'I knew someone who had three grams of speed in a night,' Steve said. 'Mind you, he did nearly die.'

'From speed?'

'No, I think one of his pills was dodgy.'

'A gram a day seems prudent,' Marina said. 'It has a prudent kind of sound to it. Jane Austen would have had a gram a day, out of a nice Derbyshire-ware dish.'

'More like three years, then.'

'I'd be twenty-six,' she said. 'Twenty-six.'

'You'd look older,' Steve said 'You'd look more like forty-six '

'Like Marianne Faithfull?'

'Worse probably.'

'Yeah, but I'll have a promising career in this really well-funded funky little media centre by then, so I wouldn't have to worry '

'Marianne Faithfull never had one of those '

'She probably lost it up her . '

'Thanks Kelvin.'

'   . up her jacksy, along with the Mars Bar and half of Mick Jagger . . '

'Yes, thank you, Kelvin, I think we've all got that now '

'You know what Ward said about it?' Kelvin said. 'I was talking to him about it in the kitchen, and he says, "Anyway, no fucking drug gets me addicted And I mean no fucking drug I give up the ciggies, didn't I?"'

'Yeah, and he started smoking dope all day And he was a complete twat for about six months. I mean more than usually Do you remember all that?'

'Anyway then he says, "It's not like it's smack or something It's just some poncy upper It's just speed with knobs on by the sound of it "'

'This is all hypothetical, though, obviously,' Marina said. 'You're not suggesting, of course, that we should do anything as stupid as take it? That can't be what you're suggesting.'

Steve and Kelvin exchanged a glance. How to say this?

'Is it?'

'Well, actually . . . '

There was a roar from the far end, where small figures were jerking about in front of the goalmouth. 'Offside!' Marina and Steve called out automatically. You either went 'Offside!' or 'Ref-er-ee!' and they'd tried 'ref-er-ee' earlier on – there wasn't one, apparently There were other things you could shout as well, but they were never quite certain about them, and Ward would never explain anything.

'Look, we don't have to have it all, do we?' Steve said, sweetly reasonable A new drug! A sex drug! 'We can just have a bit, see what it's like, then we can sell it.'

'We can mix it up with Ajax or whatever you do to make up the weight,' Kelvin said.

'Can you still get Ajax?' Marina wondered.

'John reckoned you use baby teething powder. Anyway, come on! It's a new drug! Let's have it! Let's have it today! Let's go!'

They fell quiet as the ball somehow accidentally got up to their end and the goalie raced back into position Bazza was right behind him, his thick heavy legs pumping away inside the shorts. He flailed at the ball and fell There were yells from down the field

'Those are rugby shorts, aren't they?' Marina said thoughtfully, and Steve nodded.

'Also, they're the rugby shorts of a somewhat smaller man,' he said 'A man of lesser endowment.'

'He's the flower of British manhood,' Marina said, and Kelvin bristled

'He's practically indecent,' Steve said.

They watched as Baz picked himself up and started yelling

'So what do we think?' Kelvin said. 'Are we going to try it?'

It was in Marina's hands, as usual, and she wasn't decided. Steve whispered something to her, and she giggled, then looked horrified, then giggled again. She listened intently. Then she said, 'Right Until we find some way of selling it we're going to have a bit. A bit. Right? A little bit. Are we agreed?'

They were. Ward lolloped up, flushed and triumphant, and they broke the news to him

'Fine with me,' he said, and then ran off again shouting

'I thought they'd finished,' Marina said. 'Haven't they sodding finished yet?'

'What did you say to her?' Kelvin asked Steve later, and he said, 'I told her that once she got a bit of cocaine in her, your legs would feel like Bazza's. Rugby shorts and all '

'Well, just as long as I don't end up with the face as well,' Kelvin said. 'And what's wrong with my legs anyway?'

four take cocaine

They pulled the curtains and lit candles, which seemed suitable. Kelvin made a joint and Steve and Marina opened one of the bags and took out a tiny little amount, with the smallest teaspoon, the one that Marina liked to use for her boiled egg They laid it on to a book called *200 Houseplants Anyone Can Grow* Kelvin started worrying about the music. Nothing was right somehow.

'I know what we need,' he said, and went off to look for it.

Marina and Steve placed the book on the floor in front of the television, both holding their breath and turning their heads to breathe, like swimmers. Steve chopped up the bigger lumps in the pile with Kelvin's good serrated fruit knife

'Do you think that's enough?' he said, and Marina examined it

'Do it a bit more,' she said, hardly speaking above a whisper. Their heads were almost close enough to touch

He carried on chopping, making tiny gentle movements with the knife, taking infinite pains that nothing should go shooting off the book. One of the remaining medium-sized lumps split apart and he rescued it with a quick flick of his thumb and gently brought it back to the pile Ward was biting his nails on the sofa.

There were no medium-sized lumps left now, no matter how carefully Steve sifted through the pile with the knife.

Tiny amounts were lifted up and put down, as if he were building the foundations for a miniature motorway embankment. A stray trace of breath lifted up a few grains and set them down again, and their two heads came up. Marina breathed out through puffed cheeks

'I'm geffing a stiff neck,' Steve said.

'Give us a go,' Marina said, and took the knife. She started on the small grains, chopping and sifting, until there was an approximately even white powder She lifted her head. 'That's it, I think.'

'Right, then So now we need four lines.'

She divided the pile into half and then each half into halves Microscopic adjustments were made until they were both satisfied with the distribution. She formed the little piles into lines, all going the same way A few final infinitesimal nudgings back and forth.

'That's it Do they look the same to you?'

Steve leaned forward, almost at the end of a breath The lines were thin and narrow, about two inches long.

'This one wants to be a bit longer,' he said, and she applied the knife, stretching the line out another quarter of an inch.

'Actually, that's not exactly what I meant,' he said. 'But it looks OK now '

'We're ready.'

Ward came over to look He seemed to be holding his breath too.

'Where's Kel?'

'He went looking for some music, I think.'

'Kel,' Marina shouted, 'come on, we're ready '

He came running in, clutching a CD

'Got it '

Ward took out a £10 note and formed a little trumpet, while Kelvin put the CD on.

A low, low orchestral sound, almost too deep to register Then trombones and basses, climbing up from the bottom

Ward glanced over at Kelvin. 'This is from *2001* '

'*Also Sprach Zarathustra*,' Kelvin said, and Ward glared at him

81

'*2001* music I recognize it.'

Full brass and strings, da daaaaaaa, and tympani banging out bong bong bong bong, full on. They gathered round *200 Houseplants* and Ward smiled up at them and applied his nose to one end of the tenner. The other end went to the start of one of the lines Then he lifted his head again, breathed out massively, put the trumpet back to the line and breathed . . .

after...

in, moving the tenner along the line, sucking up the powder as it travelled, leaving nothing behind it

The music went back to subliminal basses, as Marina took the note from Ward and did the same. The music climbing up, then da daaaaaa, the other way round this time, and whoever it was on kettle drums making the most of his moment, pounding away. Ward was sitting back, his eyes meandering around the room Marina finished and also sat back. Steve took the note and the music went back again, this time moving up to a new chord, a huge shimmering chord for full orchestra Then Kelvin. The chord shifted, then began to climb, slowly, inching its way to the top. Shattering climactic tutti, everything on full, full orchestra and full organ, with tympani. Drop back to organ alone, then orchestra back louder louder louder and the final smash of cymbals. Reverberation.

Ward picked up *200 Houseplants Anyone Can Grow* and flung it into the air

symptoms

'Er, does anyone know what you're supposed to get?' Ward asked after about ten minutes.

'We should have read one of that woman's leaflets '

'Well, isn't it all that increased communication and swinging your kilt stuff?' Marina said.

'I'm not swinging my kilt,' Steve said. 'Not so's you'd notice '

'Maybe you have to wait a bit more '

'When did we have it?' Ward asked, and Steve knew to the minute

'It was just ten past nine,' he said 'Twelve minutes ago '

'But I mean, do you come up on it like an E? Or does it just kind of creep up on you, like? Or what?'

'John staggered around and said, "'Ard",' Steve said

'Yeah, but then, Steve, he has been known to do that before,' Marina said. 'Once or twice.'

'And then, he did have about a gram and a half in one go. Two goes '

'Why did he have two goes?'

'Why did he have a gram and a half?' Kelvin wanted to

know. 'Isn't that a lot?'

'He couldn't be sure what it was at first,' Steve explained, and everyone said, 'Hmmm.'

'Gram and a half,' Ward said meditatively. 'How much did we have just then?'

'It can't have been more than a quarter of a gram,' Steve said, 'if that.'

'Each?'

'Between us. Sixteenth each '

'Oh, well,' Ward said. 'Maybe we need to have a load more.'

'Fuck, he's an addict already '

'It's sad, actually, isn't it?'

'Victim '

'It'll be self-harming before bedtime.'

'Hey, Ward,' Kelvin said, 'did you see that Q interview with Iggy Pop . '

'Thank you, Kelvin,' Marina said. 'That'll do '

'Anyway,' Steve said, 'apparently, quite often you don't get anything much the first time Some people don't anyway.'

'Is anyone getting anything now?' Kelvin asked impatiently. This was ten minutes later. He was timing it

No one was. Steve was reading a CD sleeve Ward was lying flat on his back staring at the ceiling. Marina was fiddling with her teeth

'I thought I was for a minute,' Steve said. 'I thought I could feel a little tingle in my gums.'

'Oooh, tingly gums, eh? The Holy Grail of the druggies' quest,' Kelvin said

'But it's stopped now '

'Erm, wasn't there supposed to be something about increased sexual experience?' Steve continued after a minute 'Because with me that's usually quite a reliable indicator.'

'We could do a test on you,' Marina said. 'We could put one of those funny wire things on your nob and measure your degree of excitation '

'Any drug that involves funny wire things on your nob,' Kelvin said distinctly, 'can count me out '

'Typical,' Marina said.

'Actually, wire things on your nob might not be so bad,' Steve said reflectively. 'Depends '

'But anyway, what I guess you're trying to say here,' Kelvin said, 'is that any hypothetical nobometer would not be registering much just at present.'

'Not a twitch,' Steve said.

'I think we need some more,' Ward repeated.

'Let's give it till half-past,' Kelvin said. They watched the clock on the video.

'Sod it '

Ward jumped up and went to get *200 Houseplants*. He scooped out eight heaped teaspoons from the open bag on the television, chopped them roughly, dragged them out into lines. Eight lines. Big, long, thick, chunky, sexy lines, two each.

'If we're going to have it,' he said, 'we should have it '

'Er, how much have you got there, Ward?' Kelvin said, and Ward said, 'How the fuck do I know?'

'I think I'm getting a little something   .' Steve said

marauding about

Everyone was uncontainably twitchy by ten-thirty. It wasn't like the hard, chemical rush of a pill, or the edgy jolt of speed, it was more like a wind that came up, lifting and pulling them along with it A geothermal, maybe It was effortless and smooth, benevolent The lights came up and the music came on and the warm wind blew. Compared to the strenuous, tight exhilaration of E and speed, it was like an ancient blessing It made them wise and powerful Invincible. It wrapped them up and looked after them, the most genial of hosts. It loved them

The wanker upstairs had started in with his ghastly evening sequence of old Gap Band and SOS Band hits. It wasn't so much the music, it was the inevitability of the thing, the same tracks in the same order. If all went according to the usual plan, this would be followed up by the entire Atlantic back catalogue, '75 to '78 or so There would be Donny Hathaway. There would be Roberta Flack. Again, the actual music was fine, but somehow the wanker made it hideous by his inability to play anything else He seemed to have got stuck somehow in the mid-seventies and would remain so, presumably, until he died It was just a depressing thought. Also he would sing along, his voice an insane, ugly parody of their sweetness Then his bath would start to overflow and ten minutes later their kitchen ceiling would start to drip

So they went marauding about. Kelvin put some fairly large amounts of cocaine into little cigarette paper twists, about ten in all. He also made up some joints and stashed the whole lot into an empty cigarette packet.

The four of them ended up, perhaps inevitably, sitting on the hard pebbles of the beach Waves crashed momentously in front of them, stupendous, their crests lit an icy ghost blue by the moon Gulls wheeled overhead, dirty white and expert The dark form of a closed-up beach-front café was a little to their right Steve glanced over at it, casually but frequently

Ward lay on his back, the waves at his feet, the great masses of cloud and sky above Brighton was crouched behind him. He felt incredibly powerful; he could move the whole stupid thing through ninety degrees if he felt like it The town would then be situated on piers over the sea, stretching out in some absurd way towards France It might be an improvement Gusts of wind were tugging, the air cool and moist Patches of sky were clear and there were stars The stars were there for a purpose, or else why would they be there? They were saying something.

Marina caught Steve looking over at the locked-up café and wanted to know what he was staring at.

'Keep watching,' he said

It was not yet quite kicking-out time, but already she could make out dark figures, just shadows, moving back and forth in front and behind it, or just standing

She cast her eyes skywards

'Fucking homos What are they all doing over there? Line-dancing, I suppose '

'No, actually I think they're shagging each other.'

'Yes Well, I suppose they have to, don't they? Who else would have them, really?'

'That makes no sense at all,' Steve said, after a moment's thought, and she giggled. Steve sat upright and threw some pebbles at the sea

'Go on, boy, go and show them what you're made of,' she said, and Steve hesitated.

'Normally, of course, I don't,' he said, half-standing.

She gave him a push

'See you later, then,' Marina said, and Steve stood and walked self-consciously away.

The three of them watched the surf, intermittently. You could see right out to the horizon. The sky was clearing fast and the air was getting fresher. Marina shuddered with a cold, clear exhilaration. Occasionally one or other of them would glance up towards where the shadowy people came and went Casually, like. It was too far, too dark to see anything. Not that they were trying to see anything, of course.

They were so busy watching, in fact, that they completely missed the first, premonitory splashings of something in the sea, somewhat to the left of them.

At first Kelvin thought it was just someone throwing pebbles, but it became clear a few seconds later that it was in fact someone in the water. Someone coming out of the sea

He emerged, from absolutely nowhere, doing an efficient breaststroke, then standing when the water was shallow enough. He was bare to the waist Dark water surged round him.

'Christ, how cold is that water?' Ward said.

The man was paddling out now, with the waves breaking round him.

'Oh,' Marina said when it became obvious that he was also bare *from* the waist. Bollock-naked, a lean swimmer's physique, panting

He rose out of the sea like a mythical beast, the cold ripples of water running down and off him, faintly phosphorescent

'He's like a, like a . ' Marina said, her voice a breathless whisper 'He came out of the sea Kel, did you see that?'

No one spoke as the man walked up the beach, then saw them and came towards them

'He's coming over here,' Marina breathed 'Do you think he's real?'

The man sauntered out of the depths, sparkling with drops, serene of purpose, oblivious to the stones under his bare feet,

91

oblivious, seemingly, to everything. He had a graceful, other-worldly smile

'He must have a message for us,' Marina said. 'From the deep.'

Kelvin gave her a pack-it-in look

They tried not to look at him as he approached. Soon he was standing at their feet, dripping, the immense sea and sky behind him.

'Hi,' he said, and smiled 'Do you think I could have some wine? My mouth's dried out from the sea.'

Marina watched him with awe. No one moved. Then Ward spoke, slowly and distinctly: 'On your bike, pal.'

Steve was back about fifteen minutes later. They had all had another joint by now, to settle themselves after the man from the deep. Steve sat down beside Marina and watched the sea

'So, how was it?' she said after a minute.

'Fine.'

'Did you get any?'

'Certainly did.'

'Who was it?'

'Big ugly skinhead.'

'And what did you do?'

'You really want to know?'

'Of course.'

'Twisted his bollocks and wanked off.'

'What was he doing?'

'He was fucking someone in the mouth '

'Uhuh. I see Yes. And everyone was happy about that, were they?'

'Seemingly '

'Nobometer reading?'

'Off the scale '

Marina looked over to Kelvin, who was throwing pebbles.

'Kel? Would you like it if I twisted your bollocks?'

'Not now, sweetheart.'

'Not now, sweetheart,' she repeated She turned to Steve 'You see? I can't just go behind a shed and fiddle about with people. I have to wait for when old sexy pants here is in the mood.'

'Go and have a look,' Steve said. 'Maybe one of the boys there is a two-way swinger I thought one of them did look a bit that way, come to think of it.'

'Really?' Marina took a quick glance at the shed, where the dark figures were shifting about. 'Which one?'

'Well. Actually he was the one with the variable-tinted sunglasses and your dad's jeans '

'Pressed?'

'Oh, yes.'

'Age?'

'Sixty-two '

'Footwear?

'Match trainers, *circa*, ooh, I'd say '84, '85 '

'Mmmm. Hey What a prize '

'I think he got driven away, though.'

'Oh, shame.'

'Yeah, this is a very fussy skinhead up there He's having no truck, basically.'

'Dammit,' she said. 'I want a shed thing to go behind and twist skinheads' bollocks I demand it. Kel, why haven't we got a shed thing?'

'The point is,' Steve said, 'that we're basically better organized than you.'

'Kel,' Marina called, 'we require better organization Sheds will be constructed and bollocks will be twisted. I have said it ' She waved a hand commandingly.

Kelvin was getting restless. He threw pebbles with greater and greater force 'Let's go and commit a crime,' he was saying 'Come on '

Ward was lying face up watching the skies. He looked distant and happy The stars, he was thinking, are in a very interesting pattern.

No one wanted to commit a crime, so Kelvin wandered off on his own The streets were lovely and wet and people passed by every so often, and he could smile at them Such a smile!

Such people! One old man stopped and exchanged a few baffling comments about carpets, and Kelvin said a few things about carpets himself: 'I like those really grey ones you get in offices,' and, 'Carpet tiles are weird, aren't they?'

What wasn't there to be said about carpets? They parted with great goodwill and mutual affection, and the old man shuffled off. I'll see him again probably, Kelvin thought, and smiled

He ended up outside the bright lights of the big 7-Eleven. They had things going on right on the doorstep, a party. People were accumulated on the pavement, with dogs· some of them wanted money, others wanted to smile and say things Kelvin patted all the dogs, every one. They were gorgeous and some of them seemed highly intelligent. There wasn't time to do proper tests,though.

The 7-Eleven was terribly, glitteringly, brilliantly lit It was like a Mediterranean cathedral at some particularly auspicious time of year. The staff were fat and torpid. Kelvin wanted to ask them things, but refrained. 'Why's it so bright in here?' and, 'I love working at night, don't you?' were some of the comments he rejected He searched one of the chilled cabinets for a can of drink He had a bit of a bad taste in his throat They were all lovely, bright and cold and impeccably consumer-tested, some new ones for the adventurous, some old ones for those in need of consolation, and some weird-looking foreign ones For foreign people presumably. He came to no decision.

This crime, he was thinking. What I'm going to do is get a cucumber or something in my pocket, and then point it at the cashier and say, 'This is a cucumber '

No, say, 'This is a stick-up. This is a robbery, I mean Please give me the contents of the till. When you get a minute.'

She might panic a bit, but I would smile and look saintly and she'd just do it I'd pay for my purchases with the money Then I'd get all the dog people in and I'd give them the money That would be brilliant.

He was wandering down an aisle which contained a promiscuous mix of household products and pet products and dried food. He lingered over different kinds of dog food, for the dogs outside. They were all fantastically nutritious, either completely balanced, or rich in some particular area. There was a man behind him, looking at washing-up gloves, and Kelvin threw a comment to him 'Wish I had a dog!'

The man ignored him, besides clenching up some shoulder muscles. He had a scar on his scalp where the hair didn't grow properly. He picked up bleach, bin bags (two packets), gloves What's he want all that for in the middle of the night, Kelvin wondered He was fascinated. Actually, he was fascinated by everything.

Kelvin picked up a tin. It wasn't the kind that had a ring-pull lid Need a tin opener as well, he thought, and went in search of one.

Marina watched a wave breaking and felt a sudden, cold thrill inside her. All time, suddenly, was here. There would be a future, but for now time had stopped and was held suspended, an endless breaking moment. She felt as if she needed to move, quickly, to get things going again

'Where's Kel gone?' Marina said suddenly 'Ward,' she said, 'where's Kel?' and Ward stirred and said, 'Who?' and reached out to touch her hand. She didn't look at him, and he laced his fingers through hers and lifted the hand to his mouth and kissed it No one said anything

'Sir?'

Kelvin looked up at him. He was very tall and spectacled He had bad skin, and a bright red shirt with a little stitched logo on the breast.

'Is everything all right?'

'Oh,' Kelvin said, and smiled. 'Oh, I see Oh, yes. Yes, you see I was just thinking about the dog food.'

'Thinking about it?'

'Yes, you know Perfectly balanced and particularly rich.'

'Were you going to buy some dog food?'

'I mean, if only you could put those two together, you know What a fucking dog food that'd be '

The young man was silent, shifting about beside him.

'And, you know, what a dog!'

'Sir, can I ask you to complete your purchases and move to the cash desk, please.'

The young man walked away and people muttered at the other end of the shop.

'Hey,' Kelvin called out after him, 'hey, have you got a dog?'

Kelvin came back just as they were going to go and look for him

'Kel, you've bought some dog food, then, I see,' Marina said, and he admitted that yes, he had. He just liked the tin, he said. And she had to admit that it was a fine tin, as tins went

They had the contents of some of the little paper twists and the last remaining joint. There were a great many things to be done, seemingly. The dope made them hungry, the cocaine made the idea of food slightly distant. Later maybe. They walked effortlessly, aided by the warm wind blowing in their heads. They could have walked for hundreds of miles, had the need arisen It would have been little inconvenience They were a bonded unit again, the cocaine held them together beautifully, and they would never leave each other's sides. The uncocained who passed them seemed small and dull and pointless. They four were special, chosen, uniquely important Kelvin and Marina walked arm in arm, and Steve and Ward took the piss from behind. The seafront was filling up with people staggering from pub to club, forming great disorderly queues outside the doors where the bouncers held sway, grimacing and fussing. Kelvin decided that they should join one of these queues, and they spent a happy half-hour getting to know the people in front and, later, behind. We've had a bit of cocaine, they told people, and everyone seemed happy to know, happy for them, happy about everything This was a brilliant club, they agreed, this was the best night. Marina gave away a few twists of cocaine, and people had little snorts off their hands.

The doorman let the others in, but stopped Kelvin.

'What's the matter?' Kelvin said, thinking, shit, this is it,

I've had it He prepared to brazen it out, and then the bouncer gestured to the tin of dog food.

'Have to leave that out here, son.'

'No dog food, eh?'

'No '

'That's the policy here, is it?'

'Absolutely no dog food inside,' he said, as if he'd been dealing with this particular problem all night. When Kelvin finally got in, the club was heaving and too hot and impossibly loud. He found the others, and they danced for hours. It was, Marina thought dimly, as the cocaine flared and retreated and flared again, in great warm waves, brilliant. Just brilliant She gave Kelvin frequent little pecks, and after a while became impatient to get him home.

weird water

The kitchen ceiling was indeed dripping lustily when they all got back home some time after five. The flat felt long-disused and strange The bags of cocaine were still there, lined up on top of the television. Ward, for whom euphoria had more or less worn away, to be replaced by a gritty feeling of depletion and general dissatisfaction with things, decided to go and give the wanker upstairs a good thumping. Marina, desperate for her bed, and prey to an intense, almost violent randiness, tried without conviction to restrain him Steve was all for it.

Ward banged upstairs and tapped on the door. Not surprisingly, given the hour, there was no response Ward waited for a moment, then knocked louder. Finally he set up a good hard pounding with the flat of his hand, which would give him trouble for weeks afterwards

The wanker appeared finally, looking bleary and bad-tempered, as he had every right to

'Ceiling's leaking again,' Ward said.

'Sorry?' The wanker appeared not to be able to believe what he was hearing

'You've made the kitchen ceiling leak. Again.' Ward had become huge and immobile, and the wanker had the good sense to avoid the confrontation.

'Oh, right. Sorry about that '

'You've made the whole fucking floor wet, actually Again.'

'Right, well, sorry . . '

'You're always doing it.'

'Yeah, there's something weird about the water up here . . . '

'There's . . ' Ward began, screwing up his face and tilting his head. He had a tense, hard little smile on his face He was looking increasingly dangerous 'Sorry, there's what about the water?'

'It's weird, it just seems to get everywhere '

Something about Ward's face, the glittering, slightly unstable eyes and the incredulous eyebrows, made the wanker think again 'I'll see it doesn't happen again,' he said. 'Really.'

Ward stayed in the doorway, not moving, an incarnation of rank irritability and pure cold hate.

'Better not happen again, pal,' Ward said finally 'This could be the last time, what do you think?'

'Sure. Absolutely '

Ward still had not moved. The wanker tried to shut the door on him, but Ward's foot and part of a shoulder were in the way Finally, grudgingly, he started to move back, and as he did so he caught a face behind the wanker's and stopped again

She had long black hair and a pale ghostly look, her eyes screwed up against the light from the hall She looked out and Ward looked in and suddenly leaking ceilings were the last thing on his mind The fury transmuted into something else that started to throb inside his jeans The woman peered out at him through sleepy eyes, and Ward allowed his face to thaw

'Sorry about, you know, waking you up,' he said, his voice gravelly now instead of icy.

The wanker shrugged, and the woman behind him hitched up the towel she was wearing, revealing for a second a creamy white neck and throat and upper chest. Ward was transfixed She was so close. He moved back another step, and the wanker shut the door Ward remained standing on the landing for a few moments. When he came back downstairs Kelvin and Marina were audibly at it in their room, and Steve was rustling about in his. Ward lay on his bed and gazed up at the ceiling, until the throbbing in his jeans decisively overthrew any rational objection to itself.

squinty woman

Everyone was difficult the next day, none more so than Ward.

Marina was up first. She'd woken remembering that it was today her parents were coming, to discuss her financial affairs, by which was meant her overdraft. There was some tough negotiating to be done. Sometime around midday, depending on the traffic. She surveyed the terrain.

The front room showed all the signs of last night's doings – candles left to burn into messy little puddles of wax, shreds of torn card and paper, ripped-up cigarettes, cushions all over the place. Ward's rolled-up tenner was still on the floor. She unrolled it and tiny traces of white powder fell out on to her hand She blew them away. The cocaine bags sat looking at her from the television. She went over to look at them The plastic was smooth and shiny, the bags were full. Even the bag they'd started last night looked full. She made sure it was properly sealed, then transferred all five bags into one carrier bag and deposited it in the fridge. She had the idea that it would keep better there And she didn't want it staring at her all day

Ward came out and joined her

'I'll mop up that kitchen in a minute,' he said.

They were reluctant to talk about the beach and the club and the cocaine, both of them It seemed like a faintly embarrassing memory, like the recollection of a particularly overstated argument. You were holding my hand, she thought, on the beach, and he thought, I was holding your hand.

'What happened last night when you went up?'

'He said sorry.'

'Did you hit him?'

'Hit the door,' Ward said, and rubbed the meat of his hand. 'I was going to go up and say sorry actually '

'That doesn't sound like you,' Marina said, and Ward gave her a hard look.

'Actually,' he said, 'actually what I thought I'd do was go up and say, you know, did he want to come down and maybe have a smoke some time, like.'

'Ward, the last time he was down here everyone was making wanker signs behind his back after ten minutes Don't you remember? He saw Kelvin doing it '

'Actually, I was thinking maybe you might be better going up than me You're more   . '

'Yes?'

'You know '

'You mean I'm nicer than you?'

'Yeah. Well, basically '

'Hm ' Marina turned the idea round 'Well, I could, I suppose.'

'And, you know, if he's got anyone staying . . '

'Like who?'

'Just anyone . . '

Marina shifted impatiently. Ward was one of those people you had to chisel information out of. She was bone-tired, she wasn't in the mood She was, she knew, going to have to clean the place up single-handed.

'Ward, has he got someone staying?'

'Woman. Long black hair Squinty eyes '

'I take it she's grossly obese, this woman, and over fifty and smells strongly of bleach and piss?'

'Not exactly '

'So you want me to go up and invite the wanker upstairs down, against all reason and established practice, so you can

101

have a go at squinty woman? Is that what you're saying? Solicit her for you for an immoral purpose?'

'Yeah '

'I'll think about it.'

'And I'll go and mop up the kitchen '

'Oh, that's supposed to make it worth my while, is it?'

'I'll make it worth your while,' Ward said, with a fair imitation of lewd intent, and Marina was about to remind him that she would not be experimented upon by ugly cunts like him, that she already had a sodding boyfriend in case he hadn't noticed, and would he please stop holding her hand on the beach all the time, when Kelvin came in and ended the conversation

Kelvin sat down at once, crossed his legs, recrossed them, finally stretched them out in front of him.

'Bit tender?' Marina cooed.

'Raw. Bleeding. Abraded.'

'Well, you would keep trying.'

'Oh, against your will of course.'

'I think I made my opinions on the matter perfectly clear at the time '

Kelvin looked pleased, and Marina gave him a disdainful glare

'Just one thing, while we're on the subject though, love,' he said 'About twisting .   '

chicken frenzy

Marina's mum and dad arrived just as Marina was finishing behind the cooker. She let them in and they came and sat in the front room and looked about at everything They looked defiantly cheerful and almost wholly out of place. Marina had tidied and cleaned things up as much as they would go, but to any sensible, middle-class outsider, like her mum, it still appeared to be some kind of appalling slum Marina insisted on showing them everything, how clean it all was, the bath and the kitchen surfaces She even tried to interest them in the place behind the cooker, but her dad was poking about in the fridge and saying, 'What's in the bag?'

She'd forgotten about the carrier bag in the fridge. Completely forgotten about it. She was silent for a minute, and the two of them regarded her strangely. She felt strange.

'Chicken,' she said finally. 'It's a chicken '

'Big chicken,' he said, still with the door open, and her mum looked in as well My, she said, yes, it is a big chicken, isn't it? How much does it weigh?

'Five keys Kilograms, I mean '

'What's that in pounds, Ian?' her mum wanted to know, and he was immediately screwing up his face and muttering aloud

'Eleven pounds, give or take,' he said.

Her mum looked at her strangely again

'Well, there are four of us and we all happen to be very into chicken,' Marina said. 'You know.'

She tried to drag them away from their poultry fixation and made them look into all the bedrooms, one by one, where she had posed everyone. Thus Kelvin was sitting at the word processor with his glasses on, looking busy He glanced up and smiled

'Kelvin's just working on something,' she said proudly.

The cushions were all stacked up nicely on the bed and the ashtrays were all hidden.

Ward was reading one of Marina's old course books, *Three Reformation Comedies* (Marina didn't want him to be seen with anything by Nietzsche – it might give the wrong impression, she said) and was sitting on a chair rather than lying on his bed. He'd shaved and damped his hair down He was all but wearing a tie and looked perhaps just slightly stiff

Steve had the paper open on his desk and was scanning the jobs pages, ringing things randomly though enthusiastically with a red pen Claire would have been greatly pleased He looked up and smiled winningly

'Hello, Steven,' Marina's mum said. 'Looking forward to your chicken tonight, I bet?'

Marina stood behind her and flapped her elbows about Steve smiled to gain time

'Yes,' he said, glancing from daughter to mother 'Oh, yes, you can be sure of that.'

Marina dragged the parents away and out of the flat, still going on about chicken

They went to the boring kind of café that her dad liked, and she fended off questions as best she could, her mouth dry and gritty with scone crumbs. How was everyone? Was Ward going to go back to college in the autumn? Was Steven going to get a job soon? They couldn't be happy just hanging round that flat all the time, could they? Shouldn't they be thinking about their futures? What was meant of course was, what about you? What are you doing there, with those people? Are they the right people for you to be with? Of course they couldn't say that

104

Marina found herself inventing the most ludicrous fantasies of future possibility for them all. Ward was indeed going to retake his first year, then he was going to get his degree and be a researcher for an MP or something. Kelvin was on the brink, the absolute verge, of getting a grant to do an art project, a really exciting one, it could really make his reputation. Steve was going to, Steve was going to play with himself until it fell off. No, no, Steve was going to finally buckle down in the autumn and take A levels, then go to university Oh, they were all going to be so successful and educated and gorgeous And of course, once she'd sorted out her finances, she was going to do her final year, starting in September She felt a warm glow of optimism start to grow inside her. She smiled and explained and improved. Her parents listened, with expressions of guarded scepticism. She directed the words to her mother, but it was her dad she was talking to

'Well, as long as you're all happy,' he said, and Marina felt her eyes start to fill up.

'We're fine,' she said, and reached for his hand. 'Honestly.'

'Look, love,' he said gently. 'The reason we came down, really, was to talk about money '

'Absolutely,' Marina said, and beamed at him They were so nice, her parents, she thought. This was going to be quite a negotiation, though Her overdraft currently stood at over £3,000 which was not a sum they could easily afford. She released his hand and straightened her face and posture, all business

'Right. Ready '

the wanker upstairs

Seattle!' said the wanker, and looked pleased with himself.

Kelvin looked at Marina and Marina looked at the floor. Steve, left alone to make a response, uttered a short, rather derisive bark The wanker seemed satisfied Kelvin rolled another one, and Marina sighed and tried to think of something to say, but she had temporarily lost the will to communicate Maybe even the will to live.

'Anyway, this other time .

It just went on and on and on, there was no end to it, no point to it, it was just the music of futility spilling seamlessly from the wanker's lips, anecdote and opinion and explanation, all of it equally self-referential, self-congratulatory, self-aggrandizing.

Ward, of course, was pointedly not looking at squinty woman, who had been introduced as Carola With an a What an unusual name, Marina said, and Carola smiled, sphinx-like (in her head), and said, yes, and wasn't Marina an unusual name too. This woman, Marina thought, has no underwear on. Baggy black combats and a zippy little top that had not been bought reduced at Warehouse. Expensive hair. Expensive boots. But somehow effortless, and not in the least alluring. And this woman, she thought, is not meant for Ward. Not in this life. Not unless Ward had hidden talents This was a non-starter

Ward wouldn't look at squinty Carola, for reasons which were obscure but compelling none the less. She had been brought down here, accompanied by Mr Very Interesting Indeed, precisely so that Ward could look at her, get a good proper look, let the dog see the rabbit. Maybe even talk to her, perhaps charm her, possibly captivate and fascinate her, to the extent, who knew, that she would follow him out to the kitchen maybe and, accidentally, brush his chest with her fingers, or allow her breasts to make brief, luscious contact with some delicious part of him. (It was a small kitchen.)

But of course none of this was going to happen. Would he so much as look at her? Marina had introduced her to him, and he hadn't looked at her, he'd just made some ridiculous sound, some kind of chimpanzee grunt sound, and looked away She had spoken a few times, and each time he had completely ignored her. She had asked him a polite question, and he had all but refused to answer.

This was all maddening enough. But the real problem was getting the wanker to shut up long enough so that another attempt could be made to get Ward to at least look, if not speak. The trouble with the wanker, though, which she had forgotten since the last time, was that he gradually ate away at your sense of the possible, he eroded your spirit, he turned you into a passive anecdote-hearing machine

' .. particularly in Seattle!'

'Huh ' Wanker

'Carola   ' Marina said

'But of course, what you have to understand . . . '

After a few minutes, you just endured You had no greater ambition than that the time should, finally, pass, that he would get up and go, that it would end Life would be good again

Kelvin was rolling the joint, as yet unroached, between his fingers Somehow or other, and Marina was not certain quite how, he managed to make the movement irresistibly reminiscent of the gesture that every male child learns, round about the age of ten. Hand loosely open, fingers curled, as if holding a fairly thick candle, say The hand slides up and down, from the wrist. 'wanker'. He looked up to see her watching him and the hand behaved itself again.

Steve watched the wanker's mouth. He was determined to get a comment in. Anything would do. Timing was all. He sensed the end of a sentence, actually a paragraph, and drew a breath.

' . . . unlike, say, Boston.'

'Yeah, it's interesting you should say that . . '

'Hey,' Ward said.

Four pairs of eyes turned on him. Marina looked startled. He seemed to be addressing Carola, though the stare could be interpreted in many ways, mostly hostile

'How long you staying, then?'

She blinked at him with her lovely dark, narrow eyes. She flicked the hair out of her face.

'Why? Do you want me to go?'

Ward flushed and muttered and stared at the floor. It was a disaster. He stood up immediately and went out to the kitchen, whence could be heard banging and muffled curses Marina heard the sound of the fridge door slamming

'   don't think they'd ever seen anything like me, not in   '

'Seattle?' Kelvin said, in a nasty sneery voice, which earned him a glare from Marina

'No, this was in Phoenix '

'Oh, really?' Steve said. 'And what time did you get to Phoenix? Was it by the time that she was waking? Or not?'

The wanker looked momentarily flummoxed, and Carola took advantage of this pause in the flow of things to go to the toilet

The passage that linked both kitchen and bathroom was narrow and somewhat dark It also had a persistent, faint damp smell, which was, to Ward, incomprehensibly but irresistibly sexy Ward emerged from the kitchen exactly at the moment that Carola was groping her way towards the bathroom, and for a second she was startled to find her way blocked by a great looming figure that, in the sudden semi-dark, she was not able at once to identify.

'Uh,' Ward said, and froze. She was inches away from him. He could smell her shampoo, almonds and coconut. In order for her to get past he had to reverse back into the kitchen. He didn't.

'Sorry, could I just . . ' Carola said, with a nervous little smile, and a few long, long seconds passed before Ward took the necessary step backwards.

'Be my guest,' he said, and she scurried past him.

Fucking weirdo, she was thinking. Fucking lurking weirdo. Ward stood in the kitchen, waiting for her to come back.

Inevitably, once the wanker took hold of the joint, that was it, and no one else got a smell of it unless they asked outright. Little gestures, stretching out a hand, or looking hard at it, got you nowhere. And, instead of smoking it, he just waved it around while he filled up the precious moments of the one and only life that any of them were going to have with his interminable bloody nonsense The wasted smoke rose up to join the pointless words. Occasionally he would take a drag, but, maddeningly, he did this right in the middle of sentences, so that (unless you were prepared to just be rude) you had to sit and wait while he inhaled, held, slowly exhaled and then continued the thought.

Marina had noticed that Ward and Carola were both missing at the same time, and attempted to put an optimistic interpretation on it. Things were going badly, true, but maybe if he could just be alone with her for a few moments he might be able to come up with something that would turn the tide Ward Ward Ward, she thought. She's so gorgeous.

Kelvin, pointedly, with great sighings and visible reluctance, started making another joint Steve was making wanker signs behind the wanker's back

They were all six back together again soon, Carola first and Ward sneaking up behind her. They were, respectively, worried and pleased. Not a good combination, Marina thought, not at all good. Not like lustful and trusting, or innocent and determined. Worried wasn't a good partner with anything, particularly not Ward There was something wolfish about his look that she didn't like at all.

Kelvin stopped making joints and the wanker decided, with much regret, that he had to go. There was an awkward huddle at the door, where everyone suddenly felt as if they should attempt to make up for the horrible conversational abyss that had just yawned before them all and try to talk to each other.

Marina, with practised efficiency, extracted from Carola some surprising information· she was a Roedean girl, her parents lived in Geneva, she herself was just back from 'a few weeks in Costa Rica', was on her way to New York with some people who were opening a gallery there. Her parents were in the process of buying her a little place in Brighton, but until then she was just sleeping on floors She was doing some rather nice little course at the Courtauld soon, the Brighton flat would just be for weekends. During this quite brief exchange she managed to use three words that Marina had never heard before

'You're fucking loaded, aren't you?' Marina said, and Carola said, oh, not really. Not really loaded. She did get a little allowance, but then she had a lot of expenses.

'God, I know just what you mean darlin',' Marina said. 'Tell me about it.'

Carola gave her a strangely inappropriate look and giggled. Marina thought she had even stuck her bum out slightly in a kind of shag-me-from-behind-guys-I'm-just-a-brainless-tart kind of way. Marina was shocked

Ward was watching all this, of course He looked pleased and hostile, even faintly menacing. Carola, quite rightly, didn't even try to say goodbye to him The wanker was still going as the door was shut on him. He could be heard continuing up the stairs and into his flat until the door slammed.

'This is the last time I do anything like that for you, Ward,' Marina said 'I mean it, that woman is strange. And what,' she demanded, 'are you looking so pleased with yourself about?'

Ward was the soul of reticence, would not be drawn. The perfect gentleman. She managed to get it out of Kelvin later, when they were having a lie-down

110

'He got a cop of her tit.'

'He got a what of her what?' Marina yelled, incensed, and Kelvin shushed her. Everyone was still slightly frazzled.

'She had to squeeze past him and his hand, accidentally and oh, so softly . '

'Yes, all right, Kelvin, I don't want all the fucking gory '

She was furious That poor, odd woman, flung into a houseful of people making wanker signs about her friend and then groping her in the hall

'So he's after her, then?' she said tentatively, and Kelvin nodded

'But he hasn't got a chance. Can't he see that? He's got as much chance of landing her as, as . '

'He's got more of a chance than the wanker.'

'Kelvin, the wanker's got zero chance. He doesn't even want her.'

'Less competition, then.'

'And what about you? Are you after a "cop" of her "tit" as well?' she said, giving the words a savage emphasis and jabbing him in the side as she did so. 'That was a flanconnade, by the way,' she said 'It's a fencing term It means a thrust in the side Carola said it '

'So?'

'Listen, anyone who knows words like "flanconnade" and has friends who open galleries in New York is not going to want something primitive and nasty like Ward pawing at her. You think for one minute that girl doesn't know what she's worth?'

'That's for her to decide, isn't it?' Kelvin said, looking smug He wanted to see Ward abasing himself in this hopeless quest, she knew it

'Poor Ward,' she said. 'I'm not sure he's really thinking straight on this one '

'He needs a good woman,' Kelvin said

'Like me.'

'Of course Everyone needs a woman like you,' he said gallantly, and kissed her neck, making her shudder He knew just how to do it

111

'Hey, I know. We'll clone me and then I can be issued to the entire male population at puberty. There could be vouchers.'

'Well,' Kelvin said, 'I think you may have cracked it there, love. Definitely.' He was keen to get on.

'We could clone Baz as well,' she said. 'And issue him too.'

'Would there be much call, do you think?' Kelvin said, his voice slightly indignant.

'Oh, I think there might be.'

'Shorts aren't everything,' he said, and began to illustrate the point.

She could only agree. They had a little more cocaine (just a little more) and she found herself agreeing with less and less reservation.

shaving mr universe

Ward was made to stand up straight where everyone could see him

'So. What do we think?' Marina said speculatively. 'What do we think about this?'

Kelvin grunted. 'Looks about right to me Got all the right parts '

Marina turned to him.

'Kel, "about right" isn't really going to do, is it? Let's just go over what we know about this woman, this Carola First thing, she's totally gorgeous Yes?'

Kelvin grunted again. 'If you go for that type, I suppose '

'You mean the totally gorgeous type?'

Grunt

'Second, she's very, very serious about certain matters which we might call swallowed-a-dictionary-have-we-darlin'-clever-bollocks things.'

'She's got a brain on her,' Ward said. 'What's wrong with that? I quite like a lassie with a brain on her, actually.'

'Yeah, and a tit or two, Ward As you, I understand, are only too well aware On the other hand, she is deeply frivolous in other ways She is a stranger to underwear or foundation garment of any kind, and she affects a sexy-kitten-sticka-my-bum-out-and-giggle kind of version of what she clearly thinks is femininity '

Kelvin shifted about in his seat.

'And she's rich. Very, very rich. So let's turn our attention to our lovely Ward here. Now. To start with, is Ward "totally gorgeous"?'

'Well, he's all right,' Steve said. 'He's what I call a good B, an upper B He's not bad.'

'No, he's not bad exactly,' Marina agreed. Ward was told to stand up straight and turn round 'He's better from the back, wouldn't you say?'

'Front, back, who's counting? Actually, I think he might almost be too much of a good thing from the back.'

'There's room for improvement.'

'Looks all right to me,' Kelvin said.

'Exactly. So where to start?'

Ward was told to walk up and down in front of the television Marina and Steve watched him closely.

'There's something a bit odd about the way he holds his shoulders,' Steve said, and Marina agreed.

'Drop your shoulders, Ward. Just drop them down a bit. You look like you haven't got a neck. No, not like that . . '

Ward moved his shoulders and his chest seemed to collapse. He looked neanderthal

'No Back as you were. We'll think about that later '

They watched him thoughtfully for a few moments.

'Marina,' Steve said, 'if you were getting ready to go out, what would you do?'

'I'd put on gorgeous clothes and fiddle about with my sodding hair for six hours '

'No, I mean what would you do first?'

'Have a bath, shave my pits, pluck, that kind of thing '

'Ward, have you had a bath today?'

Ward shook his head.

'Yesterday?'

Kelvin grunted, and Ward was dispatched to the bathroom. While he was gone, Steve and Marina courteously shared a line from the little dish on the television and discussed Carola.

'The thing I really hate about her,' Marina said, 'is that

she's a brainy tart. I don't mind if she's rich, but brainy and tart is just a particularly horrible combination of attributes.'

'She's not brainy, she just likes saying complicated things and intimidating people.'

'I wish Ward would find someone else. She's really not the thing.'

'Good body, mind,' Steve said in justification, and Marina had to agree

'Yeah, and doesn't she know it?'

'She's got no arse and her thighs are scrawny,' Kelvin said absently

'Beautiful arse,' Marina said, 'beautiful thighs,' and Steve nodded.

'She's quite muscley also. Did you see when she was opening the window, how muscley her arms are?'

'She's lean,' Marina said, 'and she's fit.'

'Eating disorder,' Kelvin offered.

'Fantastic hair,' Marina said.

'Good condition.'

'Good colour '

'Now, conversationally, would we say . . . '

'Ah, well, not easy,' Steve said.

'No, definitely not easy. Would we say difficult?'

'No, but you had to kind of get the hang of her, didn't you think?'

'Not quite completely human maybe,' Marina said, and looked thoughtful 'Kind of over there.'

'She was off her head,' Kelvin said shortly, in her defence 'She had her face in the powder Do you know how much she hoovered up?'

'When did she?' Marina demanded. She hadn't seen any of this She did, however, remember hearing the fridge door slamming

'In the kitchen Ward and her had a little line or three.'

'Was this before or after the copping of the tit?'

'What do you think? Before She apparently told Ward that she's partial to the odd gram.'

'Trapped in a kitchen with Ward,' Marina mused, 'I think I

115

might develop a partiality for any kind of escape.'

'Have they done anything yet?' Steve asked.

'No. Just the tit. He probably just brushed past her or something. It was probably nothing It probably wasn't even a proper feel.'

'Well, brushing past can be something,' Steve said. 'Depends.'

'But no snogging or anything?'

'No '

'And then of course conversation is going to be an issue with Ward, isn't it?'

'It's not his strongest suit, certainly.'

'He's not one of God's talkers.'

'He's a boring idiot,' Kelvin said.

'But hasn't the cocaine helped at all?'

'Oh, yeah, now he's a boring idiot off his head on cocaine,' Kelvin said shortly.

'Every girl's dream, then,' Marina said, and sighed.

'We'll just have to concentrate on the body,' Steve said. 'It's the body or nothing

'I wish he hadn't told her about the cocaine,' Kelvin said, 'I really do '

Ward returned from the bathroom.

'Don't you worry about a thing darlin',' Marina told him 'We can fix you.'

'Well, I think that's all we can do clothed,' Steve said after half an hour. 'I think it's kit-off time '

Ward was endlessly unwilling to remove anything. He held out for the better part of fifteen minutes, sitting stolidly with his arms folded protectively across his chest. Marina wheedled and cajoled and flattered, but to no effect. Kelvin finally said, oh, fuck's sake, Ward, show 'em what you've got, it's not that bad, and Ward, slowly, reluctantly, pulled his T-shirt up over his head.

'My God,' Marina said, and whistled softly.

What emerged was a large, heavily made torso covered from

belly to neck and across the throat in coarse chestnut hair. The hair ran down the back and across the shoulder blades, meeting up with a band of hair round the waist The only bare patches were the undersides of the upper arms and a triangular patch on each side below the armpits.

'Fuck,' Steve said, and sat back. Somehow or other he'd never seen Ward undressed before He had known that Ward was hairy, of course, from the forearms and the neck and the shins. Just not quite this hairy.

Kelvin laughed aloud and said something about *Planet of the Apes*.

Marina surveyed the terrain with dismay

'Just look at it,' Steve said distantly. 'It's incredible '

'I don't suppose anyone knows what Wonderwoman's feelings about body hair are?' Marina said, and Ward sat down and crossed his arms across his chest.

'Yeah, I do actually,' he said.

'How, for God's sake?'

'Asked her, didn't I? I says, bet you like a man with a bit of a welcome mat on him, am I right, love? And she goes, you what? in this really stupid snotty voice. So I says it again and she laughs and goes, ooooh, actually bodily hair makes me want to be sick, since you ask Those were her actual words '

'Bodily hair,' Marina said 'I like that Well, that's clear anyway ' She frowned at Ward 'Now, have you got any other little secret features?' Ward said not, but Marina had a nasty suspicion forming. She was thinking about a certain five-a-side match, and comparing two sets of legs Bazza's, which were visible, and Ward's, which were swathed in Adidas stripes right down to the foot

'Ward, I'm afraid I'm going to have to ask you to take off your jeans,' she said sadly, and Ward protested Definitely, definitely not, no fucking way and that's that

'Ward, lovely linguistic Carola is at some point, if things go to plan, going to want to see you with your kit off This is quite normal and is not to be feared But before that happens I want to see what you've got going on under there. Whatever it is, I have to see it. It may need attention Judging by the top

117

half, I'd say it's quite likely it will.'

Ward left the room muttering and returned wearing only a small white towel. He stood by the door.

'Jesus,' Steve said. 'Look at this.'

Ward's legs, right up to the edge of the towel, were luxuriantly hirsute, the same thick chestnut hair as on top, but if anything coarser, like coconut matting. He had hair on the first and second joints of his toes, hair on his instep, there even seemed to be some hair on his heels. 'In all my experience,' Steve said, 'I can honestly say I've never seen anything like this.'

Marina looked him up and down.

'Ward Ward Ward,' she said sadly, 'what are we going to do with you? Eh?'

'Hold still, tiger.'

Ward grunted and twitched. The blade was edging down his left pectoral towards his nipple. At its gleaming edge was a small breaking wave of oil and cut hair, behind it was a path of clear denuded white flesh. Marina was biting her lower lip in concentration Steve was watching, rapt. Kelvin had gone out to see an old college buddy called Neil, refusing to participate in or even observe such a barbaric ritual. Ward was stretched out on the sofa, the towel chastely round his midriff, his big hairy form oiled and still under Marina's razor. It was half-eleven, still hot. The streets were full of people yelling and staggering and arguing, their sense of the rational and the proper eaten away by heat and beer. The smell of the baby oil was thick in the hot room. Ward had been given a good big noseful to keep him happy while Marina brandished her blade, but she complained that his muscles were tight and awkward.

'Do you think a joint might loosen him up a bit?' Steve asked. 'He seems just a wee bit tense '

'Might It might just make him fear the blade.'

'Fear the blade,' Ward said distantly, his eyes screwed up hard.

'I think really what he needs is some alcohol Have we got

118

any alcohol anywhere?'

'Can of Special Brew.'

'That'll have to do it, then.'

Ward swallowed it in three long gulps, then was made to lie down again and relax Strips of body emerged from under the hairy coat. They looked white and artificial, like frozen chicken

'He may need a tan,' Steve said speculatively.

'I like a white body myself,' Marina said, after a moment, 'nice tight white body.'

'Do you think he's going to need a second going-over?' Steve said, running a finger down one of the white strips 'He still feels a little bit stubbly.'

'I never saw so much hair,' she said 'It seems a shame to touch it really, it's a phenomenon '

'It might have given him novelty value,' Steve agreed. 'This Carola might be kinky for that kind of thing.'

'What, like amputees and stuff?'

'There's a big market for amputees,' Steve said. 'I've seen it in the classifieds Callipers, orthopaedic aids, that whole scene '

'Multiple or single?'

'Oh, all kinds. Just as long as it's stumpy.'

'Stumpy,' Ward said.

The blade was travelling down his left flank now, across his side and down the edge of the belly

'That's the bit I like,' Marina said in a distant voice, 'the belly. Nice tight white belly '

She took her hand away and ran the blade down the sweep of deforested body 'Nice '

She drizzled more oil down him and massaged it in The hair was glossy and damp with it, mixing in with the sweat that was breaking out all over him, beading him.

'Everything all right down there?'

Ward nodded and she told him to be still

'This is going to take all night,' Steve said. 'I'll take a leg '

'Funny thing is, he's kept this from us all this time '

'I was thinking that,' Marina said. 'More than two years '

'You've been living with Ward for two years?'

'Two years,' she said proudly, and patted his leg. 'I must say, I did wonder. I thought maybe it was an unwise tattoo or something '

It was quarter past twelve, they were having a break. Ward was nearly finished, there were just a few rough patches, particularly round the throat and neck. He lay perfectly still, glossy with traces of hair in little streaks. His eyes were open now, but they seemed to see nothing.

'Ward,' Marina said hesitantly. 'Has anyone ever introduced you to the concept of the bikini line?'

Ward shook his head.

'Ah Well, you see darlin', we're not going to be able to stop just at the top and bottom of that little towel you've got on It's going to be necessary to, ah, go a little bit further '

'Higher,' Steve added helpfully 'Closer.'

Ward said nothing, and Marin glanced over at him He was lying motionless, his eyes locked on to the ceiling.

'Ward, what kind of underwear have you got on just now?'

No response.

'Boxers?' she called out in a determinedly bright voice. 'Mini-briefs? Tanga?'

'Pants,' Ward said indistinctly after a few moments, and Marina raised eyebrows to Steve.

'Pants usually means briefs,' he said 'I'm afraid it can mean polyester '

'Patterned?'

'All too often, I regret to say '

'High-cut?'

'Not normally. Usually years of neglect and too-hot washes mean sort of baggy and dangly.'

Marina took this in

'Ward, ah, have you got anything else?'

'I know something he has got,' Steve said when Ward refused to speak. 'I've seen it drying on your radiator,' he explained quickly

'What?' Marina asked. 'What is it?'

120

'I'll go and put it on,' Ward said, desperately trying to stave off the naming of the thing.

Marina and Steve waited in tense silence. Ward returned, still in the towel. He lay down, and Marina slowly untwisted the towel from round his waist.

Steve was made to go away to a safe distance while Marina etched away the hair from the boundaries of Ward's jock strap. He was rolled over to have his arse shaved, and a few final passes with the razor and he was finished

'OK. Let's have a look at it,' Marina said, and Ward stood.

Marina and Steve regarded him soberly for a few moments.

'Other side,' Marina said, and Ward turned slowly

'He's a god,' she said finally, and Steve gave himself a good hard squeeze in agreement.

'I'd shaft it,' he said, and Marina repeated it back to him slowly, disdainfully:

'I'd – shaft – it. Uh-hm.'

Ward ran a finger down his chest, and, reaching for his towel, winked.

'In your dreams, pal.'

noisy is the night

It was hot, even with all the windows open Shouts and bangings could be heard late into the night, a whole town seemingly unable to sleep, caught up in a single restless, sweaty, beery argument. Insomnia Central. Alarms and sirens sounded, and the throb of a sound system, miles away, sending out its subterranean four in a bar, came through the walls and floor The cars that passed also boomed, mobile parties, a sudden muffled thumping, and the occasional burst of metallic singing Tiny little black insects emerged suddenly, from nowhere, and clustered round streetlights. A vast moon appeared, hanging anxiously over the town and the sea.

Ward couldn't sleep. The cocaine was wearing away, leaving its growingly familiar feeling of restlessness and deprivation. Plus, of course, the fact that he was raw to the touch, itchy and perpetually dislodging fragments of shaved hair sharp as razors, from various crevices and crannies of his body They seemed to have some kind of navigational capacity, and their target was underneath the foreskin

He padded out to the kitchen and peered into the light of the fridge The bags of cocaine were all there, safe and sound, all wrapped up. He took one out and handled it, passed it from hand to hand There were beads of condensation on the plastic and he wiped them away with gentle fingers.

He put it back and wandered into the dark front room The

bowl on top of the television had been completely emptied, licked clean, by the look of it He returned to his hard bed. He was hard too, but nothing could be done with it, it was a stiff and painful, unproductive kind of excitement. He lay watching the ceiling. Over his head somewhere, Carola was lying, her body perhaps lightly beaded with sweat. Was she sleeping? And then above her, the sky and the great white moon. Up and up and up.

Half an hour later he was sitting up again. The room was dark, the curtains half-drawn. He lit a cigarette and lay quietly smoking. The erection hadn't abated

Back in front of the fridge again. He stroked his newly defoliated stomach The moon appeared at a corner of the kitchen window. He glared at it. Went back to his room. Lay down. The air was full of scents and cries from far away. Also something ticking, nearer at hand. He went out to investigate: the central heating clock had stuck. It said quarter to five. He tried to nudge it on, but it just stuck again, and clicked at him a few times. Quarter to five it is, then, he thought.

the lost language of central heating controllers

There were a dozen people in the room, six of whom Kelvin could name He surveyed the scene through clear, bright eyes: it was all candles and cushions and ashtrays There was a joint coming soon, he felt, though he couldn't see it anywhere Kelvin had invented a story to account for the cocaine· they'd just got a record deal, they'd just had their first advance They were blowing it on cocaine, in time-honoured fashion. People seemed ready to believe this for as long as was necessary. No one was arguing anyway

The party, if that was what it was, had been going on for some time. First the wanker had come down, summoned by booming through the floor, and squinty woman as well, of course. She was wearing a different striped zippy top with something like a ring pull on the zip fastener. She looked fantastic The wanker smirked until he was given cocaine. He clearly knew it was here because of squinty woman They didn't bring anything with them, except his big, big personality

Ward could name three of the people in the room, at a push He was lying on the floor, and talking to a woman who was wearing dark glasses. She'd been in the pub earlier, she and some others, and they'd come back after He couldn't have named her if challenged. She didn't seem to be taking much notice of what he was saying, but, then, neither did he. What was it he was saying anyway? He smiled up at her, and she directed her face towards a small dish by her side, from which she emerged a few minutes later, wiping her nose. She smiled down at him.

'What's your name?' Ward asked, and she smiled

'We've had that,' she said, 'and I've told you already, about a hundred times before. Remember? Like the television show?'

'Pets Win Prizes,' he said, and laughed when she did

Her accent was European, perhaps Spanish

'*Habla español!*' he said, and she blew a strand of hair out of her face.

'We had this. We had this already Don't you remember? About a half an hour ago. Not Spanish like Franco, but Portuguese like . . '

' . like . '

'   yeah, remember?'

'I don't know why I like you,' Ward was saying, 'because you're kind of stupid, but I like you.'

'Ho-neeey,' said Franco's rival. 'If I'm stupid . . '

'Wait a minute, we had this,' Ward said. 'If you're stupid, then I'm Butthead's arse. Was that it?'

'We need a drink,' she said, looking round for one The bottles in the kitchen were long exhausted, all that remained were the private stashes of canny individuals Ward didn't look like such a one.

'Butthead's arse's arse,' she said, smiling, and dug her ankle into his crotch. Ward smiled too, though only because she did.

'Arse's arse,' he said. 'Arse's-arse's-arse.'

The original little dish on top of the television had now mutated, cloned itself into at least five other, smaller, as it were satellite, dishes, spread round the room Someone would periodically take one of them into the kitchen for refilling Marina had tried adding cinnamon and castor sugar to improve

125

the taste, which, after a while, seemed to lodge permanently in your throat, a thick, rank, rather bitter taste They had taken to drinking Strawberry 20/20, which was the only thing viscous enough and sweet enough to do the job. The room was full of the sound of people discreetly snuffling It was like the day room of the common-cold research centre. People were talking and gesturing, smiling, passing things to and fro Someone had brought a new Playstation game, 'Frogger', which only really made sense when you had a bit of cocaine in you. Otherwise it was perplexingly stupid. It involved frogs crossing a road and getting squashed by cars. Everyone was getting better at it.

Marina found herself sitting by Carola, who was holding a cigarette very tightly. She looked determinedly bright.

'Having a good time, darlin'?' Marina said, and Carola nodded tightly. 'Listen, I just thought I'd should apologize for my pig the friend over there.' She nodded her head in Ward's direction· the Portuguese woman's foot was moving round in his crotch, and Ward was stroking the ankle

'Apologize?'

'Yeah, you know.' Marina gestured towards Carola's breasts, and Carola glanced down, confused.

'I hear that he copped a bit of a feel.'

'Did he?' she said. 'Oh, well, I didn't really notice, to be honest Is he all right?'

'He's harmless enough.'

'Is he your . ?'

'God, no,' Marina said, and backed away slightly. She tried not to watch Ward's curiously slow-motion ankle work 'No no no, that one's mine ' She gestured over to Kelvin, who was grinning broadly at a woman who was speaking very rapidly in his ear He nodded vigorously

'And I'm sorry about the, you know, the wanker stuff.'

Carola again looked blank, a bit of a bad habit in Marina's opinion She pointed in the direction of the wanker, who was explaining something to someone who was walking away from him rapidly

'You know, the . ' Marina made the gesture, and Carola watched her, astonished What was she suggesting?

126

'I don't really know what you're talking about,' Carola said, and Marina patted her arm and said to forget it, it was nothing

'Have you had any . . ?' she said, pointing to a dish She found that she was speaking to Carola as you might to a foreign visitor with slightly imperfect English Perhaps someone like Ward's ankle woman

Carola nodded and smiled. Marina detected controlled panic and guessed that she'd had too much

'I'll go and get you a joint,' she said. 'Would you like a glass of milk?'

It took a long time to get the milk, partly because there seemed so much else to do and partly because she kept on meeting people – some new, some old, they were everywhere. Everyone appeared to have what they wanted, or know where they could find it anyway. She found herself laughing hugely, and couldn't remember what she was laughing at The laugh stopped abruptly

Milk. She opened the fridge and the cocaine bags flung themselves out at her and knocked her over. Well, not exactly, but they were certainly very much there She went to take out the opened one and found, to her amazement, that there was now a just-noticeable surplus of plastic wrapping it She averted her eyes and took out the milk

Carola was talking to someone when she returned with the glass Or was listening to someone anyway The person speaking seemed to be an old friend of hers, he was murmuring confidentially, and they laughed easily Marina sat down beside her and her friend slipped away Marina gave her the glass.

'Who was that?' Marina asked, and Carola shook her head, don't know She sipped the milk

'Why have you brought me milk?' she asked abruptly, and Marina found that she had absolutely no idea

'You're being such a hostess,' Carola said. 'In fact you're being an air hostess '

'God, am I?' Marina said, and realized that it was so. She was, she realized, rushing round the cabin fetching cushions, looking after people, seeing that everyone was all right, until the co-pilot could bring this baby down in one piece.

'Are you displacing something?' Carola said, and Marina gazed at her in awe.

'Am I doing what?'

'You know. Instead of doing the thing you want to do, you do something completely different to disguise it. Displacement '

Marina glanced over at Ward. He was no longer there, nor was the woman with the beguiling ankle. Then Marina noticed a part of a body, a patch of elbow and forearm, sticking out from behind the sofa She stood up and tiptoed over to have a look Ward and the woman with the slightly imperfect English It had progressed from hands and ankles; now it was tongues and bellies and thighs moving against each other. Ward's jeans seemed, somehow, to have become slightly imperfectly fastened. She came back to Carola

'No, I don't think I'm doing that,' she said. 'Do you think I'm doing that?'

Steve crashed in at three o'clock with two others

'I found them on the seafront,' he said, exuberantly drunk. 'They're fantastic ' He showed them to Marina, who got them settled and found out what they wanted.

'Tea?'

They didn't smoke No, they didn't want any cocaine, thank you. They smiled and were impeccably polite They were both dressed mostly in black. The older of the two had a big, Australian cop-style moustache and a good-looking knitwear- catalogue-model's face The other had an oddly confidential look, as if he was bursting to tell you some secret he'd been carrying round with him all day

'They're from Crawley,' Steve said proudly 'They've come all the way from Crawley '

'From Crawley,' Marina said, 'really?'

'They just crawled out,' Steve said, whispering hotly in Marina's ear. 'Like slugs '

'I see,' she said, smiling at them as she felt Steve's spittle landing on her cheek.

They were looking round, signalling something to each other, a subtle matter of raised eyebrows and little twisting movements of the hand. She couldn't decode it exactly. The catalogue model smiled handsomely at her.

'And what are they for?' she whispered.

'They're for love,' Steve whispered back wetly. 'They're the love slugs.'

'Why have they come from Crawley?' Marina asked.

'I don't know, but try not to do anything startling I think all the tall buildings have confused them.'

Steve wandered away to find cocaine cocaine cocaine and found Kelvin sitting in a chair with his head thrown back and his eyes open. His mouth was slightly open also There was some cocaine on a saucer behind him, and Steve reached expertly round and retrieved it. Ah!

Hours later The music was some ambient nonsense of Kelvin's, the room was still full, still snuffling. Marina was talking to a big man with a square, ugly face and the most obscenely lewd eyes she had ever looked into. Light blue, the whites slightly bloodshot, heavy lids, the visible area of eyeball curved down at the ends, dolphin-shaped Very small pupils, despite the cocaine They blinked very infrequently, and slowly, these eyes, rather like a cow She had the unsettling impression of someone who would take pleasure in watching an animal being tortured. He had an almost disgusting carnality about him His smile was small and rather unvarying. Little teeth. Great thick irregular pitted nose. His voice had a pronounced Manchester accent He took little sips out of a small bottle of brandy he had stashed in his back pocket, and took very small, but quite frequent, snorts of cocaine. There was a small scar on the back of his head, where the hair didn't grow properly

Kelvin wandered over, looking lost, and said, 'Hey, I know that face '

They discussed it for a few moments Marina's man was polite but certain that he'd never met Kelvin before Kelvin wandered away again, feeling quite unmistakably dismissed, and the man turned his pale-blue sex eyes back on to Marina. He took her hand and placed it on his groin, which she had tried to avoid noticing The smile didn't flicker, and the raspy accent continued He was half-stiff and enormous, rubbery. He closed her fingers over him, squeezed, and the eyes narrowed just perceptibly. Marina felt a shudder of pure sex and put his free hand on her crotch. He took the hand away and lifted it to his face, sniffed it, ran his disgusting wet tongue all over the thumb, put it back in her crotch He had a very big, very thick, square thumb, traces of paint or ink under the nail. His eye didn't leave her She opened her mouth slightly and her eyes lost focus.

The party, if that was what it was, went on for hours, until full daylight, mid-morning. People drifted away, some slept on the floor and in the hall. Steve and the love slugs could be heard moving about in his room, which must have been uncomfortably crowded – things seemed to keep banging. They were having quite a time by the sounds. The house quietened down in the afternoon. Siesta time Ward came out to the toilet and the central heating clock clicked merrily at him as he passed. He waited for a second. It was silent. Then it clicked, twice Then once He gave it an absent-minded tap and went on his way

Half-past five and Kelvin was back in the kitchen, spooning out cocaine into a dish and settling in front of the television From the look of the bag in the fridge, he estimated that, so far, they had used somewhere between twenty and thirty grams – £1,000 to £1,500 – in one night. Who had all those people been? He pinched his nostrils and sniffed, wiggling his fingers. His passages felt cool and open, ready and waiting. Before you ever had cocaine, he thought, you were in perfect equilibrium Then you put it in, and immediately and permanently you were in disequilibrium, staggering from having it to wanting it to having it again, seeking a point of rest

He'd almost got there last night He'd been thinking about

130

art, about making an artwork. Something he'd hardly considered seriously since the débâcle of his degree show almost two years ago. Last night ideas had started coming to him, unbidden. Some kind of ultimate art object. He'd had the feeling that he was right on the brink of it, on the edge of something, he just had to reach a bit further. Almost there. He hadn't made it, though, and the moment had passed.

A line of cocaine, he thought, wasn't really a line at all, it was just the start of a line, a much longer line. You had a snort, you waited a bit, then the wind started to blow and you came up to this exhilarating place, just above the surface. Twenty minutes, half an hour in and you were plateauing, pure pleasure, total control, then it started to dissolve. Before you began to come down again you had another little snort. He was getting better at timing it so that the plateaus all joined up seamlessly. It was almost an artwork in itself, he thought, such skill. No, a line was just the beginning, the real line was several feet long, stretching out from the first one at regular intervals. It had its own rhythm, you just had to let it go to work. It lasted about twenty hours or so, then you were ready for a break from it. And then there was nothing for it, of course, but to try it all again. Get there, get closer, get more. When a whole roomful of people were doing this, Kelvin thought he could almost hear it, the roaring of the cocaine as it came alive, took over, took control. The individual people were just a vehicle, an expression of the cocaine's will Three days on, maybe two off, then on again On and on

If it was a party, it was well under way again by eight, and continued, on and off, for the next two days People came and went, faces became familiar, and disappeared again Ward decided that he needed to work the door: he stopped letting people in and politely menaced those leaving to minimize theft, which had probably been considerable already. Carola came and went, circling round him He gave her various blank looks, which he intended to express something but which, all in all, didn't. He felt cool and solid and heavy, perfectly controlled, a rock The flat reeked of stale smoke and old beer and sex fluids Great exuberant sticky stains materialized on the carpet and the furniture. At some stage the sink in the bathroom got cracked. Another time, Ward cornered Kelvin by the front door and started explaining something to him: Kelvin had no idea what it was, it was something to do with the central heating clock, which was speaking in code or something. He wasn't sure that Ward recognized him He was close, he was closer, he was nearly there. The curtains stayed adamantly pulled against the banal glare of daylight and the trivial world outside. Kelvin found that he was uncertain as to the day. He went out for cigarette papers and realized that he hadn't left the house for seventy-two hours He could barely open his eyes it was so bright out here. The headlines were all stories that were completely new to him Meanwhile candles dripped and melted into the carpet, bottles and cans filled up the corners and bin bags appeared everywhere, full of more bottles and cans and the contents of ashtrays. Kelvin found a quarter-ounce bag of grass thrown away By the end of three days they had used at least a hundred grams – £5,000. More than he'd had to live on last year. And that was still only a hardly visible dent in just one of the bags By this time the feeling of being on the brink, just one more snort away from something, nearly there, had become very familiar, but the art object hung still over his head, just out of sight. He still hadn't got there. The frogs jumped the cars, and the cocaine roared. On More.

Ward woke up in the middle of the night, and the flat was oddly silent Something had woken him up, though. He pulled his jeans on and stood in the hallway, listening

There. The central heating clock, ticking again. He'd been hearing this in his sleep, he was certain, for hours, and he'd been decoding it. He listened again.

'Two, then three, then one,' he said, and waited The clock was silent, then clicked twice. Then three times 'Come on,' he said, and it clicked again. Once. He gave it a good hard look and went back to bed.

the flood

The sound was coming from the kitchen It took about two minutes for the other three to gather, bleary and disorientated, their heads poking round the kitchen door. Ward was in there, hopping.

'Ward?' Marina said, slightly fearful.

'Just take a look at this.'

Marina looked where indicated. One of the cocaine bags was on the counter by the bread bin, open, on its side The plastic was slack, sagging, crumpled. Inside it there was a certain amount of thick white sludge. Coming from it was a long, white smear, like a comet's tail: there were dribbles down the front of the cutlery drawer and a pale white puddle on the floor Beside the puddle, the imprint of a foot, toes and heel, several steps, a couple of messy, dragging, partial imprints, drips, splashes. Everything very wet.

Ward looked as if he was hyperventilating, and Marina rested a hand on his shoulder

'Easy, tiger,' she said, but he ducked away from her and made for the front door She went after him Steve and Kelvin looked at the cocaine slick Kelvin heaved up a big sigh.

'Fuck,' he said 'The cocaine had an orgasm.'

Ward was filling the bath. The wanker was sat on the toilet. He had been advised, in his own interests, not to move.

Neither was he to speak. Particularly not speak. Not a word. He wasn't arguing. Squinty woman was nowhere to be found, much to Ward's chagrin. Marina was watching nervously from the door, ready to intervene if things took an actually psychopathic turn

'Now this,' Ward said, turning to the wanker, 'this is what we call "filling the bath".' His accent had thickened and deepened; his movements had become even slower and more deliberate than usual.

Water gushed from the taps. The wanker communicated messages of panic by writhing His mouth moved but no sound emerged. It was torture for him.

'Now just sit still there Don't be moving about No one's going to hurt you. Not much anyway. Not scared of a bit of water, are you?'

Marina had never heard him speak so much. Nor had she seen this particular look. It was the kind of look you had nightmares about. He was not wholly human. The wanker used more body language, to communicate distress.

'Water,' Ward said, 'it's really interesting, isn't it? What it does and that D'yous want to play with it a little bit? What d'you reckon? Yeah?'

The wanker opened his mouth, shut it again. The room filled up with steam.

Kelvin declared the kitchen a no-go area and took Steve out for breakfast to a nearby fry-up café.

'Ward might kill him,' Steve said, as they were choosing between breakfasts of varying degrees of enormity. 'There might actually be a death.'

'It wouldn't be a true death,' Kelvin said, 'because there wouldn't actually be a real live person involved at any stage Just a wanker.'

'Yeah, but I wonder if the police would think about it that way, Kel,' Steve said, and Kelvin considered this.

'Police can be bought,' he said at last, 'particularly with drugs Specifically, with cocaine.'

'Right, yeah, let's do it,' Steve said sarcastically, and Kelvin looked surprised.

'Yeah?'

'No, Kelvin. You need to know what you're doing with things like that. Ward isn't going to kill anyone anyway He's just letting off a bit of steam.'

'I had a dream about Ward,' Kelvin said. 'He had some animal in his room and he was experimenting on it.'

'Yeah, I had a dream about Ward, actually,' Steve said 'Not the same one you had, though, obviously '

Their breakfasts arrived hugely.

'Anyway, whatever Ward does, that's the wanker's problem. We need to think about how to retrieve the cocaine from its present wet condition,' Kelvin said. 'We need a plan.'

'And you just happen to have one?'

'Well, now you come to mention it . . '

The bath was full, right to the rim. Ward had blocked up the overflow hole by stuffing a face cloth into it. He swished the water around.

'See how when you move something in the water, even if it's just a little bit, it makes the water move as well. At the same time You watching now? Do you see the connection there? Between the two things? Nod if you do '

The wanker nodded.

'Do you see all the little waves and ripples, like?'

More nodding.

'Ward   ' Marina said, but he wasn't listening.

'Now, what do you think would happen if I put something right into the water? What d'you think might happen?'

'Ward, you're making me tense,' Marina said

'Can you think what might happen if I did that?' Ward had adopted a wheedling voice and manner, one that Marina found more worrying than his you-want-this-bottle-in-your-face-pal look

The wanker tried desperately not to speak, despite the provocation of the repeated questions His mouth writhed and twitched

'Shall we do a little experiment?' Ward said 'Just to see

135

what happens? Would you like to do that?'

'The problem with using any kind of absorbent material,'
Kelvin was saying, 'such as a cloth or paper, is that it will be
impossible to retrieve the cocaine from it. It'll just adhere,
and we won't be able to reclaim it. We could lose quite a lot
that way. Possibly thousands of pounds' worth. That's also
the problem with any kind of crude mechanical retrieval
programme.'

'Kel, sorry to interrupt, but do you think you could try
sounding a bit less corporate?'

'Was I? Sorry.'

'Actually, you sound like Claire, my benefit woman '

'Sorry. So, for instance, using a mop or brush of any kind is
out.'

'I know,' Steve said. 'I've got it. We need a team of cats. Get
the cats to lick it all up, then get them to be sick back into
the bag.'

'Look, there's a lot of money at stake here Potentially '

'Oh, come on, we've lost some, that's all We can just scoop
up what we can and bugger the rest of it We've probably got
just about enough for the time being, wouldn't you say?'

Kelvin looked shocked. 'What do you mean enough?
Exactly how much is "enough" cocaine?'

'There's tons of it.'

'Do you have any idea,' Kelvin said, like a shocked parent
confronting a prodigal child, 'how much we've got through
over the past four days or so?'

'Hardly any?'

'At least a hundred grams. At a conservative estimate. Now
at that rate what we have will last us .   hold on, two
hundred days.'

'Yeah, but Kelvin, we're not going to go on like that, are
we? Anyway, my God, that's nearly nine months Nine
months like last night? I'm not sure my dick would last that
long I think that might just be enough.'

'That's no reason to waste any,' Kelvin said primly, all but
adding 'young man'

Steve sighed 'Anyway, you haven't told me your plan.'

'You're going to love it.'

'Of course I am.'

Kelvin smiled up at him, loving the conspiracy, the whole thing, and leaned closer in. 'Allow me to demonstrate,' he said

'Let's start,' Ward said, 'with a hand. Just a hand Just put your hand in the water.'

The wanker didn't want to put his hand in the water. For one thing, it was hot. And for another thing, he just didn't happen to want to, just at that moment.

'Come on now.'

'Ward .'

'Just your hand, that's all I'm asking.'

The wanker approached the bath. Ward was standing beside it smiling, like an infant teacher cajoling the shy one to have a go in the sandpit The wanker didn't want to.

'All right, look, I'll put my hand in first, how about that?' Ward said, and dipped his hand into the water The level tipped up fractionally and a tiny glassy ripple slid off the edge and on to the floor

'See? Now you.'

The wanker moved his hand closer to the bath. Ward smiled and nodded encouragingly. His hand hovered over the water.

'That's right,' Ward said. 'Nice water '

The wanker dipped his fingers in and a few drops spilled out over the side

'Oooops,' Ward said, and punched the wanker on the side of the head 'Did you see what happened then?' He grinned like a maniac 'Shall we take a little look, like?' He pushed the wanker's head down until they were both bent over double 'Do you see? It's gone on the floor It came out of the bath and then it went on the floor. Now then, my question to you is, why do you think it did that? Hm?'

'Look, that'll do ' the wanker started to say, and was silenced by a sudden shove on the back of the head which bent his head uncomfortably into his chest. 'Fuck .'

Ward lowered his own head to the wanker's and held a finger to his lips. 'Shhhhh. Now,' he continued, 'let's see what happens when we put your fucking head in the water, Archimedes.'

Kelvin had made a puddle out of salt and tea, and had pulled it into shape with the tip of a teaspoon. He outlined his procedure to Steve, illustrating his point by reference to the sticky mess on the table.

'Kel, it's brilliant. It has all the hallmarks of your genius,' Steve said finally, and Kelvin nodded in modest acknowledgement.

'Not too complicated?'

'Perhaps a little bit complicated. But elegant.'

'Thank you. Listen,' he said, suddenly confidential again 'Look, I want to ask you something. About Marina.'

'What about Marina?'

'Well, is she – what I mean is, is she serious about .. you know?'

Steve was genuinely mystified. 'Serious about what, Kel?'

'Nothing.'

'No, go on.'

Kelvin sat back and looked out of the window, and Steve abruptly felt rather sorry for him, he wasn't certain why He seemed to have a cloud around him.

'It's just that she keeps on mentioning it,' he said, not looking at Steve

'Kel, you have to tell me what it is, because I don't know.'

'Bazza's bloody rugby shorts, since you ask '

'What?'

'She keeps going on about Bazza's shorts, Bazza's bloody legs, Bazza's arse .   The flower of sodding British manhood or something.'

Steve couldn't help himself and laughed out loud He reached over and patted Kelvin on the neck. 'Kelvin, look, it's not Bazza you've got to worry about,' he said, remembering Marina's sure hands travelling down Ward's oiled body, and stopped.

'What do you mean?'

'Nothing. Nothing. Look, Marina's mad about you, she's always telling me. All the time.'

'Does she talk about my legs?'

'Ceaselessly! Does she talk about your legs? She talks of nothing else, obviously. If I had a pound, Kel, for every time . . '

'I mean, they're not bad.'

'You've got fantastic legs,' Steve said, indignant that any other possibility was even being aired. He lowered his voice when he noticed that they were attracting looks. (Taxi drivers used the place.) 'I mean, all right, perhaps they're less . '

'What?'

'I don't know I think the word I want is "Wagnerian". They're perhaps, maybe, just a whisker less Wagnerian than Bazza's '

'So?'

'That's what I'm saying! So what? Could Baz have come up with your plan just now?'

'I suppose not.'

'Of course not Look, I'll get you another cup of tea. Stop worrying about it. In fact, stop worrying about everything, Kel Really '

Ward watched with folded arms as the wanker sat, fully clothed, in the bath.

'I can still see your head,' he said.

'My head?' the wanker said, and Ward leaned forwards.

'You got a problem?' he said.

The wanker shoved his head under, then came back up. 'OK?'

'Fine,' Ward said 'Now you can come out again.' The wanker started to lever himself upright

'There's just one thing,' Ward said, running the tap so that the bath was again brimming at the edge 'You can come out, but only if you don't spill one more drop of water. If I see one more drop of water on that floor,' he said, now more parent than infant teacher, 'then I don't know what I'll do I might have to hold your head under again I don't think you liked that last time, did you?'

'How can I get out without spilling water?' the wanker said

Ward shook his head sadly. 'Yeah Bit of a problem that, I have to agree.'

The wanker moved and water sloshed, and Ward belted him on the side of the head again.

'Oooooops,' he said

'Ward,' Marina said, 'would you say that you're experiencing any of the following irritability, mood swings . . '

Carola's face appeared round the door, behind Marina's.

'Is everything all right?' she said, and Ward straightened up.

'Why is he in the bath with his clothes on?' she whispered to Marina, and the wanker looked over at her.

Ward looked at the wall behind Carola's head.

'We're just playing,' he said finally, and Carola snorted and tossed her hair a little. 'All in fun,' he said, and she shook her head.

'Are you, like, holding him in there?' she said, her voice more exquisitely disdainful than ever before. 'Does he want to be in there?'

'I'm not stopping him if he wants to get out,' Ward said, holding up his hands and sounding indignant. 'Do I look like I'm holding him in there?'

Carola snorted again, and Ward stood back, breathing heavily, hands dripping. She looked at him for a moment, then went away, with Marina following.

'Listen,' the wanker said, clambering out and dripping everywhere. 'Listen. Word of warning I think you're having a bit too much of the white stuff '

'You do, huh?'

'Oh, yes I've seen it before I'd wake up and smell the smoke if I were you ' He started towelling his hair

'You would?'

'Oh, yes I really would.'

'You were good,' Marina said, as she and Carola sat in the kitchen 'I was impressed.'

'So, look, is he some kind of weirdo or something?'

'What, our Ward? Well, now you say it like that, I suppose

'He just seems a bit unbalanced.'

'Hell, no, he's just . . . ' Marina cast about for a word and realized that 'weirdo' was actually it. 'He's a lovely boy,' she said. 'In fact I wanted to talk to you about that some time, when you've got a minute.'

There were wet sounds from the bathroom and some muffled thumping.

Carola listened to what Marina had to say with a look of incredulity

'But he hates me,' she said. 'He keeps asking when I'm going.'

'Well, actually, no. You see, Ward – well, he's not very highly skilled at speaking. So when he said, "How long you here for, then?" what he wanted to say was, I'd like to go out with you and maybe get to know you a bit better before you leave And not, how much longer have we all got to put up with you, then Which, I agree, is how it might have sounded.'

Carola eyed her steadily.

'You're saying he wants to go out with me?'

'That's it.'

'With me, and not with you?'

Marina laughed. 'Me? I've got one already, remember One's enough.'

'Oh,' Carola said, obviously confused 'You know I just thought, I mean I'd picked up the impression . '

'No no no And no again. No, it's you or bust for our Ward. So to speak.'

'Well,' Carola said and sighed deeply. 'Well, I could, I suppose '

'What can it hurt?'

'Yeah,' Carola said, though she sounded less than convinced. 'Well OK, then. I suppose.'

'Don't worry,' Marina said confidingly. 'I'll have him all ready for you. I'll see he gets a bath '

Carola smiled bleakly 'Oh. Great '

operation clean sweep

'Phase One,' Kelvin said, and produced his first prop from the table behind him, a dust mask: 'Regularization. One person – me – will go into the room marked Extreme Caution! Expensive Drugs All Over The Floor! He – I – will centralize all the cocaine mixture into one pool using – ' a flourish inside his shirt – 'this palette knife The wet residue still in the bag, the dribbles on the counter and down the sides, all of it will be expertly gathered together, and amalgamated with the main deposit, on the floor. I, as I say, will be responsible for this crucial procedure.'

'Why you?' Marina said

'Because I have the nerves of a surgeon and the hands of an artist '

'And great legs,' Steve added, and got puzzled looks

'Now, Phase Two '

Kelvin rummaged behind him and swivelled round

'Kelvin, why are you holding a phaser in each hand?'

'Not a phaser, sweetheart, a hair-dryer '

'Hair-dryers on stun,' Steve said automatically 'Perm me up, Scotty '

'Now,' Kelvin continued, 'I have found two hair-dryers in the house One of them is Marina's The other one . '

He paused, and eyes gradually turned to Ward.

'Ward,' Marina said, 'I didn't know you had a hair-dryer '

'Well, you know what that means,' Steve said. 'Has he got a handbag as well? Is that where you found his hair-dryer?'

'May I continue?' Kelvin said archly, and switched both hair-dryers on in one smooth movement

'Phase Two· De-liquefaction. We very, very gently and slowly blow warm air over the cocaine slick. After a while the consistency will begin to change Instead of being a liquid, it will begin to take on the properties of a paste.'

He had to shout over the noise of the hair-dryers. He switched them off again and rummaged behind him.

'Phase Three,' he said, and turned round brandishing a toothbrush. 'Compaction Once the cocaine solution is thick enough, we will brush it, slowly and cautiously, using a toothbrush, just like this, into a smaller, more compact shape. The puddle will be transformed, over whatever period is necessary, into a neat, manageable heap of cocaine paste '

He handed the toothbrush to Marina to inspect. She cast her eyes to the ceiling and passed it to Ward, who flicked it back at Kelvin It bounced off his head.

'Phase Four Retrieval Using – ' more rummaging – 'very small spoons and a knife, such as these, the paste will be scraped up and placed in a suitable container, which I would suggest to be – ' rummage – 'this margarine tub. Which will take us, effortlessly, to the fifth and final phase . . '

This time he took slightly longer His audience shifted about. When he turned round he was holding a large white metal object.

'   twenty seconds on medium in this microwave. *Fini* Questions?'

'Yeah,' Ward said 'Why does everything you say and do have to be so totally tedious, Kel? Just bin it and start another bag. Who gives a fuck?'

'Irritability,' Marina said excusingly 'Ward's got things on his mind '

'His what?'

'Yes, actually, our Ward here,' she said, proudly patting his leg, 'has got a date '

'Oooooooh,' everyone said, and Kelvin looked incredulous

'With what?'

'Guess,' Marina said, hardly able to contain herself.

'Not the Weird Woman From Upstairs,' Kelvin said.

'Lovely Carola, that's right.'

'Why?'

'Well, why do you think, Kel?

'Rather her than me,' he said, and gathered up his props.

Ward stood up and left the room. The taps in the bathroom came on, seemingly all of them at once.

Steve regarded the assorted implements and shrugged sympathetically. 'Maybe the cats would have been better,' he said.

fucking irish

Ward and Carola sat in Rosie O'Grady's. Ward hated it, the beeriness and the senseless bellowing and the thumping, leering, violent music that shredded the nerves like cheese wire Carola was in her usual combats and zippy top. They were drinking fast, pints of Caffrey's. Even the very short delay during the 'settle' period of pouring seemed awkward

'He's just letting it settle,' Ward said, and Carola tried not to look anxious They spoke very little. 'Have you ever been to Ireland?', 'Have you ever been here before?' and 'How long are you staying?' were the best Ward could do. She was staying for another week, then she was moving into another flat with her friend Mal, then after that she was . . 'What's Mal short for?' Ward wanted to know, and had to say it three times before Carola could hear him. She shouted the answer back He couldn't hear it. He didn't care anyway They both looked away It seemed to be getting more Irish every minute. The floor was bare wood, and every time one of the stompy fiddly records came on feet would, obediently, start stamping. Hands would hit the tables. Everybody was on percussion. Everybody was Irish Ward looked belligerent. He kept meeting people's eyes and holding them.

'Fucking Irish,' he said, when they had sat down. It was exactly this kind of comment, he remembered, that had made him first realize that he had no place on a modern history and politics course. It had been something of a shock at the time. He'd just naturally assumed that everyone thought the Irish were a waste of space, that the French were pathologically submissive, that the only nation worthy of respect were the Germans He could still remember some of the faces they'd pulled. Unbelievable. Carola cupped a hand to her ear, smiling

'Fucking Irish,' Ward said again, louder. 'I said fucking Irish.'

'This isn't real Irish,' she yelled at him, 'this is just Oirish.'

'What?'

'Oirish!'

'Fucking right,' Ward said emphatically, and sat back. It was her turn to get more Caffrey's, but his glass was empty and hers was a quarter full. There were going to be an anxious few minutes He decided to take advantage of the delay by going to the toilet. 'Slash,' he said, and pushed his way through

He tried to think of things to say to her on the way, but all he came up with was 'Are you staying long?' which, of course, had been asked and answered already. Not that he could remember what the answer was He hadn't been listening. He had a crafty little snort in the toilet, balancing his twist of paper on the cistern, and snorting off the back of his hand. Not all of it found his nose. He elbowed his way back and surprisingly soon the light seemed to clarify and the music opened up and there was more perspective and more depth and more time. He slapped the table and smiled She was staying for ages, apparently. There was lots of time.

'Git Gwaaaan!' Kelvin stood in the doorway, masked and gloved, and flapped his hands at the cat who was licking delicately at the pool of cocaine The cat looked up at him coolly – I'm sorry, did you want something? – and dipped its head back into the puddle Its tongue was perfectly adapted for the task. By the look of things, Kelvin calculated the cat had so far had about £200 worth

'Marina,' Kelvin called, 'could you give me a hand a minute?'

Marina brushed past him and picked the cat up, stroking its head as she carried it to the open kitchen window There was a trail of little pussy prints in bright white cocaine solution across the floor and over the dirty dishes by the sink There were also neat little piles of pussy sick here and there. The cat was clearly in two minds about the cocaine.

'Someone seems to have left the window open. All day. Kelvin.'

'Fucking animal,' Kelvin said.

'And, by the look of the prints, this wasn't its first visit I think it may have developed a taste for it '

'Well, at least we know what it was cut with,' Kelvin said 'Lactose. Powdered milk, basically '

'That cat,' Steve said, 'had exactly the same idea as me I think it must be some kind of telepathic supercat '

'It could be a specially trained police cat,' Marina said. 'They train it to sniff out drugs and eat them, then they tag it and follow the trail of sick back to the house '

'Cats are vermin,' Kelvin said shortly, 'and they should be clubbed to death wherever practicable. Particularly the telepaths '

The animal in question was hanging round on the window ledge, turning in tight little circles and rubbing up against the window.

'I think we might have a pussy junky on our hands here,' Marina said 'That cat wants rehab '

'That cat wants clubbing,' Kelvin said. 'And I'm not clearing up the sick.'

Operation Kelvin-bollocks was going fairly well, it even seemed to be working. Steve and Marina were playing the hairdryers over what remained of the cocaine slick, while Kelvin watched He was, at least in his own mind, supervising

'It's a shame there aren't any cormorants tangled up in this,' Steve said, 'or we could get *Nature Watch* here '

'It's always cormorants,' Marina said. 'They should look where they're going. How come they don't know an oil slick when they see one?'

'They have failed to adapt to their new environment, which is an oil slick and a camera crew, and thus are destined to disappear,' Kelvin said 'We really shouldn't interfere with nature.'

'Let's club them too,' Steve said. 'Club the whole lot of them. We could call it a sport.'

They fell quiet. The hair-dryers whined softly.

'I've been thinking,' Kelvin said suddenly 'I think we should be a bit more careful about things. We've got to stop having parties all the time That cunt upstairs hates us now, thanks to Ward's stupid little tantrum. He could just go and ring up the police or those bastard *Crimestoppers* people and tell them that there are always drugs here. People were just turning up, did you notice that? Well, who were they? We're lucky we haven't got every cokehead from here to Balham banging on the door We've even got cats hanging around, for God's sake It's beyond a joke We could get raided any time, and cocaine is Class A, which is gaol time, first offence or not. We should just tell everyone that there was some and it's all gone now, and we should be a bit quieter about it generally '

Marina and Steve looked up at him. He was right, of course, and why hadn't they thought of it? They were getting sloppy

'Tell you what else I think, I think we ought to divide it up Four ways straight.'

'What, this down here?' Steve said.

'No, I mean the whole lot I think we should take a bag each and divide up whatever we get off the floor . . Because, thinking about it,' he carried on after a minute, 'someone left it out on the counter in the first place. Someone's being careless. We're all being. It's so expensive, this stuff. Would be, anyway '

'Who gets the cat sick?' Marina asked.

Ward and Carola stumbled in late and found the cocaine all cleared up from the kitchen floor Carola opened the window to clear the smell of sour milk and vomit

'Ward,' she said, 'why is there a dead cat on the window ledge?'

straight line

Carola came down the next evening. They were playing 'Doom' and no one spoke much. Marina told her to help herself to the cocaine, and she took a few delicate sniffs Ward, of course, would neither look nor speak, and Marina was obliged to keep smiling and offering cups of tea.

Ward scratched a bit and then went away, into his room. He was very close to finishing *Ecce Homo*; after that there was nothing for it but *The Satanic Verses*. He lay down on his back and held it up It weighed several tons It was going to take some reading, he could tell just by the smell of it.

Carola looked at Marina, who shrugged and gestured that she should go and follow him

'No good waiting for an invitation, I'm afraid, darlin',' she said. 'He wasn't brought up proper '

Carola tapped almost silently on Ward's door and he grunted She sneaked in. Ward put the book down and lay looking at the ceiling, hands behind head *Ecce* There was no hiding his mounting excitement

She giggled and told him to be still There was a subdued shout from the next room as Kelvin got on to the next level, finally It had taken him long enough, Ward thought

Ward was fully erect, perfectly stiff, aching He was still fully dressed. Carola gave him a bold look and unfastened his

149

jeans, easing him out, with some difficulty. He watched her impassively. Carola carefully unfolded the wrap until she had a pouring edge, then laid out a line along his cock. It was of necessity a nice long line. She rerolled the wrap and took a fiver off his bedside cabinet, slowly rolled it into a tube She pushed her hair back and lowered her head. Ward stiffened further, twitched, and a few grains rolled off. She took the whole line in three snorts, starting at the base, ending up at the glans She sniffed it all in, then laid out a second, thinner line She licked a finger and slowly, gently, worked the cocaine into a paste and worked it into the flesh of his cock The skin cooled, then all but froze.

'That'll slow you down a bit, big boy,' she said, and lowered herself on to him

'Good God,' she said, 'you're not tellin me you're like this all over?'

''Fraid so.'

She had accidentally revealed an area of belly, and was now stroking it in amazement. He was stubbly for as far as the eye could see. She took off her zippy top and he undid the first two buttons of his shirt and pulled it over his shoulders. She rubbed against him. 'Good fucking God,' she said again, distantly Smooth didn't seem to be all as far as she was concerned.

Ward lay still, eyes on the ceiling. He didn't feel terribly involved, somehow.

She stopped suddenly and sat up He pulled the duvet over both of them, and she rested her head against his neck, fiddling with his stubbly jaw.

'It's all right if you don't want to,' she said.

'I do, honest,' he said, but the evidence was against him.

'Do you think Marina's listening outside the door?' she whispered, and they laughed. 'She seems to be more interested in this than, well, for instance, you.'

'What do you mean?'

'Well, I mean, this must be how those pandas feel. All the warders watching and taking their temperatures and

150

everything, but they just don't feel like it. I don't know. Do you feel a bit manoeuvred?'

Ward lay beside her and stroked her hair, and she fell asleep He wanted to wake her up and talk to her but she was out cold. Maybe she'd wake up again a bit later on. Mind you, what it was that he'd talk to her about, he had no idea. Pandas maybe. After a while she started to snore gently, and Ward patted her leg and got up. He went back to the front room and sat watching the others play 'Doom' Kelvin was getting slaughtered on his new level

Marina raised an eyebrow to see him back again, but he ignored her, and she said nothing.

the difference between 'sleeplessness' and 'insomnia'

'All I'm saying,' Kelvin was saying, 'is that we should not have any for seven days.'

'Why seven?' Steve wanted to know

'Because it's a nice number. Seven days we don't have any, then we can have some more. We all need a rest. And we need to, you know, just quieten down a bit We're drawing attention to ourselves.'

'It'd need policing,' Steve said, 'or I'd cheat. And she would.'

'We hide it again. Like before.'

No one spoke.

'We've been whopping it. Every day for twenty days now. I've counted. Does anyone want to know, approximately, what we've spent on nasal gratification in the last twenty days? Would have spent Approximately, not counting wastage due to telepathic junky police cats, etc '

No one did

'He's a cunt isn't he?' Steve said, and Marina nodded.

'He's the king of cunts.'

'Cunt,' Ward said.

'Would anyone care to hear the World Health Organization definition of "addiction"?'

'Would anyone care to hear the World Health Organization definition of "cunt"?' Ward said.

Kelvin glared at Ward, who glared straight back, and Kelvin subsided.

'OK. Listen. Twelve hours. No one has any for twelve hours, that's twenty to eight tomorrow morning. If we manage that, then we can keep it. If we can't, then we lose it for a week'

'Then what?'

'Then we divide it up'

'So what you're saying,' Steve said, 'is that in order to keep it we've got to stop having it.'

'Yes'

'Kel, were your parents in some kind of weird cult or something?'

'Something made him like this,' Marina said, 'it's not his fault'

'And the worst thing about him is that he's right That's what I hate about him.'

The cocaine was put back on top of the television, four fat puppies now and a bag three-quarters full of a slightly caky white cocaine composite, not the nice fluffy white flaky powder as before The drying out had not been completely successful

They played 'Doom' again Muffled noises of random slaughter and perpetual menace from behind, against a continuously modulated machine hum of claustrophobic panic. Fast, scuttling, insectile movement. At nine they went into Rosie O'Grady's and downed tequila and pints of lager Kelvin started to say something about how much they were spending on alcohol and shut up fast There was no shortage of money anyway. Steve had found someone to sell the odd, very approximate, gram to. It's true, he said, incredulous You really can get fifty a throw for it Unbelievable They could drink all night if they wanted to. All week

They fell out of the pub at half-eleven, grim-faced, gritty round the eyes, but not really drunk, it just wouldn't happen

Ward was looking evil. Kelvin seemed fidgety and apologetic, and Marina held his hand. They got back to the flat, and the cocaine was still there. They watched T. J. Hooker on television and opened a bottle of wine. The time passed jerkily They called it a night just after three.

Steve couldn't sleep He'd given up trying and was flicking through the contact pages of a mag he'd picked up somewhere recently. The ads were a lusty mixture of things: arch, coy, obscene, insane, desperate, all sorts. Many of them were composed almost entirely of codes and strings of letters, which gave them the quality of short poems written in a foreign language or descriptions of second-hand cars.

'Ex-services, 6' 3", 10", No. 1. Into boots and used jocks, seeks guys any age for regular training sessions in fully equipped playroom. CP, TT, yellow,' for instance. Some of the codes Steve knew, many he didn't CP was corporal punishment, TT was tit torture, yellow was pissing. He was happy not to know too much about it. GSOH, which came up all the time, was 'great sense of humour', and invariably accompanied the saddest of the ads, such as 'Mature, cuddly bear, likes pubs, restaurants, GSOH, seeks twenty-yrs or less for good times and maybe more. Could you be the special one?' Decoding this was slightly more of a challenge, but it went something like 'Old, fat alcoholic, into self-pity, with no sense of humour at all, wants very young men and is willing to pay '

Steve read idly on He'd never had even the most jokey intention of answering one of these things

'5' 3", gym-trained, wants you to use my hot filthy arse, into piss shit and recycled lager, use me like a pig. Fuck me with your huge stiff fat cock. Piss in my mouth. Bigger the better ' This decoded as 'I have an overheated erotic imagination and like to talk dirty I have an obsessive cleaning fixation and my house smells of bleach.'

'Cute, slim, GSOH, seeks similar for safe fun and maybe one to one ' Skinny git who giggles all the time and only wants to snog all night. Has not got the body of a man

Perhaps has undescended testicle.

Then Steve read this: '6' 1", No 1, chest 56", biceps 20", cock 9" Leather/military. 43. Into pain, obedience, discipline No time-wasters Time is short.'

It was the last three words that caught Steve's attention. The urgency of the thing appealed somehow. He dialled the number, left his number, and then settled down to try to sleep again. He was working tomorrow

Ten past five For God's sake. He got up, laid down, read a book, stared at the ceiling. The question circled endlessly round and round his head, like a little electric train, fuelled by cocaine. Was this 'sleeplessness' or 'insomnia'?

He was awake all night and went out as soon as it got light, pausing only for a little snort from the open bag on the television Kelvin could fuck off with his puritanical nonsense

Kelvin heard the door slam. He'd been awake for about half an hour. His hand had been jammed into Marina's crotch for some reason, and he pulled it free She was sound asleep beside him He'd been dreaming of his artwork It wasn't enough for it to be just some dumb object, it had to be a completely new type of object He'd been so close to it when he was on the cocaine, now it seemed to have sunk down into his brain again, and was only surfacing in dreams which he couldn't remember He sat up in bed and reached for paper and a biro He made random marks, but the shape, the look of the thing, was eluding him. All he could come up with was a box It resembled a coffin

It looked as if they were going to make their twelve-hour deadline anyway, which meant that they were going to keep the cocaine, for the time being. He was glad and not glad. In a way, he wanted just to be rid of it, all of it It was fantastic, it made you feel like a god, it turned lights on all over your brain, parts you hadn't even known were there It was the best sex drug he'd ever had And yet The image that that funny leaflet woman had used crept into his mind. someone, a guest, just sitting on your couch and eating, eating, eating, on and on

Eating, he thought, something about eating, but the thought fell away again like a wall collapsing The artwork had something to do with eating. It would come, he was sure Maybe when he'd done it, then he'd just finish on the cocaine. Marina could do what she liked, but he'd had about enough of it. Nearly enough anyway. He tried to get back to sleep.

the biggest jeans ever manufactured

Ward had been to the club once, several years ago, and had not liked it. The building was a long-deconsecrated church, a hideous Victorian red-brick thing with half-hearted Gothic embellishments. Perhaps inevitably, the club nights were called things like 'Blasphemy', 'Ritual'. There was a shoddy, amateurish feel to all the proceedings Much use was made of large strips of grubby white cloth and spray paint. The décor was a kind of cosy urban brutal, with a lot of mock-graffiti and dim lighting and bare plaster It was entirely unconvincing and, frankly, silly, but perhaps precisely because of this you could get in on a Saturday night and nobody felt obliged to try to dance When Ward had been there last they'd played REM and even Dexy's Midnight Runners. Defiantly unhip, it was paradise for people who liked plastic glasses of lager and swaying in T-shirts with lists of tour dates on the back.

Ward hesitated outside. It was early yet. There was a rickety A-frame sign with the word 'Blacka' on it in blurred, misaligned lower-case letters The blurring and misaligning were, obviously, intentional. Ward had seen posters with this on all over town recently, in the all-night cafés and the second-hand clothes shops. Underneath 'Blacka' were the words 'Soul–Hip-hop–Ragga' All it needed was a line stating, 'This is a black club and what's more it is much trendier than you are,' to make the message entirely explicit to any trembling white boys that might chance by.

Ward rang the bell, and a few seconds later the door scraped open. A large black man, well over six foot six, gazed out, not at Ward, but at the patch of wall over the street from him, above his head. He was dressed completely in black. Black black black, Ward thought, and fretted over his trainers (not black! green in fact!).

'You open, then?' Ward asked finally, and the doorman sniffed the night air. He held the door slightly wider, and Ward crept apologetically in.

There was the usual foolishness with signing in Admission was surprisingly reasonable, Ward thought, as he handed over the money to the woman behind the rickety walled-in enclosure They'd changed the layout since he'd been here last, and the whole of the downstairs seemed to have been closed down Ward didn't know where to go. The ticket woman watched him neutrally.

'Er,' he said, and she nodded to the stairs. The vast doorman and the woman watched him go up. The stairs were as he remembered them, uneven and with an overdesigned hand-rail that snicked little bits of flesh out of your palm from time to time. Everything was chill to the touch, everything felt damp Big white sheets were nailed up, bellying in and out, with the 'Blacka' logo on them. Others had hugely stylized pictures of a gun, a syringe, a record and, puzzlingly, something that looked like a frozen chicken. Ward worried that he ought to know what the chicken meant, but he didn't Something to do with cold turkey maybe?

The stairs turned, and suddenly Ward could hear something thudding from behind a door In front of the door were three men, all black, all dressed in black, in huge jeans and loose jackets with big pockets and big stitching all over them. The three watched him as he came towards the door. One of them looked away, and Ward felt criticized, menaced, made a fool of, he didn't know why. He wasn't supposed to be here He had green trainers on, for Christ's sake!

He edged past one of the three and came to the door to the

158

main bar. The sound whumped up to meet him as he went in, and from inside the room he felt eyes fasten on to him.

He remembered this room from years ago, though it had seemed far larger then. There was a bar at one end, some tables, then the dance floor, with the DJ's enclosure high up and to one side. Much of the internal partitioning was of old MDF, chipped, ragged Everything was painted black. There were more sheets, though not, as far as Ward could tell, any more chickens. He headed directly for the bar, looking at nothing and no one. The barman had to come back to the other side to serve him. Ward asked for lager and received a plastic glass of Fosters that smelled, somehow, as if it had been around for years. The barman moved slowly, and it took what seemed like minutes for Ward to get his change, in fact he'd already turned away, as if it was no big deal (change from a ten!). The barman immediately came back round to the customers' side of the bar and carried on talking to a small white man with a ponytail, whom Ward took to be the owner. Ward lifted the glass and the pressure of his grip slopped some of the contents down his shirt and on to the floor. Ward's eye found a table against the far wall and he aimed for that, looking at no one

Sitting, he felt safer and looked around him for the first time At another table there were four girls, all very young, all blonde, dressed in hooded tops and baggy jeans Everyone else in the place, with the exception of the owner, was male, black, dressed in black, standing or leaning, motionless, silent, smoking and, Ward was certain, watching him when he couldn't see A man from the other side of the room held his eye for a second, and Ward recrossed his legs, uncrossed them, spread them out, placed one foot on top of the other, panicked (my shoes! my shoes! they're green!) and put it on the floor again He fastened his gaze on the back of a man a few feet away The man had a big reflective patch on his jacket, which seemed to say ON/ON in metallic letters. Or it could have been ONION ONION, Ward felt, was less likely

The music, now he had a chance to attend to it, was indeed ragga and hip-hop and all the rest of it It was all of the above, irreproachably cool. There were two roaming spots, each

159

fitted with a prismatic filter; there were all the appurtenances of a dance floor, but no one was dancing and you knew that no one would dance, not for all eternity. They would stand, and lean, and watch.

Ward finished his beer in an astonishingly short time, and needed to go to the toilet

Going to the toilet was, of course, an integral part of his plan, such as it was He was going to make contact with someone at this club, probably in the toilet, discreet conversations were going to be had, and he was going to be ushered away by a Mister Big. The strategy had been reluctantly approved at a somewhat fraught house meeting They would attempt to sell one whole bag, and divide up the proceeds One step at a time Ward had self-selected as the agent of the sale, because he was 'cool' whereas they were 'crap'. No one had been able to actually improve on Ward's hang-about-in-the-bogs plan, even though no one seemed to be able to take it terribly seriously. As long as he didn't try to actually take the cocaine with him and sell it on the spot, no one could legitimately object.

He made his way out of the room and down the stairs The toilets were painted in surprising shades of lavender and plum Ward hung around for a few minutes, pretending to piss, but no one came in He was just zipping up when a figure joined him at the trough. Ward glanced quickly up The man was tall and heavy, and was wearing a pair of the biggest jeans Ward had ever seen or even imagined They had little patches stitched into them, leather and leopard skin and shiny material of some kind. Huge, sagging, denim marquees

'All right?' Ward said, and the man stared ahead of him and had nothing to offer. It abruptly occurred to Ward that this big figure beside him might not be in the habit of talking to men in toilets It was certainly not one of Ward's practices More in Steve's line really, he guessed. 'Listen,' Ward continued regardless. He had come this far, he wasn't going back now 'Listen, er, wonder if you can help me out?'

The man regarded him for less than a second, an appraisal of absolute finality

'See, thing is,' Ward continued, and the man watched his water splashing against the steel trough 'See, thing is, I was wondering if you knew anyone who wants to buy any cocaine, like?'

The man's piss hitched for a second, then continued. 'You're having a laff, aren't you?' he said, his accent mostly Liverpool, overlaid with little bits of *EastEnders* cockney.

'No, really. I've got some to sell, if you know anyone wants some '

'Yeah, well, I know one or two fit that description,' the man said. He finished pissing and made his way out again.

Ward didn't know what to do next. Hanging around here was making him jumpy, but he couldn't just go upstairs and start offering it round, could he? He ducked into the lock-up and had a quick inaccurate snort. He waited in the cubicle until he could feel some effect. It made him jumpier. He didn't want to come out of the cubicle.

'Hey, in there.'

Shit! Ward froze, trying to pretend he wasn't there, even though the lock-up was obviously locked up, from the inside

'Hey, in the bog!'

Ward fiddled with his clothes and pushed the flush, then unlocked the door.

It was the man with the little ratty ponytail from upstairs, the man he assumed was the owner Shit! He was going to get thrown out now.

'Friend of mine said you were talking about something down here,' ponytail said, looking carefully at Ward as he cowered in the door of the lock-up

'Oh, yeah?' Ward said.

'Yeah, er, actually friend of mine said you were talking about selling something.'

'Did he?' Ward said, trying to look innocent. He brushed anxiously at his nostrils, and ponytail laughed.

'What exactly is it you're selling down here?' ponytail asked, managing to make it sound as if Ward was trying to sell sexual services.

'Cocaine,' Ward said, before he had a chance to think about

it. 'I'm selling cocaine. Anyone want any?' He met and held ponytail's eye, and ponytail laughed again Ward realized that they were both as nervous as each other.

'OK. You're selling cocaine Maybe'

'If you want me to leave, I'll leave,' Ward said. 'There are other places I can go to. So, you know'

'Now don't be in such a hurry,' ponytail said, and leaned in the doorway. 'Let's hear what you've got If I like it, then maybe I might want to buy' English was not this man's first language, that much was clear.

'I've got cocaine,' he said shortly. 'Just that.'

'Well, now I can maybe find someone who might want a gram Maybe two. Three maybe. Some of my friends they like it, it helps them relax, if you know what I'm saying. Sometimes I like a little myself When I'm with friends'

Ward believed he knew exactly what the man was saying

'I've got more than a few grams,' Ward said, unable to keep the pride out of his voice 'I'm after a bigger sale than a few grams Actually.'

'How much you got?' Ponytail said, accompanying the remark with a frank stare that managed to combine hostility and amusement

'Kilogram,' Ward said, resisting the temptation to call it a key

'Woh, slow down now, say again how much?'

'Kil-o-gram,' Ward said slowly and clearly 'I've got a kilogram to sell Do you know anyone?'

'Sure I know people I know a lot of people. I've got a lot of friends'

He leaned in the doorway, watching Ward.

'So?' Ward said at last, unable to bear the silence.

'If you're yanking my chain, I'm not going to be pleased,' ponytail said

'I'm not yanking anything,' Ward said, and then winced slightly at the words 'It's up to you Either you know someone or you don't, like Entirely up to you'

'OK,' ponytail said, and laughed longer than seemed necessary 'Come up I'll make a phone call If you're pissing around, then now's the time to say Me you don't have to worry about '

'Oh, fuck off,' Ward said, his patience finally at an end with this git. 'Make your fucking phone call '

Ponytail courteously gestured for Ward to go first, and Ward did, aware that he was being scrutinized from behind. Without intending to, he tightened up his thighs and buttocks and walked with more of a swagger, then worried about looking bandy, and tried to adjust his gait back again, but ended up just looking constipated Ponytail guided him up to the office, and gestured for Ward to sit in an ancient steel and foam-rubber swivel chair. The seat felt sticky. Everything was battered and chipped. Everything looked like it was made of MDF, even the phone and the chairs Ponytail dialled and spoke in a low voice, then raised it.

'Alex?' He listened, then laughed hugely, smiling at Ward as he did so 'I'm afraid it is,' he said after a moment, and laughed again. 'No, nothing like that. No, I was wondering if you had a moment to come over to the club?' Alex said something, and ponytail continued to scrutinize Ward, as if trying to fix him in his memory. 'It's just a little business thing It's in your line ' He listened some more, cleaning in between the numbers on the phone with a finger 'OK, Alex.' He hung up and smiled at Ward. 'All fixed. He'll be here in half an hour and you can sort things with him then, all right? I guess you haven't actually got it on you?' Ward shook his head. 'Well. There won't be any trouble, nothing to worry about ' He fell silent, picking his teeth and rocking on the MDF swivel chair. After a minute or two he leaned over his desk and looked down at Ward's feet. 'Fine pair of trainers you've got there,' he said, and winked.

time is short

He was coming at nine. Steve, was it? Or Dave? Something like that Terry cleared round the playroom, emptying ashtrays, removing beer cans, towels. One of the light bulbs had gone; he replaced it. The weights round the gym were messed up, and he stacked them neatly into piles, brown and blue and red.

He checked oil oil OK The toys were all stacked in size order against the wall, straps, belts, paddles, dildoes, whips, wrist restraints, leg restraints, manacles Also leather pieces, cock rings, candles.

He flicked over the mirrors Last quick check He caught a flash of himself in the full-length mirror bolted on to the wall by the multigym. He looked at it for a moment He put off the light.

Steve rang the doorbell just before ten past nine It wouldn't do, he thought, to be quite on time, and he'd walked round the block a couple of times just in case. His nerve had failed him temporarily and he'd needed a biggish snort off his hand behind someone's garage before he could march up the path and ring the bell He was well equipped, cocaine and dope, both ready to use and in reasonable amounts. Two grams and three joints That should do it.

*

164

Terry had just got his mother settled for the night. He'd changed her and fed her, then read to her for a few minutes. She would probably need changing again later on

Terry opened the door, and Steve was surprised. He actually looked a little like his ad, a big, well-developed older man, huge across the chest and shoulders and in the arms. He had a polite but basically blank face. Steve smiled, and his blood backed up and thumped hard against the chambers of his heart, then sent down a few preliminary licks to his groin. He felt weightless and his bladder tingled He felt good Terry opened the door wider and gestured him in They sat in the front room, which retained just the last traces of daylight Everything was clean and polished and dusted. There was an antiqued map of the world in polished copper on the wall, there was a stack of CDs which Steve flicked quickly through while Terry was getting him a drink from the kitchen. Dory Previn, Harry Chapin, Levellers (puzzlingly), Phil Collins, as well as the inevitable Streisand and Middler. S and M indeed

They drank, cans of bitter Terry was polite and distant, Steve was instantly bored and wanting to get on He flourished a joint. You don't mind if I   . ? Tery didn't mind; he produced a small pottery ashtray from the kitchen. He didn't want any himself. He was in and out of that kitchen, Steve thought

When the joint was finished, Terry said, 'Do you want to bring your drink?' and led the way.

The focus of the playroom was an upright scaffolding pole, concreted into the floor and bolted into an exposed joist at the top Around this had been fastened a padded fixture something like a corner pillar in a boxing ring Steve stiffened at the association There were also a mattress and a lot of cushions.

Terry was in the far corner, doing something to his clothes When he turned round he was in leather shorts and vest Army boots Steve regarded him soberly He himself was in floppy jeans and big T-shirt, and he had on only very dull underpants He felt terribly underdressed. They looked at each other for a moment.

165

'I should have put something on,' he said, and Terry shrugged. 'Listen, let's have another joint, yeah?'

Steve lit up another one, the leathery man sitting beside him on the mattress. Steve took the opportunity to look around, took in the groovy track lighting and the recessed wires, the orderly racks of equipment. Serious.

Leathery man talked about Munich and Amsterdam and Manchester, places Steve had never been. They sounded good. He put a tentative hand on to leathery man's leathery leg, and they fell on to the mattress and kissed for a while. He was a good wet kisser, but somewhat immobile.

Steve sat up after a few minutes and needed the toilet He noted small framed prints and oak-effect kitchen fittings, cupboards with tiny little glass panes and criss-crossed leadwork on his way back. He was somewhat off his head, which, he thought dimly, might not be such a terribly good idea, in the circumstances. He furtively sniffed some in the toilet, but the blood just didn't seem to be getting to where it was needed. He scrutinized himself severely, flicked it about Nothing doing.

When he came back, Terry was standing, motionless, in the middle of the big low room, just standing. Steve really only wanted to lie down; he'd gone off all the pain and obedience stuff, just for the moment. Also Terry had a rather off-putting listlessness about him.

Steve came and stood beside him, awkwardly, and Terry pulled off the T-shirt and jeans He hardly seemed to look at the body underneath, it was just another body. Terry took him under the arms and lifted him physically over to the padded scaffold pole.

'You haven't done much of this before, have you?' he said, and Steve shrugged He was getting desperate for a cup of tea more than anything.

'We need a codeword. I usually use "Endgame". Can you remember that?'

Steve nodded and grinned

'Endgame' he said, and Terry nodded seriously.

'Try not to forget it.'

166

'What do I need it for?' Steve said stupidly. Apart from anything he was starting to want to break Terry's stride just a little bit. The man was a sex machine, but he only seemed to have one setting

'Well, it's what you say to stop me. It's the only word I'll obey. If you just say stop or whatever, I'll carry on.'

'What if I punch you in the throat? Will you stop then?' This was intended as a joke, but GSOH was not a code that Terry seemed to recognize.

There were large hooks screwed into the joist above the pole with straps attached. Terry fiddled about to get the right length His last guest must have been about two foot taller than Steve He attached the straps to Steve's wrists, breathing heavily through his nose as he did it Steve watched him, fascinated He was so boring. Steve struggled to think of things to say while this was going on but decided he couldn't be bothered. Terry didn't look like he expected much in the way of talking, so Steve just stood against the padded pillar, waiting for Terry to finish fiddling about. He seemed to be having a bit of trouble with the left-hand strap. It had got twisted up somehow.

When he had finished, Steve's arms were secured at more or less head height, bent at the elbow He still had his uninteresting underwear on, and there was nothing going on inside, not a twitch. In fact he felt himself shrinking further than usual, telescoping back into the scrotum What remained external felt about the size and shape of an acorn or the little turned-wood weights you sometimes get on light pulls. Terry went away to fetch something, and Steve watched him, trying to get some charge, but he was just a rather lumpy man in fancy dress. His legs from behind were doughy and freckled. His shins and calves were white, hairless, bony-looking He obviously neglected his lower-leg exercises, preferring instead to concentrate on getting further out of proportion across the top

Terry came back with something that looked like a table tennis bat, but broader and with a longer handle. He stood in front of Steve, a few feet away, and turned the thing over in

167

his hands. He slapped it a few times against his wrist, and held Steve's eye. Steve got the wearying impression that he was supposed to do or say something. He avoided Terry's gaze, which was still conveying nothing at all.

Terry tapped him across the face with the paddle, quite gently, once on each side. His eyes never left Steve's face Steve struggled to look interested. The joints were making him sleepy What he really wanted, he realized suddenly, was more cocaine That would wake him up, it might even allow him to take some interest in proceedings.

'Hold on a minute,' he said, and waited for Terry to put the paddle down and undo the straps. Instead, Terry took hold of Steve's left leg by the meat of the thigh and slapped the paddle across the back of the leg, hard.

'Fuck's sake,' Steve said. 'Listen, you want to stop a minute? I just want to do something.'

Terry scrutinized his face, wearing a look of mild amusement. He twisted Steve's lower body out, straining his arms, and used the paddle more. No one stroke was particularly hard in itself, but they quickly added up to something that was more than a little irritating.

'Terry, just stop a minute,' Steve said, directly. Terry stalked back to his equipment corner and returned carrying two roughly cylindrical objects. One was a thick tube of lubricant, the other a dildo. Steve didn't know if it counted as big or small, but it certainly looked big enough

Terry held it out for Steve to see It occurred to Steve that he might have some wish for Steve to lick it or something, but he had no intention of doing anything of that kind. Terry folded his fingers round the thing and wanked it up and down He pulled a condom out of a small pocket in his shorts and rolled it over the tip of the dildo The thing was looking bigger all the time; it had very pronounced veins and a big helmet Black latex. Terry smeared it all over with lube, then pulled off Steve's uninteresting underwear Steve was terribly conscious of the absurd little acorn between his legs, which just made it contract further It didn't seem to belong in the same class of objects as the black latex dick that Terry was

168

waving about Terry was slapping lubricant round Steve's arse and balls, with a thoroughness that was profoundly unerotic. Steve felt fingers probing his arse, was unable to relax, and flinched

Terry watched his face intently as his fingers went in and out, one, two, three, then an attempt at three and the thumb. Steve pulled himself away as best he could and Terry pulled out. He stepped back a pace and squeezed himself: the leather shorts had packed everything in very tightly at the front and he looked like he was carrying something that did belong in the same class as the dildo. 6' 1", chest 56", biceps 20", cock 9". Was that more or less than the dildo? Steve couldn't gauge it, but he found himself hoping that Terry had exaggerated.

Terry came forward again and kissed him, slobbering over his mouth and neck. Steve felt the cold, lubricated dildo being moved about in between his legs, felt the tip being pressed against his arse, flinched again, and the thing sank in, an inch, two, three, then a sudden jabbing pain.

'Shit, hold on a minute,' he said, and tried to pull himself away, but Terry was intent. He pulled the dildo back, then thrust it in again.

'Fuck,' Steve said. 'Fuck, just stop a minute, it's not quite   '

Terry stood closer and rubbed himself against Steve, grinding his crotch into him. He started to say things, just little murmured phrases, oh yeah, you like that, I've got what you want, fucking well in, give it me. Steve fixed his gaze over Terry's shoulder Still no message from his cock, not a whisper. The dildo slid in another inch, another. The jabbing pain was gone but the fear of it returning was strong. Terry stood back again and watched the dildo slide in. He was handling himself frankly now, he undid the shorts and pulled himself out, a long, thick cock, slightly flattened across the top, skewed to one side He looked between his cock and the dildo, up to Steve's face This was clearly a private matter. Now that the pain had gone Steve found himself getting rather bored There was just nothing exciting about any of it. It was so bloodless. It all seemed to be about control rather than losing control The pain was administered in tiny little doses, like sherry at a christening. It was doing something for Terry though, clearly; he was now fully upstanding. He stripped off the shorts, leaving him in boots and vest, and started to lubricate himself all over, belly, cock, balls, thighs. More rubbing, more murmuring. The dildo was pulled out and a big foul smell came with it. Steve looked away, and Terry busied himself with a hand towel, wiping under Steve's legs and round his balls, he even poked a towel-wrapped finger up his arse. He threw the towel into a wicker laundry basket and returned. The smell was strong. He stripped the fouled condom off the dildo, and put it into an open plastic bag by the door.

He was drooping again when he came back, and some vigorous rubbing and murmuring was needed to get him pumped up again. He twisted one of Steve's nipples, one way and the other, watching his face closely.

'Come on then,' Steve said, 'fuck's sake.'

Terry lifted Steve's legs and rubbed his cock between his thighs, dragging his balls and scrotum back. Off again to find another condom and more lubricant. A few paces back while he pulled the condom on and smeared lubricant over it Then he was nosing his way in, gently at first, then much less gently. He was lifting Steve up from the hips and thrusting in at a slightly awkward angle. He lifted his upper body clear and Steve saw a patch of lividity start to form round his throat and over his chest. Terry was panting now, his breath pulsing straight into Steve's face. Steve screwed up his face, in the hope that the pretence of pain might spur Terry on, which it did. He came almost immediately with three great thrusts and pulled out at once, panting, red-faced, looking furious. His cock started to droop at once. Steve glanced down: the condom was thickly covered in shit, the smell was much stronger than before. Terry stepped back, breathless, heaving

'You might want to look away at this point,' he said, as the smell reached its fat fingers up and out He pulled the condom off with a sharp elastic smack, then he took another hand towel from a rack and again wiped Steve's arse and legs and balls. He looked scrupulously away from Steve's face as he did it He had some moist wipes ready, which he used. Steve got the distinct feeling that this was a part of proceedings Terry particularly liked

Terry took quite a long time over the arse wiping, it even turned into a little finger game of its own. He wouldn't meet Steve's eye. He got dressed in boxers and jeans, then came back to untie Steve from the pole

Steve was so bored he didn't even feel relief particularly. All he wanted to do was have some cocaine and a cup of tea.

'You should have stopped when I said,' he said, though without rancour – he couldn't even manage that much interest

'You said stop, you didn't say "endgame",' Terry said, smiling, and Steve sighed.

'How about if I punch you in the throat now?' he said, and Terry looked politely concerned.

'Hope I wasn't too much for you,' he said, with a smirk which suggested that he thought he was a bit too much for anyone and proud of it

Steve smiled back and punched him in the face, hard, knocking him off balance, and he sprawled on the floor

Terry put a hand to his face and felt blood trickle from his nose Steve let himself out.

The whole thing had taken no more than forty minutes from start to finish Nothing had occurred Steve got the feeling that in that house nothing ever did. And now, now it was no longer needed, his body started to send back the cocaine pleasure signals, and politely suggested another snort He sighed

esoteric drum and bass

Ward was sitting in a deep black-leather chair, at least ten feet away from an identical chair, in which sat Alex The room was dimly lit by tall uplighters, and Ward felt rather than heard the presence of at least one other person. He had no idea of the layout of the place, but it looked hastily assembled, like a stage set. It also looked as if it could be struck, equally rapidly, and transferred, if the run was successful.

The cocaine was banging on all his doors, and he was also feeling the effects of three cans of Export, but the thing that was actually activating his nerve endings was the music. It came from a satanically beautiful stereo stack, the sleekest, blackest, most twinkly stack he'd ever set eyes on The speakers were *ridiculous*. It was turned down low, and even so the sound was physical, creating little draughts and eddies round his ankles and ears. The definition, the clarity, the brilliance, the depth, the resonance, he'd read about sound like this in *What Hifi* waiting for his Chinese, and now he was hearing it It was menacingly beautiful, predatory, cold, sumptuous

Alex sat watching him for a few minutes Not, Ward guessed, in any attempt to gain a psychological advantage or to intimidate or anything like that, but rather just because he didn't know what to say Ward could empathize with that The cocaine made him empathize He even felt a little sorry for Alex, rattling round this absurd fantasy flat with this almost entirely fictional stereo. He smiled ruefully.

'This is great music,' he offered finally.

Alex leaned forward. 'You like it? I'm pleased. Really.'

'What is it?

'Oh, well, you know. 303.'

Ward must have looked blank. Alex waved a hand. 'You know. Drum and bass.'

'Yeah?' Ward said, nodding comfortably Certainly there was quite a lot of both drum and bass in the music In fact, thinking about it, there was very little else, except occasional vocal samples and the odd synthesizer sweep.

'Yes, er, friend of mine, he helps produce it Or he has something to do with it anyway. It all gets quite technical,' Alex said

'It sounds great.'

Actually, he thought it sounded deranged. It stuttered and puttered and stopped and started continually, a machine that had run out of all human control and was just fizzing to its own preoccupations, little wheels spinning and tiny servos humming, oiled but arbitrary Tiny little electronic sounds pittered and pattered and coalesced for a second, then spun away again, like figments It was so delicately made that it hardly seemed to exist at all for seconds at a time But it was also immensely heavy, the bass seeking its way through floor and foundations, down into the earth. Ward followed a bass line as far as he could, then it disappeared and he started to feel the shaved skin of his ankles tickling. It took up residence amongst the plumbing and joists, it inhabited the walls and the floor completely. Alex regarded him gravely

'Esoteric,' Ward said, without the least idea of what he meant, but Alex leaned forward attentively, a look of tremendous surprise on his face

'Esoteric?' He remained leaning forward for a few seconds, then sank back into the leather

Ward tried to feel as if he had not said something laughable

'That's an interesting word Esoteric drum and bass Yes, it is That's what it is '

Ward felt a glow of pleasure start to smoulder inside his abdomen.

'It'll take me one hour and one phone call to arrange things,' Alex said, out of nowhere, 'is that OK?'

Ward waved a hand dismissively 'Of course.' Anything was OK. He'd just invented a new category of music. What was there to not be OK?

Alex took a joint from the breast pocket of his jacket and flashed a pink plastic lighter. He was certain now that Ward wasn't police Their men always tried to be so cool about everything, but this was strictly amateur. Ward was so obviously out of his depth it was almost touching.

'You need this,' he said, 'for the music. You need to stop trying so hard. You're trying too hard.'

Ward smiled, though he had determined that he was going to keep his head clear until this was over, but hey!

'May I see it?' Alex said after a moment, and Ward was confused for a second.

'Oh, the . . you mean the cocaine, like.'

'Yes. I'll have to do my little tests, you know – weigh it, that kind of thing. Now, I'll need to use a gram for an ammonia test. Of course if it's good, then I'll buy the test gram as well Just take a few minutes. That's OK, isn't it?'

'Oh, yes.'

'You do have it?' Alex asked after another short gap.

Ro-ro-ro-ro-ro-rock da house da house da house

'Of course ' After meeting Alex at the club Ward had run home and grabbed a bag. It was snug in the inside slash pocket of his jacket, and he gave it a little tap. 'Right here.'

Thump. Rattle-rattle-rattle-rattle-rattle-rattle thump Rat rat ratatatatat-t-t-t-t-t.

'May I see it?'

Ward pulled it out. The smell of linseed was very strong in this thin, pure, esoteric air.

Alex received it respectfully, turned it over to where the sticker was, raised an eyebrow and glanced back to Ward. Oh yeah? He passed the joint. Ward took a pull on it and watched Alex, who was squeezing the package gently between his two hands, not looking at it now He looked familiar, like the kind of family member you only see at funerals.

'OK Like I say, I'll just go next door and, you know. All that. Just next door. Come and watch if you like. I'll be, I don't know, ten minutes? Maximum Then, if everything works out with it, I'll make my phone call, maybe forty-five minutes, maybe an hour, the money will arrive and we're through. All right?'

He spoke with deep concern, gravity, solicitude. He's like a dentist to the stars, Ward thought, and smiled at the image

Ward nodded. 'Of course.'

'Enjoy the music Be at home Anything you want? I have some whisky somewhere, I think No?'

Ward shook his head, and pulled on the joint again as Alex went into an adjoining room.

Thump thump booooooong at-at-at-at-at atatatat It was so intricately patterned, but you couldn't see the pattern all at once. It was like trying to look at a butterfly wing through a magnifying glass. You had to step back slightly from it, hold it in your mind, see it spin. See it rather than hear it, Ward thought, that's how esoteric it was Ward took another drag. It wasn't all dope, he thought, with interest There was something else, sweeter and heavier. Opium? It was too lovely He sank back into it and the darkness gathered around him for a moment The music spun

He heard someone speaking quickly. Someone had taken his cocaine away and he suddenly needed to see it again Time had gone weird, it was clotting like cream Creamy The word spun in his head.

Kitchen?

He wanted the kitchen suddenly, he wanted a drink of water

The music seemed to spin itself into a tight little vortex and disappear, the words 'doctor da joint' echoing away into some infinitely vast space. Ward felt moments passing like heavy lorries He sat a little straighter.

'Hey!'

The sound came out of his mouth unbidden.

He really did have to find the kitchen He managed to find his feet and went through a door, another door, into a hallway. There was a light showing at the far end, and he made for it He pushed a door. Alex and another man were standing at a table. Alex was talking quietly on the phone. The bag of cocaine lay between them on the table, opened carefully at the top, and there was a saucer, the contents of which Alex was studying. There were also bottles and teaspoons, and an item like a large calculator, which Ward recognized as digital scales

Alex turned and smiled at Ward. 'I'll get back to you, Trev,' he said, and hung up. Ward was shaken by a wave of nausea and paranoia Who were these people? His cocaine was sitting in plain view The two men watched him as he swayed in the doorway Alex no longer looked like his long-lost uncle Danger danger danger, said Ward's head Let's go now Let's go right now.

'I've changed my mind,' Ward said, and Alex gave him a look of great sympathy and understanding.

'Well, that is a pity '

Ward shucked his eyebrows

'Are you certain?' Alex asked, still with his celebrity dentist manner in place 'I'll be giving you a very good price You don't have to worry about that.'

'Yeah, well,' Ward said, and shrugged 'Sorry I thought I wanted to But I don't '

Alex shrugged and sealed up the bag again

'It's very high quality, almost 80 per cent. Exceptional. See?' He showed Ward the contents of the saucer, where the cocaine had been precipitated out by the ammonia into a single jagged lump

Alex scooped up the precipitate and expertly jigged it into a little sealable plastic bag He returned this to Ward, along with the big bag

'Of course, I won't ask you where you got it,' he said, and Ward shrugged 'Well, if you change your mind again, you know where I am,' he said, and Ward shook his hand. 'Be very careful,'

Alex said. 'Be extremely careful. Be more careful than this. You could have got into trouble here, really quite easily'

Ward handed him back the joint, and made his way out The music twitched and spasmed at his back. The cocaine nestled inside his pocket, warm and substantial. How could I ever have thought I could give you away to that man? How could I, Ward thought Exceptional, Alex had said. Whatever had been in the joint drew layers of curtains over his eyes as he walked, and he slowed down to enjoy the air It was thick and creamy and benign. He sat on a garden wall and breathed the gorgeous stuff in. Exceptional, he thought. Exceptional. He smiled at the small growing things in hedges and gardens.

'Trevor? Alex again.'

'So can you talk now? It turned up?' Trevor was in his cluttered office/spare room in Solihull He was trying to assemble some Dexion shelves; the socket spanner was giving him grief and he kept banging the meatier parts of his hand against angled sections of perforated steel

'Well, yes, it turned up'

'And?'

'And then it went away again. He got the horrors and left.'

'So who was it? Let me guess, one of Paul's little helpers, yeah? That what's his name, Carlos?'

'Costas No.'

'So who?'

'No one I've ever seen. Big retarded-looking boy He kept scratching himself.'

'There's no new operation down there though, is there?'

'Again, not to my knowledge This looked very freelance anyway I couldn't quite make sense of him.'

'Not the police, though?'

'Oh, God no, nothing like that No, just some funny little independent thing I fancy. God knows really'

'So where is he?'

'Well, he's gone, Trevor I could hardly hold him here I don't really have the facilities. I'm not set up to receive guests. I wouldn't meet fire regulations for one thing'

Trevor sighed. I don't owe you, Alex was saying. This is strictly courtesy. Just good business relations, nothing more

'So what you're telling me, Alex, is that my consignment is being touted round Brighton by some retard with a skin problem.'

'In essence' Alex wasn't trying very hard to keep the amusement out of his voice.

'And everyone knows it'

'Well, Trevor, you did rather tell everyone, now didn't you?'

'Great That's great. Truly great'

'I knew you'd be pleased I sensed it' Guffawing in the background.

'Yeah, well, I owe you one, Alex,' Trevor said in a steely voice, and Alex demurred Ah, no You don't owe me, I don't owe you, let's keep it that way.

'Of course, I can always help you out, if you're short,' Alex said, and Trevor laughed along with him.

'The day I buy from you, Alex my friend, is the day I cut my genitalia off and feed them to the dog.'

'Woof,' said Alex

More dumb laughter. Trevor called him a cunt and they hung up He kicked the partially erected shelves for a bit, then went back to the phone and dialled an Amsterdam number

'Jaap?'

'No, it's Georg here.'

'Oh, right Listen, it's Trevor in Birmingham Can you get Jaap to give me a call when he gets back I want to put in an order'

'Another one? So soon? Didn't we just .'

'Yeah, you did You'll never believe what's been going off at this end, mate, I tell you Unreal, I'm not kidding Totally'

'So you need another one the same?'

'Certainly do You can sort me out, can't you?'

'Oh, sure No worry'

'Going to put a bit of a kink in my end-of-yearlies, I can tell you'

'You're an unlucky man.'

'Amen to that A-fucking-men to that one, my friend' He rang off and went to find a drink.

those little bags

Ward stood in W H Smith fingering hole reinforcers and Tipp-Ex thinner. He scratched absently at his chest and belly; the hair was growing back with a vengeance now and it was itching like a swine.

It had been decided that Ward would buy the little bags. They were going to divide it all up into one-gram deals, share them out and then after that they could do whatever they wanted with them: sell them, snort them, feed them to the cat Whatever. If they couldn't sell it wholesale, then retail it would have to be Kelvin had insisted that this was the only sensible course. And anyway, only by actually measuring it out in this way would it be possible to monitor exactly how much they were using. There was something more than a touch obsessive about this, as Marina had noted, but Kelvin won the day. We need to know exactly how much there is, he said, and how much we're using, day by day, and the only practicable way of doing that is to have it already weighed. He was going to start keeping a graph: each person would have their own colour He had it all worked out. He had the pens Accurate information, though, was clearly going to be a problem.

So they needed four and a half thousand little plastic bags

There must be a name for them, Ward thought. The kind of bags you got eighths of dope in or sometimes if you bought more than half a dozen pills at a time. Small capacity, clear thick plastic, with a snap fastening at one end

Ward approached the cash desk. The woman was very friendly.

'Listen, er,' Ward said confidentially, 'you know those little bags . . '

They were called minigrip bags. Ward wanted the 410 by 350 mm size. The woman went away and found a bag of twenty-five for him: 60p. Ward thanked her and looked dubiously at them

'Need a few more than that, actually,' he muttered, and the woman looked sympathetic and inquiring. 'Yeah, I'm going to need about fuffunuffunuff '

'Sorry?' she said, and Ward met her eye.

'Four and a half thousand,' Ward said, and the woman raised a tiny bit of a eyebrow, but just for a second. Working in stationery had made her broad-minded.

'I doubt that we've got that amount in stock,' she said, regretfully, smiling at the floor, 'but I'll just go and have a look.'

She went away and Ward did a quick calculation. If twenty-five were 60p, then 250 were £6, a thousand were four by £6, equals £24, which meant that four and a half thousand would be, would be . . It was some utterly ridiculous amount of money

Ward stood by the cash desk and felt furtive. It suddenly occurred to him that she had perhaps been trained to watch out for just such purchases as this Unusual patterns of demand or something. She was probably on the phone to the police right now Those little plastic bags, is it, miss? We'll be there straight away Keep him talking.

He fidgeted and looked at ring binders and lockable files. If challenged, he would say he wanted the bags because he was opening up a bead shop That was what he needed them for. Yeah, I'm opening up a bead shop actually, he said to himself, and fled for the door, before she could come back to keep him talking

*

They changed the plan. They wouldn't divide up the whole amount into deals. Instead they would just take a whole kilogram bag each and divide up the open bag, which was now actually a big margarine tub, into deals. These they would share out. Kelvin nominated himself to take charge, principally because Ward had failed in the matter of the minigrip bags and Marina and Steve just looked blankly at him, a trick Marina had learned from Carola and taught to Steve. Anyway, he was the one with the digital scales. They would use wraps instead of bags. Cheaper anyway. Kelvin organized a sweatshop, and quickly came up against the problem that no one knew how to fold up a wrap.

'It can't be that difficult,' he said, and started to experiment. 'It's just a matter of figuring it out.'

Half an hour later he'd got through a whole page of the *Observer* Life section and had yet to produce anything that didn't fall apart, leak, look ridiculous or just not work.

'Hold on now,' he said, and had a good big snort. 'Hold on just a minute now.' He surveyed the heap of folded and crumpled paper in front of him. 'Let me think.'

Marina came over to look. 'Oh dear,' she said. 'I don't think you've got that quite right yet, have you?' and wandered away again. She and Steve were being uproarious in the kitchen

'Ward,' Kelvin called out, and Ward dutifully ambled over and sat on the floor He started to fold and tear a sheet of magazine

Ward folded and thought and folded again, opened it up and put some cocaine in, folded it back up. Shook it. Shook it in Kelvin's face

'Like this,' he said, and chucked it on to Kelvin's lap

Kelvin took it apart but then couldn't retrace his steps, and Ward, with insulting patience, drew him a series of diagrams Six steps, from a large diamond to a small rectangle, lots of dotted lines and little arrows. Fold flap A up, then take shaded section C and fold across Kelvin went over it a few times and got the hang of it Ward sat quietly on the floor tearing up the required squares of paper. At last, he thought, a use for the *Observer* Life section They needed about five or six hundred.

Say sixteen to a page, that was – he couldn't do it in his head and went to look for a calculator.

Thiry-seven and a half pages He settled in to the job and was pleased with the stack of neat little squares as it grew beside him on the floor. Kelvin was folding, one at a time, then weighing, jiggling tiny amounts back and forth with a knife, and then closing them up. His mind wandered freely. He shared little snorts with Ward from time to time and after a while the thought came to him: the world did not need another artwork That was in fact, perhaps, the last thing it needed, there was far too much already. What it needed was something else An anti-artwork perhaps, like a little piece of anti-matter? He nudged the idea around. The sound of tearing paper at his feet was oddly stimulating.

Ward and Kelvin finished at twenty past two. Ward had quite a few paper cuts and Kelvin was crotchety from squinting at the scales The wraps were all stacked neatly into a shoe box. Ward counted them up: 688

'That means we've used 312,' Kelvin said, and calculated quickly. 'That's £15,600.'

'Can't be,' Ward said, and Kelvin glared at him.

'That's if we were paying fifty a gram. We'd probably get a little bit of a discount for bulk '

'Close to £4,000 each,' he said, and Ward played with the shoebox full of wraps. They stacked rather nicely, like little flat bricks.

'Can't be,' he said again.

the decline of the west

Saturday Kelvin had a number of pictures mounted on cardboard, and a sheet pinned up, behind which, like this year's Astra, was his all-new art thing He was keyed up, his voice was higher and faster than usual, his gestures wider He'd been up, snorting, for more than forty-eight hours putting this together, and the strain was starting to show His audience were more laid-back It would take a lot, Marina thought, to impress anybody here. She remembered a previous art idea of Kelvin's, completed soon after his final show, which had been basically a continuous, round-the-clock performance by a troop of eight singers and dancers of 'Another Rock and Roll Christmas'. This routine was to be installed in a gallery and performed, twenty-four hours a day, with continual changes of cast as necessary, until the end of time. Whoever bought it bought also the responsibility of maintaining the performers It had mercifully remained a concept only She waited with subdued anxiety for whatever he had hidden behind the sheet He got so caught up in these absurd ideas that she worried about the effect on him of their inevitable failure. He really did think he was an artist, at least sometimes. He definitely did now. She wasn't happy about him at all just at the moment. She wasn't entirely happy about any of them.

He held up his first picture· an Assumption of the Virgin by Agostino Carracci

'Artwork,' he said 'Also a masterpiece. Characterized by consummate technical skill. Value several million pounds. Currently owned by a private, anonymous collector, who is thought to possess more than a hundred such pieces.' The Virgin in question, a matronly figure by this stage of her career, was being borne aloft by a team of husky cherubim who were clearly struggling with the weight. She wore an expression of mild worry, as if she was thinking, did I pack my mascara?

Kelvin chucked it away behind him, and it bounced off the sheet.

Next picture an Andy Warhol car-crash print.

'Another artwork, another masterpiece. Technically not of any great interest, but important because of its subject matter and its status as an icon. Each print worth many hundreds of thousands of pounds.'

Picture three. Damien Hirst's sheep in a tank

'Away from the flock. Questionably a masterpiece, no great technical innovation, but perhaps the most talked-about artwork in the last decade Important perhaps more for its value as a provocation than any particular visual quality, although many people have found it beautiful and disturbing, even spiritual, with a profound message about mortality '

'Shag,' Ward said.

Kelvin archly cupped a hand behind his ear: I'm sorry, could you perhaps enlarge on that?

'It's just shag,' Ward said. 'He's a shag merchant '

'Shag. Yes. I see ' He carried on. Ward said 'Shag' from time to time. 'Now, what all these items have in common is that they are accredited artworks They are immensely valuable, they are the subject of much discussion, and they have an undisputed place in the Western canon '

'Kel, sweetheart, you've turned into the Open University again,' Marina said, but he wasn't hearing her. He loved the words 'Western canon'. It was a kind of spell He was also loving his own voice saying it.

'Now, in order to do anything new it is necessary first to go beyond the old In order to create a new kind of art, it is

184

necessary to rethink what an art object should be and what it should do. All of the above examples exist in galleries of some kind, they do nothing, and they have no actual relationship with each other. In a sense they are like tropical plants in a greenhouse, separate, immobile, protected from harm, maintained by professional staff.' He paused and pointed to the sheet. 'Now, what I have behind here is something that is completely unprecedented in art history. It is a new kind of art object. There is far too much art in the world, and it is this problem that my artwork addresses. As you will see.'

He grabbed a corner of the sheet and it fell down on the floor, revealing something that resembled a large fish tank.

'Hey, it's a fish tank,' Ward said. 'Hey, it's a revolution in fucking art history, let's all go fucking apeshite.'

'Actually, it's something like the opposite of a fish tank,' Kelvin said. 'Allow me to explain. This is an art predator What it does is it eats artworks. It is a tank which will be filled, not with a preserving solution, but with a weak corrosive, like dilute sulphuric acid Into it is placed an existing artwork, preferably a masterpiece. an Assumption, for example ' He picked up his print of the Carracci and dropped it inside the fish tank. 'What happens next, of course, is that the artwork starts to corrode. This may take some considerable time, depending on the materials used and the strength of the corrosive solution. It might take years. A condition of sale of my art eater is that it must be fed continuously, so that as one artwork is digested, another is placed inside This will happen in full view, in a gallery It will be available in a range of sizes, to allow for large sculptural pieces, and indeed whole installations, to be accommodated Once inside a gallery it will, like a new predator in a hothouse, eventually destroy all the other artworks. Ultimately, there will be no other art in the world except my art eater, and then it will die Unless, of course, something is devised which can stop it. I have invented the art food chain It signals the end of art history, and the end of art ' He was flushed and euphoric. He stood beside his fish tank and smiled

No one spoke for a few seconds. Then Ward said, 'Right, well, that's art sorted out, then,' and went into the kitchen.

Marina patted Kelvin on the hand and followed him out

Steve shrugged his eyebrows. 'Take no notice,' he said, 'they're just philistines.'

Kelvin stood beside his tank looking at him

'By the way,' Steve said, 'how much is it?'

beyond the bikini line

Ward was slumped in front of the television. He'd turned the sound off The pictures were a flickering irritant in front of his eyes. He really just wanted to sleep but there were still fragments of chemical to be metabolized, the brain was still being fooled into allowing too much serotonin to wash about. It would take hours to wear off completely, and unfortunately by that time he would probably have had a tiny wee maintenance dose Just to stop it wearing off

It was after nine o'clock, still light. The day had been an anxious one. What to do? There was nothing, inside or out Hours and hours of slightly edgy nothing. The long evenings merely served to prolong this anxiety as to what to do in the day until well into the evening. The light continued to fall into the room, seeming to demand movement, purposeful activity and cheerfulness Seven o'clock Eight o'clock Twenty past eight He thought about going down to Bazza's

He heard a key in the door· Marina He shifted about and made a badly executed effort to look less bereft He held the paper up in front of him

'No footy today?'

'Couldn't be arsed '

She came to sit with him. She'd been out buying something It was some tiny scrap of green material Looks nice, he said, without the least idea what it was. Cheap, she said. Reduced. Bargain.

He scratched, thighs now as well as shoulders, belly, throat. She watched him.

'Little bit itchy, are we?' she said, and Ward muttered.

'When was it I shaved you?'

'Three weeks.'

'I guess it's grown back a bit.'

'It has '

She paused for a moment. 'Did, er, did Carola like it?'

Ward shifted about. 'Oh, yeah,' he said absently 'Actually,' he said, after a few minutes, 'I was wondering.'

'Were you, darlin'?' she said.

'Yeah, cos actually I was wondering if you'd mind doing it again.'

'What, shave you again?'

He nodded, staring at the silent television.

'Yeah, if you want,' she said.

He said nothing for a moment. Then: 'I like it when you shave us actually.'

'Oh, yeah?'

'Yeah '

'And it wouldn't have anything to do with being nice and smooth for the lovely Carola?'

'Carola,' he said, 'likes me stubbly. She was very clear on that point.'

'Really?' Marina said. 'She's quite a girl.'

'I'll give you that '

She said nothing for a minute. 'Have you still got that, er, that   . ?'

'You mean the . . ' He gestured to his groin. The jock strap.

'That, yes.'

'Oh, yes,' he said.

'It just makes things a bit easier when we get to, you know.'

'You could go a bit further in this time.'

She looked at him. 'You mean . . . ?'

'You know, you could take a bit more off like.'

'You mean beyond the bikini line?'

188

He flushed and fell quiet again.

'Well,' she said, and giggled. 'I could, I suppose.'

Kelvin and Steve were both out. Steve had taken pity on him and let him come along to his Saturday night session at the Legover Arms, where he fed him surreptitious free halves and watched him getting everything wrong in the quiz He didn't seem to know anything about anything. He looked faintly bemused by everything.

Marina drew the curtains Ward laid himself out on the sofa and took off his shirt.

'My,' she said. He was covered in dark bristles, twelve, fifteen mill She stroked them one way and then the other. 'Now you're quite sure?' she said.

He dispensed with both towel and jock strap this time, and she did indeed get well underneath the bikini line with her razor, right in She took her time, smoothing the oil into the skin, cleaning off the debris with a towel

'You do realize,' she said, 'that you'll need doing again in a week or so?'

Ward lay perfectly still, a big stupid smile on his face. The television talked to itself in the corner, flickering meaninglessly

They ambled down to the beach, at Marina's suggestion She was determined to get him out of the house, at least once every twenty-four hours. Take his mind off the you-know-what, which she was starting to loathe It tasted evil and it had no manners, it just came barging up to you and commandeered you It was certainly starting to mess with Kelvin, and Steve's episode with dildo man wasn't like him at all He'd tried to make it sound funny, but it was clearly nothing of the kind, and he was quite obviously furious about it She wished he'd be a bit more careful out there. Carola, meanwhile, was wandering around like a very expensive zombie

She herself was miles behind with her reading for next term, which she wasn't even certain of being able to do unless her parents came through with the money. She had dissertations piling up to be typed. And what was she doing about it? She was swanning about in the sun and putting everything off She was obsessing periodically about Bazza's shorts and the contents thereof. Meanwhile, she was also allowing Ward to flirt with her in the most flagrant manner Kelvin seemed not to notice; he seemed to notice less and less all the time in fact. He'd barely spoken to her for three days. And now this ridiculous art thing What was the matter with him? And all anyone seemed capable of thinking about was cocaine.

On the beach some people had a bonfire going and Ward and Marina lay back on the pebbles and watched the sparks fly.

'Ward,' Marina said. 'About Kelvin.'

'Yeah?'

She was quiet again She felt his hand feeling for hers, and she lay still as he locked fingers with her.

'What about Kelvin?' he said, sitting up on one elbow

There was a big shout from the bonfire people and then cheering. They were having a ball, seemingly

She said nothing, and he lay back again

'You mean you don't want me, you want him You don't want to leave him, like?'

Nothing

'You mean, you've seen what I've got to offer, like, and you've seen what Kelvin's got to offer, and you've compared the two and you've decided in favour of Kelvin '

'Yes, actually I did a kind of blind tasting while you were both asleep You know, I had a bit of him and a bit of you . . '

He laughed and they listened to the uproar from the bonfire.

'You know, I've been all over the place lately, Ward And I'm not really happy about Kel. I think he's losing the plot a little bit '

'Me an' all '

'What do you mean?'

'Losing the plot I'm getting really, you know In here.' He pressed a hand against his stomach. 'But I think that's as much to do with you as it is with the cocaine, like. I really like you.' He couldn't look at her; he was gazing out to the astonishing horizon

'I know.'

He was quiet beside her, steady, calm

'I mean, I really do, I really like you,' he repeated carefully, as if he hadn't said it right first time. Saying it differently might make a difference.

'No good with Carola, huh?'

He shook his head.

'I mean, she's a really nice girl and everything.'

Silence

'But. It's not her I want '

Marina sighed and lifted his hand to her mouth, and kissed it

'You'll find someone. There's some big-chested girl out there with your name on her.'

'What, actually on her chest, like?'

'Of course '

'I'm not fussed about chests.'

'Obviously not, if you're fancying me '

'You've got a nice chest.'

'Yeah?'

'Well, I think so anyway '

She was quiet again.

'Listen I'm going to get rid of the cocaine,' she said, and as soon as the words left her mouth she knew that she'd been thinking this for days, weeks even Ward didn't respond; he was sunk up to the knees in some mouldering ditch of apathy. 'And I'm not shaving you any more '

He was still looking out to sea

'Well, all right, I can still shave you If you like,' she said. 'But I think we might have to stop at the bikini line in future You can do the rest of it yourself '

'Yeah, well, it'll give me something to do on long winter evenings anyway While I'm sitting there, all by myself, like.'

'And you could collect the shavings and make pictures out of them.'

'Like a hobby, kind of?'

He was quiet again

'Summer,' he said, finally.

She was full of regrets now she'd turned him down. Why couldn't she have him as well? Why couldn't you ever get all of what you wanted? It seemed to be built into everything You acquired a colossal quantity of cocaine, it made you weird and dissatisfied and wanting more. You had a boyfriend who was funny and loyal and intelligent, then you got an offer from some other man, and he had a body. A damn good body, to be exact. And you were supposed to choose between them! It was ridiculous. Obviously you wanted both. Meanwhile, any attempt at obtaining pleasure would be severely punished, though there would be no reward for good behaviour

Ward sat up and threw pebbles into the sea. He was getting fidgety for cocaine, she could tell He'd lost the slightly glazed, wide-eyed look of an hour ago and was now seething dully

'You want to head back?'

'Not really '

'No?'

They walked along the front slowly, still hand in hand. She tried to talk him into going back to university He conceded that it was possible, maybe. He wouldn't get a grant to retake the first year, though. He'd have to get some money together. Sell some cocaine, then, for Christ's sake, she said There must be some way Some time, he said When he had nothing more pressing on, like

They washed up at an all-night café, just opening for the night, and Marina talked to everyone, with Ward solid and quiet beside her. Later they walked along the beach and watched the lights on the water and the people drumming under the West Pier, dogs and children and people who didn't care if they could dance or not, they were going to do it anyway.

Fuck it, she thought, I'm having him as well Definitely

192

I'm having him and Kel and any other bloody thing I happen to fancy. I'm having everything.

The cocaine would have to go, of course. But not just yet. Not straight away anyway. She would know when

snowstorm on mount desolation

Saturday, night. Marina was back home, Ward had gone to Bazza's. He didn't want to come home, he'd said. Not just at the moment Anyway there was big footy on Sky.

Marina and Steve were sitting by the open window A warm breeze bellowed the curtains in and out, but the heat in the room was still oppressive. The streets were quiet apart from random outbreaks of yelling and banging and deranged, violent singing, distant, then closer The television was on, the sound off

'Him?' Steve said, gesturing to a gangly youth passing by below

'Yeah,' Marina said. 'Him '

Steve reached across and found a wrap, and leaned out of the window

'Hey Catch,' he said, and chucked it out. The youth caught it, looked up puzzled, and Steve indicated his instructions for use by putting a thumb to a nostril and inhaling. 'Yeah?' The youth looked at him wide-eyed for a moment and went on his way He was the fourth tonight.

'Listen,' Marina said, 'I've been thinking. I want to get rid of the cocaine '

'Why?'

'Why? Steve, maybe I've got this all wrong, but weren't you telling me the other day about some little incident involving

194

you, a pervert, a very big thing and some confusion about the meaning of commonly used words like "stop"?'

'I think "sexual hobbyist" rather than "pervert",' he said. 'Anyway, so what? I was just unlucky, he just happened to be a bit of a wanker. And they were his rules, and he did say in advance and all that, so it was my fault really. You've got to be careful, that's all.'

'Yeah, exactly, and you aren't being. If you weren't so wired up with cocaine the whole time, you'd never have set foot in the place Would you?'

She passed him the joint.

'Well, anyway. It's just, no one seems to be having any fun any more. I'm getting sick of it, to tell you the truth. Kel's on this stupid art thing, he hasn't talked to me for three days, Ward's gone all *Sturm und Drang*, you're turning into some kind of – '

'Let's choose our words now . . . '

'Well, what's next? Nailing sandpaper to your bollocks or something?'

'Are you sure you're not getting sex mixed up with DIY?'

'Anyway, you know what I mean.'

They were quiet for a minute. Steve took a sip of water and carefully poured the rest of the glass out of the window. (There was a drought on, as always.)

'When do you want to get rid of it?' he said and inhaled.

'Two days,' she said.

Steve tipped his head back and regarded her as he held the smoke He exhaled slowly, luxuriously.

'Five days,' he said.

The television was showing pictures of a riot in Leicester Square. Some football stupidity. England had lost or won or some such result, he wasn't certain Germany were involved somehow as well. Ward was round at Bazza's right now, yelling at the television at the top of his voice This was the kind of international relations he understood. To Steve, it mostly seemed to be a lot of meatheads screaming at riot police, who were wound up tight, eager for it all. England lost the footy so the fans attacked the police. There was a pleasing

195

disregard for logic about it. Bottles rained down, the camera took a dive and suddenly everyone was running and yelling and falling down

'Jesus,' she said. 'Just look at them.'

Steve turned his attention to the screen.

Something was on fire, police vans screeched about disgorging hordes of tubby men in bullet-proofs and helmets They held shields like Roman soldiers. They advanced, fell back, got tangled up in writhing legs and arms, drew truncheons

'Christ,' Steve said. 'Have they got enough armour, do you think?'

The camera cut to a scene of complete madness, a solid heaving wall of bodies, waving flags, painted faces, red and white for Saint George, shaved heads. Jumping up and down, mouths open, dancing and yelling and launching things into the air. Faces contorted into jeering masks One figure disentangled himself and stood out front, legs and arms spread in an attitude of crucifixion

'Shall we hear him, their leader?' Steve said, and found the remote. He released the mute and started the video recording at the same time

'Ayyy ayyyy ayyyy,' the meathead was saying, 'yayyyyyy yayyy!'

Steve was transfixed

'Come on, then!' the dickhead was screaming, through the damaged barriers to the police line, who stamped and fidgeted and flexed as flames roared behind them and all hell broke loose in front 'Come on, then!'

He strutted and grimaced, big meaty mad bastard, a person from whom rationality had, at least temporarily, wholly fled, to be replaced with something hotter and purer by far He was just a body now, two fists, two boots, teeth, and a voice for taunting

He flung his arms aloft and screamed something, it could have been 'In-ger-laaaaand', but then again it could have been something entirely different

'Animal,' Marina said, and Steve licked his lips

196

'Fucking right,' he said. 'Just look at him '

The meathead started to claw at his T-shirt, and managed to tear it half off. He was gleaming white and hard The writhing mob behind him gibbered and provoked. More bottles in the air. He raised arms aloft and stood, half-naked, half-mad, half-animal.

'Fuck,' Steve said.

He and Marina watched, passing the joint back and forth Shouts and breaking glass reached them from the open window, and the great surging sound of drunken idiots all trying to sing something at the same time, coming unsteadily closer.

The report moved on. A wobbly close-up of someone lying on the floor by a phone box, his head trickling blood from a wound on his scalp, people milling round him, someone was lifting his head up and he was nodding groggily, licking his lips, trying to explain something.

A messy, straggling scuffle, a meathead with no shirt and a vigorous sense of having been unjustly used being restrained by three policemen and a policewoman. He writhed and kicked and thrashed, delirious, off his head, going down hard, taking the bastards with him. A great absurd tangle of fat-arsed police and bits of his body flying about. His face a twisted rictus of something, pain or delirium

'He looks like he's going to come any minute,' Steve said. 'Look at his face.'

'You're enjoying this far too much I think it might be bringing out the worst in you.'

'Fucking right.'

'Anyway, listen, about the cocaine . . . '

'The what?'

'Steve, could I have your attention for just the tiniest moment?'

Later Have a bit more, Kelvin thought, lying in his bed, have a bit more I wouldn't mind a little bit more actually. Now he'd finished the artwork, what else was there to think about?

Have a bit more, then But then, an hour from now or two

hours or half an hour, it'll be the same thing, won't it? So just imagine that now is the half-hour or two hours from now Here we are, and you're thinking, I just want a bit more. There's no end to it, is there?'

He looked across at the cocaine.

'There's still at least three-quarters left, it's going to take for ever to get through it.'

Then later 'It's nearly half-gone. I've had so much of it It's nearly gone.'

He lay racked, strung out, wanting a bit more, not wanting any more, and with an awful lot of little bits more nearby. Years' worth, possibly. There was no end to it in sight It just went on and on He picked up the bag, sealed it carefully and shoved it into the inside pocket of his parka. He picked up some cans from the fridge and left the house quietly, pulling the door very gently as he left He heard low voices from the front room It was right in the middle of the night

He found a taxi by the open market and gave directions. The taxi swung round and took a main road out of town, up, on to the Downs. There was no other traffic around, just the occasional police car They climbed, away from the bright, noisy, sweating town, out into the open, dark fields on either side, the lights of the town falling away beneath them The driver's radio squawked periodically.

They came to the brow of a hill and Kelvin told the driver to stop.

'I'm just getting out for a minute,' he said, and asked the driver to wait He gave him £20 worth of good faith The man shrugged and put the interior light on. He had a battered *Belgarath the Sorcerer* to read

Kelvin walked a few hundred paces away from the car He sat on the hill and looked.

The whole town lay beneath him, huddled into the hollows and hillsides, all streetlights and traffic lights cycling endlessly through the night From this distance it seemed quiet and still He traced the progress of a lone truck as it moved across town. It just never stopped. Stars but no moon

The sea was a flat black patch against the sky The breeze blew tears out of his eyes and the lights blurred together.

He opened the bag and had a big snort, then another, sealed the bag and waited. It started to come on. He opened the bag again and had some more, more than he would normally have at one time. It was difficult to be tidy about it because of the wind and the absence of a nice flat surface. But he managed It buzzed and hummed inside his veins, it prickled against the backs of his eyes. He could taste it creeping down his throat, followed by a wave of coolness. His nose was running, he snorted it all back in violently and swallowed, several times He started to feel cold and colossal. He pulled open a can and let it foam on to the dark grass.

Perfect pessimism, he realized, meant believing that, at any given moment, things were as good as they were ever going to be, because they could only ever get worse. This was cause for rejoicing of some measured kind.

'This is it,' he said, out loud, his voice pulled away by the wind, his eyes stinging. 'This is it. This is as good as it gets.'

He sat back and watched the traffic lights, cycling, cycling, on and on until there was no more traffic or electricity or people with enough determination to make it all work, until everyone just gave up and laid themselves down to die He just wanted it to be over. There seemed to be no end to it, any of it.

He stood up and opened the bag, and shook it hard, into the wind. The powder skittered away, in bursts and trickles and flurries, it took about two minutes for it all to blow away over the black grass and into the black sky. Kelvin watched it all fly away He let the wind take the empty bag as well. He went back to the taxi.

'Right, then,' he said, and they descended, back down into Brighton The driver had opinions and a country and western tape Kelvin chatted to him, and tried to understand what he'd just done

Kelvin seemed to have disappeared so Marina went round to see Julie, a uni buddy who had recently returned from foreign parts. She got the feeling that Kelvin was trying to avoid her as well as Ward.

Steve sat in front of the video. The leg swung round as flames flared. It swung in slow motion, a great powerful arc with a boot on one end and, eventually, a policeman's face on the other. Boot connected with bullet-proof vest and as it did so a bottle fell nearby and shattered, splinters flying up and out, slowly, gracefully. Too much light, a dazzle, the picture was colour-saturated for a moment, movements outlined in prismatic auras, the screen flaring, then whiting out in patches, then back again. The policeman doubled up, falling, his head twisting as he fell.

Steve sat, one hand on the remote. 'Fuck,' he said, as the kicker lurched forward and made ready to kick the head. 'Fuck.' He freeze-framed, advancing the action bit by jerky bit. He held one frame for several seconds, a frame in which the face of the kicker suddenly came into view, hard, bony face wrenched up into an expression of ultimate hate, mouth open in some silent obscenity Wound back to the beginning of the sequence and watched it again. He swung his own leg in imitation. He was fiddling about with a bag of cocaine, he had a few things to do He measured out about half a kilogram and sealed it Then a second bag, with the other half. He had a quick call to make, then out Time was short

a lifetime of pain

Two-fifteen a.m. Steve was feeling most odd as he came out of the noise of the club and into the cool of the corridor, most odd, he thought to himself. Yes, indeed He seemed to have been taken over by a peculiarly efficient buzzing entity, perhaps an alien life form which had taken up residence inside him and was buzzing, efficiently, for reasons of its own Marina was threatening to get rid of the cocaine, and knowing her she just might do it. He'd managed to track Ward down to Bazza's but hadn't found Kelvin anywhere. Emergency measures had been taken with half a kilogram. Meanwhile, he was going to have lots until she did. Lots and lots And then lots more. In fact her two-day threat had provoked in him a kind of desperate monomaniacal passion for the stuff, and he was high and rolling. His nose was raw and stinging. He was carrying the other half-kilogram around with him with a quite reprehensible disregard for common prudence He felt sufficiently unlike himself to swagger and smile, patting people on the back, smiling ruefully as others passed, the man of the moment He had no doubt whatsoever that the pitiful crew he was leaving behind in the club (who hadn't had any cocaine, none at all, losers!) were talking about him D'you see him that just went out? Brilliant bloke, I was talking to him in the bogs. Dead witty

Steve turned the corner, down three steps, and was in the

home straight, at the end of which stood the bouncer, Dave.

Dave was, of course, a familiar figure, but from this distance, and with this degree of chemical interference in his perception, he actually reminded Steve of that bastard with the dildo from the other night. Terry, was it?

Dave was talking to someone, a woman, and Steve stopped on the last step down and stared at him The bouncer looked briefly over, looked away, carried on talking. Steve approached a few paces, past the coat-check window where the man regarded him with obvious concern, then planted himself on the blue carpet and stopped. He felt roots growing into the carpet. It was here that he was standing and it was here that he was going to stay. It was a brilliant place to stand.

'Oi.'

The word (word?) was accompanied by his new look, his witty-bloke-in-the-bog look The roots dug into the low pile of the carpet and knotted themselves into the grain of the floorboards. It would take a diligent combination of carpenter and arboriculturalist to get him out.

'Oi Mate.'

Mate Now this was a word that he had never previously, to the best of his recollection, ever attempted to use. He had heard it used, of course, along with 'pal' and 'cunt', but he had never assayed it himself. It seemed to come out OK

Dave the bouncer glanced over and diagnosed the situation in less time than it takes to say 'wanker' He turned away again and avoided eye contact.

Steve pulled up his roots, with some difficulty and not a little regret and proceeded, step by swaying step, towards the door Towards the bouncer. Dave, Big Dave The man-mountain The coat-check man watched, increasingly worried Steve was completely out of control, swaying about all over the place, pale and clammy He looked like death. White, thin, trembling. Somewhat unwashed also He was a mess He was going to need help getting home

'Davo! Y'cunt!'

This really was unexplored territory. Davo? Most unlikely. Where had that come from?

'Oi, Davo, you queer cunt.'

Ah, now this was richly entertaining, he thought! Calling the bouncer a queer cunt! Dead witty! Maybe he was a queer cunt, who knew? He didn't actually look it, just at this moment, but who was to say? Eh?

'I've seen ya, y'queer . . . '

His feet followed each other down the carpet, which had narrowed to some kind of tunnel, and at the end of it, instead of light, was Davo, the bouncer, the queer cunt. A great, solid, scarred shadow in a black bomber jacket with 'Security' on the tit and black jeans, black boots, black hair, cropped short, number one. He was still looking away, fastidiously. He had narrow little slits for eyes, a scar over one eyebrow, pockmarked skin. His mouth pulled down at one end, always, and had made a little fold of skin in his cheek

'Fucking .'

Steve was almost at the door

'Hey!'

Dave had to look now. He raised inquiring eyebrows – how can I help you, sir? A face learned from a half-day course in security management or whatever they called bouncing these days

'Ya . '

Steve leaned himself against the door jamb and smiled. Ignore this, then, you queer cunt, his look said, security-manage this, ya .

'Night ' The doorman was saying 'Good night', he was opening the door and using his body to manoeuvre Steve on to the other side of it.

'Brilliant fucking club this,' Steve was saying, leaning in, to express his point more clearly. 'Only one thing wrong with it, though . '

The bouncer nodded minimally, turned away, started talking to the woman again She nodded briefly in Steve's direction, and they were both silent for a moment. The bouncer seemed to be gazing away into the distance, into some dull, orderly world without wankers and pissheads

'I tell ya what's wrong with this fucking place,' Steve said, into this contemplative silence, and the bouncer nodded again, slightly.

'Said I'll tell you . . '

'Maybe time you were on your way, pal.'

The bouncer's voice was a deep rumble, a low sound, the sound an elk might make in the depths of an eerie Alaskan wilderness.

'Only one thing wrong with it . . . '

'OK, mate.'

'And that one thing is . . '

The bouncer turned half-way, giving Steve the view of half a nose and an eyebrow. The nose was broken, the eyebrow scarred, the flesh deeply pitted from adolescent acne, topped up with adult acne from steroid use. A lifetime of pain. All this should have deterred Steve. It was features such as these that had secured Dave the job as bouncer in the first place.

' . . that it's full of . . . '

Dave regarded him sadly. The unscarred eyebrow twitched, and the mouth also, as if a smile was in preparation somewhere.

' . queers.'

'That right?'

'Oh, yeah Full to the fucking rafters I mean, even the fucking bouncer . . '

'Yeah?'

'Fucking begging for it up the . . . '

'That right?'

'Gagging for it Right up the . . '

'Probably best if you were on your way, pal.'

' . . fucking . . '

'OK You need a taxi, right? You go out here, up to the corner, up about fifty yards. There's a rank . . '

' . fucking shit stabbers . . '

'That's all I've got to say,' the bouncer said, and again manipulated the distance between him and Steve to place Steve on the outside of the door.

'No, wait a minute, wait a minute, now I'm not saying, right, I'm not saying . . ' This came out like. 'Wayamn, waymin, rye? No'sain . . . '

Dave shook his head briefly, leaned in to Steve and smiled. 'Had a bit of a night, eh, pal? On your way now.'

'Oh, yeah? And you're coming right behind me, are you? Fucking . . '

'On your way.'

Steve turned to the woman. He couldn't exactly focus, but she seemed blonde and pretty.

'He leave you alone quite a lot, I guess? Off out at night, eh? Ever wonder what he's shagging? Eh? Did you ever wonder where all that shit on his cock came from . . . ' They were both silent, the bouncer seeming to chew something inside his cheek, the woman hunching away from him. She and the bouncer exchanged a few words.

'   fucking . . '

'OK, pal,' Dave said, with energy mixed with some regret. 'Ohhhh-K. We're going to get you into a taxi OK? It's this way '

'Don't you want to hold my hand, y'big fuckin' . . '

Dave's mouth twisted down again, he took hold of an arm, just above the elbow His voice was now a hiss, no more. 'Right. All right You want it, you got it,' he said, and led Steve round the corner and into the goods entrance at the back

The coat-check man had come out to find him and called an ambulance, stayed with him, held his hand until it arrived. Steve kept muttering about something in his pocket, but he was so out of it he wasn't making any sense, and his mouth didn't seem to be working quite right. His whole face was swelling up

He had something wrong with his back, apart from some cracked ribs and much bruising· the back had been twisted in some way, moved in a direction for which it was not designed. His face was all sorts of unusual and striking colours, Vermont in autumn. Both eyes half-closed

He couldn't recall it all There was a moment, he thought, somewhere at the back beside a dripping fire escape, everything very quiet except the bouncer's laboured breath and water

205

dripping off iron. The bouncer was standing over him, legs spread, saying, 'All right? All right?' and Steve was struggling up on to one elbow and grinning, putting one finger to a tooth, checking, saying something. That the best you can do? Or something equally witty. He remembered waves passing through him, crashing round him. It was quiet and unreverberantly damp. He struggled up and had another go at him, aiming mostly for the head and belly. Back on the floor again. His head rang. There was something leaking from a pocket. Cocaine, disappearing into the puddles of rain. Blood also, pale pink in the water. His tongue explored his mouth. He tried to stand up again. Couldn't.

Sunday. He lay in the hospital bed, and spoke quietly, with a voice that seemed to come from far away.

'Well. This is new,' Marina said, sitting on the side of the bed, and regarded him with high disdain. 'I just hope we've got it out of our system now. I hope, Steven, we won't be having any more of it Hm?'

He assured her that he had no further ambitions in that direction, just at the moment Would she bring him in some you-know-what though when she came next? For some reason he couldn't quite seem to remember what he'd done with his. Government drugs were deeply disappointing, he told her, apart from the oxygen, which was, so to speak, a gas.

'No more,' she said. 'No more, Steven, I mean it. This is it now. Look at you, for God's sake. Tomorrow it all goes. All of it.'

'Do nothing till I'm out of here,' Steve said, and passed her the mask

She took a deep drag on the oxygen and felt the room expand to the size of a small planet. She reached for his hand to anchor herself 'Golly,' she said, mildly, and fell silent. She was still flushed and giddy when someone arrived at the bedside

'Hi. Remember me?'

Steve looked, but couldn't quite place him. Thirty-five or so, receding at the front, cropped, a pleasant, capable sort of face

'No? Well, I can't say I'm surprised. You were monged off your face.'

'You're not the bastard . . . ' Marina started, and he grinned at her.

'No, love, I'm the one who got him out of there.'

'Coat-check man,' Steve said, and smiled.

'Coat-check man. How do you do? Name of Darren.'

'Darren,' Steve said, and shook his hand.

'Yes, well,' Marina said, rising oxygenatedly to her feet and staggering hilariously away. She felt about the size and shape of a Richard Branson publicity stunt. 'See you tomorrow.'

'So,' said Darren. 'When are they letting you out of here?'

Steve didn't know. Not for a day or two anyway Weeks, probably

'Well, I'll come back tomorrow, then, shall I?'

'OK,' Steve said, surprised. 'Yeah.'

'Anything you want bringing?'

Steve struggled with the urge to ask for cocaine Darren didn't look like the type, somehow.

'Nope.'

'Sure?'

'Well, unless you happen to have a spare bit of cocaine lying around somewhere.' He tried to make it sound like a joke. It wasn't.

'Oh, I see That's what you were on the other night, yeah?'

'Amongst other things.'

'Let's see now, that would be the night you made a total wanker of yourself in the club and then provoked Dave into kicking your teeth down your throat, and nearly got yourself killed. For absolutely no reason at all. Yes?'

'I was expressing myself '

'That's one way of putting it, certainly.' Darren watched him for a moment. 'Well, I haven't anyway.'

'No harm in asking,' Steve said

'Get off it,' Darren said. 'Get right off it right now ' He stood up to leave, then, before he could think better of it, leaned over and kissed Steve on the less swollen cheek 'You're nicer off it '

A nurse came round after Darren had gone, and Steve

207

recognized him as the one who had first settled him in.

'Listen, er,' he said, and beckoned the nurse in close.

'When I first came in, what, er, what happened to all my stuff?'

'Your clothes are in the locker,' the nurse said. 'You didn't have anything else.'

'Yeah, but there was something in my jacket pocket,' Steve said urgently, quietly. His back was starting to hurt again.

The nurse raised his eyebrows. 'What kind of something might that have been, then?' he said, and Steve realized at once what had happened.

'Listen,' he said again, 'I'll share it with you, but I want it back, understand?'

'You've had a nasty concussion,' the nurse said, 'messing about with rough boys. Maybe that'll teach you '

Steve took a good look at him and recognized something in the eyes What better environment for a petty sadist than a hospital?

'I'll report you,' Steve said, 'to the fucking BMA.'

'No,' the nurse said contemplatively, 'no, somehow I don't think you will.'

'OK, OK. Look, just give me a little blast now.'

'I don't think that would be entirely ethical, do you? I mean, it's not as if it's on your chart now, is it? Nil by mouth, but anything you can get your hands on by nose?'

'Bastard. Bastard! All right, give me painkillers, my back's kicking off again.'

'You're not due for another . let's have a look, oh, a good hour and a half yet.'

'I need it now.'

'Is that right?' the nurse said, and started to go.

'Maybe I might bring you something,' he said, turning back

'When?' Steve demanded, trying not to sound too pathetically grateful, and the nurse looked thoughtful

'Well, I'm a little bit busy just at the minute Soon. When I feel like it ' He walked away. 'Maybe,' he called from the end of the ward 'Maybe not.' He rubbed a finger under his nose and winked

juzza leetle beet

Ward had borrowed Kelvin's scales and the remainder of the *Observer* Life section and had disappeared into his room. *Sunday Times* would have been preferable, the Magazine section was glossier and less porous, but there were limits to what they were prepared to do. This was eight-thirty, Sunday evening. He hadn't had any now for hours. He was fine, except that he couldn't think about anything except cocaine. Kelvin was nowhere to be found.

Carola came round at ten, and quickly made her way into Ward's room. He said hello, then ignored her completely while he got on with tearing up squares of paper. She offered to help, and actually did tear a few sheets, before she decided that this was not actually what she wanted to be doing of a summer evening. Did he want to go out somewhere and eat? He looked at her briefly, turned back to his paper. She left him alone He heard the door shut behind her and carried on tearing. He needed one thousand sheets He made himself comfortable on the floor in the corner of the room nearest the window.

By three o'clock, Monday morning, he was ready to have a break He wandered into the kitchen, where Marina was sitting with Julie, who was in the middle of some story about five days she'd spent in a basement in Osaka with seven New

Zealand backpackers. It was a long and rather pointless story, but at least it didn't involve any chemicals. Marina was flipping through an old Penny Plain catalogue as they talked She smiled hello to Ward, and he said hello back, but he didn't seem to be entirely there, somehow. He looked suspiciously at Julie.

'Where's Carola?' Marina asked, but he didn't seem to know. 'You're not telling me you've gone and lost her,' she said, and Ward shrugged. 'Have you got any idea how much that woman costs?'

Ward sat and scratched He hadn't seen Kel, he said. No idea.

'Did you hear what happened to Steve?' She gave him the bare bones, but he didn't seem to be listening.

'One down,' was all he'd say 'One down, three to go. Not me, though.'

'Having fun in there?' she said, and he said no. 'Stay and talk to us for a bit, then. No one ever talks to me any more Everyone's so busy.'

'Got to get back,' he said, and retreated to his room and his paper. He couldn't think about anything else just at the moment.

Marina kept Julie up late, until it started to get light, then they went out. The sky was quite astonishingly high, and there was a stiff breeze off the sea. Real summer now They watched some spry old men in hitched-up-high trunks taking a dawn dip How come they found it so easy to have a good time, Marina thought What was their secret? All they seemed to need was cold water and a few old buggers like themselves They smiled and waved at Julie and Marina, and one of them called something out, something innocent and jolly· come on in, the water's fine. The waves were bouncy and full of fun Monday morning high jinks.

Marina had always found Julie just a tad on the tiresome side, but not now It was such a relief to talk to someone about something other than sodding cocaine for a change. And it gave her a rest from thinking about Kelvin. She smiled indulgently as Julie burbled on about the world she had just been all over, a place seemingly composed exclusively of people exactly like herself who all kept on turning up at the same places. The names fell casually from her lips: Shanghai, Macao, Bangkok, Sydney. Next year she was going to South America. Marina counselled caution about native products.

Later, after Julie had gone, Marina reluctantly came home and tiptoed to Ward's room and tapped on the door; no answer. She turned the knob and poked her head round. He was cross-legged surrounded by torn-up paper. His hands were working, slowly, methodically; his eyes were facing the window, the first light.

'Ward?' she whispered, but he didn't hear her or at least didn't respond if he did. 'Ward?'

Nothing. She pulled the door shut again and went back to the kitchen and the Penny Plain catalogue. Everything in it was equally horrible, it was quite astonishing. It was like some kind of inconceivably vile pornography

All day Monday he didn't come out, except to go to the toilet and make cups of tea. I'm coming off it, he said. Fucking right. His hands were covered in powdery paper residue. His eyes were bloodshot and deeply set. He finished the tearing by mid-afternoon, and immediately started the folding.

It took him about twenty-six seconds to fold one. As he did them he began the calculation of how long it would take to do one thousand. He was on number fifteen before he got a figure he trusted – seven and a half hours, give or take. He glanced at his clock. it was ten to three. So he'd be finished with the folding by, by, about twenty past ten or thereabouts. He hadn't had any cocaine now for more than twenty-four hours, and still he wasn't asleep. He was depleted and bored, but he wasn't asleep. Every hour that passed made his hands shakier, his bowels looser, his eyes grainier, his mood bleaker. His head was thumping; he felt as if he was going blind. The time passed in a way that seemed deliberately designed to provoke, in a kind of taunting dance. Slow, slower, slowest. There was nothing to do inside it but fold. He needed to see them, one thousand wraps He needed to pass the stuff through his fingers, one gram at a time, see each one, feel how many a thousand were. One at a time they were easy. Little bastards. He processed the squares of paper from the messy unfolded side on to the nice neat ranks of folded on the other side. The time droned away in twenty-six-second units, ticking away its stupid interminable self, and soon he began to forget what day this was. What had he done yesterday? He couldn't remember. There was a big pile of torn paper beside him, but it didn't seem to have anything to do with him. He started licking his lips incessantly. Biting little dried bits off. They started to bleed. The web of skin between thumb and hand was covered on both hands with little paper cuts that stung for hours. The paper squares carried traces of dried blood. The powdery paper dust got into his nose and sinuses and eyes. Soon his nose was running incessantly, he swiped at it with his sleeve. Someone was speaking to him but he couldn't hear them. *The Satanic Verses* lay unopened on the bed, still waiting.

He finished folding at eleven-thirty p m , a good hour behind schedule but he'd started to slow down somewhere in the middle; his hands were shaking like a drunk's.

He went to listen to the central heating controller but it had nothing to say to him. He let himself out of the house and went down to the beach, lay on his back, looked at the stars. They didn't seem to be in any particular pattern; they had nothing to say either. The darkness was thin and incomplete. He went back home. The urge to reward himself for his prolonged, miserable abstinence with just one little snort was suddenly so overpoweringly strong that he'd never felt a need like it It took him by the bowels and twisted. It screamed and tore at him, for minute after minute, and he stood in the passage by the kitchen astonished and terrified by the suddenness and the ferocity, the clenching of the stomach, the weakness in the limbs, the freight of sheer total misery. He sobbed, leaning against the kitchen doorjamb, minute after minute Every bit of his face was aching and leaking some kind of fluid. What you warnt to sleeep for anyhow, the cocaine said in a stupid cartoon South American accent, sleeep when you dead, babee. Oooh aaaah, juzza leetle beet, don't you theeenk, stoopid, stooooooooooopeeeeeeeeeed?

He came to; he was slumped against the wall in the damp-smelling corridor. He wiped the snot and the tears away, he blew his nose several times. There was something thick and sticky on the skin of his thighs. He made it to the toilet just in time and evacuated with much splattering and a worse stink than he had ever imagined possible; he was almost proud of it He cleaned himself up and went back to his room. It was time to read *The Satanic Verses*. By the end of that, he'd be off it.

It was heavy, apart from anything. Marina's mum had bought it for her, new, in hardback, one Christmas, with a little inscription in the front, a slightly embarrassing though very touching message of fondness. Ward only ever read books in paperback, and only ever second-hand (or stolen).

Big book, 547 pages big, and each page covered in words He lay back in bed and allowed it to rest in the tent of his raised knees. He read the front and the back, the reviews He looked briefly at the author photograph and looked quickly away again. If anything could put him off, he thought, it would be that face, that repulsive dog-ugly face, that leering smug fucking .

He looked away again. He fingered the cool sleekness of the dust jacket, slid it up and down an inch or so, revealing the sober grainy blue underneath.

Come on now.

Page one. Chapter one The first sentence. *'To be born again,' sang Gibreel Farishta tumbling from the heavens, 'first you have to die. Ho ji! Ho ji!'*

He read it through, and then his eyes flew up to the ceiling; seemingly without his will, they just flew off the page. He dragged them back again. Now come on.

'To land upon the bosomy earth, first one needs to fly Tat-taa! Taka-thum . .'

Oh, for fuck's sake, Ward thought, it can't go on like this, can it? Fucking prancing around. Fucking jessie. And how is the earth 'bosomy' anyway? Bosoms are soft and bouncy and the earth, notoriously, is hard. The analogy hardly seemed apt, as one of the dinner-party monkeys might have said. Maybe it improved. He stuck with it, grim, determined.

Ten minutes later and he was wondering about whose was the bacon in the fridge. He knew it wasn't Kelvin's, so it was Marina or Steve If it was Steve's, then he wouldn't be wanting it for the time being. He could go a bit of bacon, just at the moment. He could just nip out and make a quick sarny, then be back in bed with Salman in no time.

He reached about for something to mark his place (Marina didn't approve of dog ears) and found that his place was on page two.

You couldn't just stop at page two, it wasn't right. He flicked quickly through; thirty pages to go till the end of the chapter He tried to find his place again, but his eyes wouldn't recognize it, they wanted to go back on the ceiling again. He shifted about and found that, somehow, despite the tented knees, the weight of the book was giving him an erection He defied it. The Triumph of the Will.

On page eight he found a little slip of paper, marking someone's place Marina, who said that it was brilliant, had in fact got as far as page eight and then stopped. It had to be her, there could be no other interpretation of the slip of paper. The lying cow hadn't read it either. He was on his own now He tried to read on, but the heart had gone out of him. He longed to start *Ecce Homo* again. Or *Moby Dick*. Or anything. He thought about cocaine.

He found that he had put the book down, face down, on top of the duvet tent, and was scrutinizing the cuticles of his nails, biting off tiny shreds of skin One in particular was engaging him He went too hard and tore a miniature wound on the finger, and a bright drop of blood welled up He sucked it with grim pleasure The movement dislodged the book, which slid sideways, annoyingly He grabbed for it and crushed or creased three pages. Shit Marina was not someone who liked her books to look used, she liked them neat and shiny. And shelved. He smoothed the pages out as much as he could. He sighed, a sigh deeper and more protracted than any he could ever remember. It seemed to bruise his chest.

Now. Perspective. He'd read worse than this, and got through it. He wasn't the kind of person who was defeated by some bloody book. He had stopped smoking, he was packing in the cocaine, and he was going to read the book. What he started he finished, always, even those bloody books about women and their sodding mothers that Marina always seemed to have lying around. Even that Anita Brookner. Josephine *Hart*, for God's sake. Nothing had ever defeated him before.

Nothing.

By page ten he had squirmed himself into the most uncomfortable position he had ever found, and one arm had gone to sleep from leaning on it. The other arm was cold and tingling He was getting an ache right up in his neck. Page eleven. he was chanting the words to himself, chanting them in a childish singy-song, making nonsense out of them and pulling sneery faces. He quickly calculated how long he'd taken to get this far (fifty minutes), calculated how long it would take to reach the end (five minutes per page, 540-whatever pages, he needed Kelvin here really, hold on, it came to, oh fuck it, who cared, what did it matter, about 2,700 minutes, which was, I don't know, more than twenty-four hours anyway, more like forty-eight) . . .

He folded the book up carefully, marking his place with a kingsize Rizla packet. He'd try again in ten minutes. He went off to the front room and fiddled with his nails a bit more The book waited for him, grinning, capering. Ho ji! Ho ji!

OK He was back now, knees neatly tented, refreshed, ready. He breathed deeply. The Rizla packet sang to him of joints and sleepy sleepy bed, but he was adamantine. This was a book like any other and he was going to read the bastard.

Three hours later he found himself collecting papers and

lighter and keys, also a wire coat hanger, throwing his jacket on and leaving the house quietly, the book sleek and solid and respectable (and unread) under his arm. It was late, no one about. He threaded the streets down to the pier, which was all locked up, the rails chill and sticky with dew. He stood underneath and watched the waves lapping at the great columns. He lit a cigarette, then untwisted the coat hanger and made a crude armature to hold the book in. He broke the top off the lighter and carefully splashed the fluid over the book, taking care to get it into the inside pages as well. He held it away from him and carefully applied the lit cigarette.

After some initial anxiety, there was a sudden blue whoof of fire, and after that the book burnt very satisfactorily, though he had to let go long before he wanted to. The horrible charred thing fell into the water and hissed, little flickers of flame still playing with the edges of the pages and at one end of the dust jacket, little purple and blue flames. Burn, you bastard. He watched it for a while, then gave it a good kicking and turned back home. He tried to think what to tell Marina about what had happened to her book. Fuck it, he thought, I'll tell her it spontaneously combusted. It caught fire and, actually, it burnt very nicely. Very nicely indeed.

banana toothpaste

Kelvin had turned up. He'd been found wandering about outside the hospital. He was incoherent and improperly dressed; he'd lost control of his bladder, amongst other things. He collapsed in the car park, and they brought him in. He'd taken an overdose of something, he couldn't tell them what. Marina got a phone call

She went in to see him and Julie went with her. Julie said she was dreading it, but she put on lipstick, something she only ever did otherwise for parties, and wore her best leggings and black silk top.

The men were the familiar shuffling, amorphous mob seen on countless documentaries and the occasional late-night art film Kelvin was in the television room, and Julie was surprised that he was fully, correctly dressed, and was shaved and groomed She'd expected pyjamas and nylon slippers, maybe a dressing gown, certainly stubble. Kelvin stood up when he saw them and smiled Marina pecked him on the cheek, and Julie followed suit, though with a perceptible hesitation. He had a slightly stale smell about him. Marina passed over her gifts: books, peanuts, tapes Julie gave him a toothbrush shaped like a banana and banana-flavoured toothpaste, which she'd picked up in one of her endless trawls through the Sunday market. Kelvin accepted gracefully, then paid no further attention to her. She was clearly not sufficiently skilled in visiting to waste time on.

It had been agreed in advance that Marina would not bring him any cocaine, no matter how often he asked. She was getting rid of it tonight anyway, she'd decided. In the event, he didn't ask; the antidepressants were making him forgetful, which was a blessing. Marina efficiently asked the questions and was answered informatively and fully. A session with the psychiatrist, sleeing, eating. Constipation, movement, etc. She tried not to appear as she felt: furious, upset, even faintly disgusted, but relieved also that things had come to a head like this. She tried to be the patient wife. Julie was appalled by the mundanity of it. She'd steeled herself to come here, had tingled with the anticipation of grief and hopelessness, or at the very least some dark sorrow piercing a crack in the armour of forced jocularity Julie realized she was staring at Kelvin, and fidgeted with her bag made of carpet material She was desperate to say something.

The suicide attempt had happened to Kelvin quite suddenly, early Sunday morning, a long, straggling, pointless night, straight after his lonely epiphany up on the Downs, without any particular warning. There'd been no one in. He'd drunk more brandy than he intended and put himself to bed. He had woken up in the middle of the night and found that he'd wet the bed He then went to the bathroom and ate half a bottle of Marina's paracetamol and some of her contraceptive pills as well, with water from the tap, as well as about two grams of cocaine It took about eight minutes to get all the pills down, he reckoned. Then he went for a walk, he said, and he couldn't remember after that. He woke up as they were pumping his stomach. Marina glared at him like he was a dangerous animal or a man who had just exposed himself to her He could furnish no reason, but conceded under questioning that he might 'do it' again.

Kelvin's voice stopped, and Kelvin examined his nails
  'So what do you do all day?'
  The voice was Julie's. Bright, cheerful, appalling. How

could she have said it? She wished she was dead, just like when she went to her first ballet lesson, aged six, and found that no one else was wearing sandals, but tidy little pink leather pumps with flat leather soles She formed the words in her head – 'I wish I was dead' – and for a second thought that it was she who had had the sleeping pills and the wet bed, the stomach pump, the banana toothbrush, and was being visited by Marina and Kelvin.

Kelvin laughed, and made the situation all right

'Oh, you know. Shuffle Urinate. Watch Richard and Judy and the weather forecasts. Pretty much business as usual, really.' He went to his locker and brought out some pieces of paper 'Actually I've started drawing again,' he said, and showed the sheets to Marina one at a time

They were all of concentric rings of stackable steel chairs in front of a huge television which was mounted high on the wall There were a few scattered figures in the chairs. They wore expressions of insane pleasure, great toothy smiles. The television showed a similar face, grinning vastly and holding a little blue and purple pill to its gaping mouth Nurses with trolleys circled in the background, distant and alluring and oddly menacing.

'Good,' Marina said as each one was exhibited. 'Actually, these are very good, Kel '

He nodded glumly and put them away again, and they ended the visit early. Julie went on ahead. Looking back from the double doors, she saw Marina sitting beside Kelvin on the bed She was holding his hand and speaking to him, very seriously He was nodding bleakly, and she rubbed his hand and they sat silently together for a moment Marina and Julie made their way out. They went straight home Marina was quiet on the bus

the great wall

Tuesday evening. Marina had told Ward about Kelvin.

'Two down,' he'd said, a weird glee in his eyes, and retreated to his room.

He lay motionless, eyes aching, fixed on the ceiling. Over forty-eight hours now. The tearing and folding were finished; the weighing, gram by meticulous gram, was finished, each wrap was precisely filled and tidily closed. He had piled them up haphazardly in a corner. In the night, still sleepless, he had gone to look at them. He had started to rearrange them, not fully consciously at first, then with a greater sense of purpose. They were flat and regular, and he laid out a layer of them, five across by twenty long He laid another layer across, with the wraps at right angles to the ones below for stability. Another level He built slowly, carefully. It took more than three hours to complete, a thick solid monument, a great wall He regarded it with dull satisfaction One thousand wraps, each in its place, all accounted for You couldn't move any one of them without seeing the gap Controlled He went back to bed and slept at once

He woke up an hour or so later; he had no idea what time of day it was He lay on the bed listening Some fucking thing had woken him up and it was still going on. An engine revving outside, going forwards, reversing, forwards again, the crack of tyre scraping against kerb, seemingly for hours. Whatever the driver of the van was on, it was reacting badly with his parking. He just couldn't get it right. He was directly outside the house, the windows were open, it was all getting a bit much.

Ward levered himself out of bed and went into the front room, shoved his head and shoulders out of the window.

'Hey! You want a fucking hand parking that van, pal?'

He felt things bubbling up inside him, an interesting feeling. For a few seconds it actually interfered with his breathing, and he clamped a hand to his heart. He didn't recognize it. It was a bright exhilarating thing; it filled him with power and joy and inviolability. It ran righteously everywhere and seethed; it clenched its fists into his stomach; it boiled up into his mouth; it turned his muscles to steel. It was pure rage.

'Hey, pal!'

The engine revved and stalled. The driver couldn't get it started again easily, and the sounds of starter motor failing, again and again and again, drove Ward back from the window and into the room again, searching for something, he didn't yet know what. He took hold of the television and tried to lift it clear, but there were wires all over the place, aerial and video and mains, and it was just too complicated He wanted something self-contained

He found Kelvin's artwork, the large fish tank that was going to bring about the death of all art. He grabbed it. He found it surprisingly heavy; the glass was thicker than it looked He stumbled with it over to the window, he balanced it on the ledge, half-in, half-out. The (assumed) Virgin in the tank looked back at him with tranquillized eyes.

'Hey! CUNT! NEED A FUCKING HAND PARKING THAT FUCKING VAN, DO WE?'

He shoved the tank with muscles newly liberated by rage, and the thing sailed out with astonishing speed and heaviness, landed fair and square on the windscreen, smashed the glass, smashed itself, bits of it bouncing away off the bonnet and on to the road. The revving and the stalling stopped immediately. The sound seemed to reach him a moment later, a chaotic splattering of broken glass.

Ward looked at the mess from the window, then sighed heavily. Fuck. He left a note for Marina, returned to his room and took a wrap off the great wall, carefully but with some distaste pushed it up into his arse, then got his jacket and keys and went downstairs. Someone had already called the police. Ward sat in the back of the police car and was soon fast asleep again

breath

'Need a hand parking that fucking van, pal!'

The door shut, keys turned in locks, gratings were scraped open and then shut again.

At first Ward couldn't understand the size of the room. It seemed impossibly small. He felt there must be another bit, a room off it or a door to another room, this must just be a kind of lobby or anteroom. There was another person in here as well, but he would presumably be going in a minute to make room There wasn't enough room.

The other person was breathing, which was of course perfectly understandable, and no objection could be mounted against it Breathing in the dark Ward could see nothing of him, since there was no light either, except a faint bluish-greenish tinge towards the ceiling The breathing was steady and regular, deep, throaty. Ward found himself listening to it intently. He didn't know where he was supposed to stand. The other man was standing in the corner, in the dark, no more than two paces away Ward took a step forwards and banged his shin on something hard He reached down to rub the injured part, found himself off balance. He hopped forward half a step, and was caught behind the knee by whatever it was that had knocked his shin He fell, his arms grabbing for the wall. It was a bed, or at least a kind of

223

platform. He landed awkwardly, banged his head on the wall. There just wasn't enough room. He sat upright on the bed and rubbed shin, knee, head. The heels of his hands hurt from banging against the wall.

Breath. No other sound.

'Need a fucking hand, do we!'

Ward swallowed, and the sound seemed extraordinarily loud. The bed was solid and cool, covered with a smooth, shiny vinyl. There was a smell which was faint but disheartening, stale, not strong, not stale enough to be strong or to be anything except mildly noticeable and faintly disheartening He swallowed again.

Ward thought, perhaps I should say something. Hi, my name's Ward, how do you do, sorry to barge in on you like this, like What you in for, then, armed robbery? Don't mind me Important to get the tone right. Genial, but tough. Or no, hard, ironic, unapproachable. He particularly liked the idea of unapproachable So just something like, er, hi, my name's Ward. Just that. That was plenty The other man didn't seem like a chatterbox, so there was little danger of unwanted intimacy

Of that sort, he added immediately, unwanted intimacy of that sort.

Or any other sort, he appended firmly, after a further moment's frantic thought.

He sat straight up on the bed with his back to the wall He pulled his feet in, but the bed seemed to be solid and there was nowhere to tuck your feet under. It must be like a kind of plinth or dais, he thought, both words seeming inappropriately exotic for the bare shabby little construction Shelf was more like it.

The other man moved, not his feet but his body; he leaned in slightly then back Christ, what's he doing, Ward thought, what's he up to? Ward felt the movement more than saw it, felt the heat from the man's body approach by a few inches, then retreat again There was a momentary interruption in the breathing while this happened Ward held his breath as well, only realizing that he was holding it when the other man's started up again. Ward exhaled. His shin hurt He wanted to rub it a bit more, but felt totally inhibited from doing so. Maybe it was one of those things you just didn't do. One of those things everyone knew you didn't do. What, you didn't rub your shin, did you? Christ's sake, what did you expect?

So so so. Someone would presumably come in a minute to let the other man out, then Ward could relax. Rub his shin if he wanted to. That must be why he's standing there, Ward thought, he's waiting to be let out

Then suddenly the other was on the move, properly this time, feet and everything. He moved quickly past Ward, the cuff of his trousers brushing against Ward's trousers, to the door, then back again to his corner. A quick convulsive movement. A little trip. Ward froze, and his breathing stopped again in the draught from his movement. The air moved about, all over the place, washing about the cell, brushing over the walls and ceiling Ward felt it on his face Only when it had settled did he start breathing again He tried to breathe more quietly, which translated into quick, shallow breaths After a few of these, though, he needed to sigh deeply, which was noisy. He tried to go back to breathing normally but found he had forgotten how Another swallow. How do you breathe, he thought, usually? He tried to remember occasions when he had breathed naturally, normally, without thought, and while he was thinking his breath stopped again, and he had to hike it back into action He took several deep breaths to make up for it, and found that his chest, his lungs, ached from the exertion. He didn't normally breathe quite that deeply, then Somewhere in between.

He heard another sound, which he knew, without knowing how he knew, was the sound of the other man's tongue moving across the other man's lips. He was licking his lips. For Christ's sake, why?

Was he looking? Was the other man watching Ward as he worked on his breathing method, watching him and licking his lips?

225

You looking at me? You looking at me, pal? Eh? What you fuckin' looking at? Eh?

Ward didn't dare look over to that corner to see. What if he looked and caught the other man looking at him, looking full on, what then? What if he licked his lips while Ward was looking, what if Ward saw the tongue come out from between the lips and move, slowly, wetly, a sly, luscious, insidious bivalve, round the mouth, then go back in again?

Another sound. Ward didn't immediately know what this sound was. It didn't suggest anything straight away.

I wish he'd just lie down, Ward thought. Maybe if I lie down, then he will too. Maybe he's waiting for me to first, like some kind of bloody game or something. Perhaps it's part of the etiquette, or it shows dominance or something.

That other sound again. It had a rhythmic quality to it.

Ward took a chance and moved round, so that his head was against the other wall and he was lying at full stretch on the bed. He swung his feet up too They'd taken his shoelaces so his shoes slipped off and one of them fell on to the floor. The sound made him feel braver

That other sound now . . .

The other man was suddenly close, right close up, Ward could see his face, could see black stubble round the chin and mouth and down the throat, could see lips, a mouth, heavily formed, and a great thick nose. There were shadows round the eyes, eyelashes. The face turned slightly and Ward could see marks, cuts and a trickle of slow blood. The face was bruised, the nose looked broken, the eyes were puffy underneath, half-closed. The hair on top, from what Ward could make out, was cropped short.

'Got a match?'

The man was holding out a tiny little cigarette, itself not much thicker than a match.

'No, sorry, don't smoke,' Ward said, quickly, his throat so clenched with tension that his voice was a funny cartoon version of his normal register. 'Sorry,' he said again, but the face showed no sign of moving, and then the tongue came out and moved slowly, sensuously, round the lips. Ward again

226

heard the scratch of tongue against stubble. He couldn't look. He felt the face move away, and then heard the man lying down on his bed, on the other side of the room, which was about three feet away. If either of them had reached out their arm, they would have touched. Ward tried to make himself smaller. His heart was banging in his chest. Breathe, he told himself, breathe. That's all you have to do.

'Don't smoke,' the other man said after a few minutes and made a small, derisive sound

'Sorry. No,' Ward said. 'I've got some cocaine, though.'

They both had a noseful, and the other man had another one as well. They sat facing each other for a few moments, then the other man swung himself back on to his bed Ward heard the sound again, the rhythmic sound he'd heard earlier. It stopped for a second, hitched, then started again, now with a new quality to it, a slightly wet quality, slurring like an old man's gums, slick and sticky The speed was quite regular, a steady, medium-paced, efficient sound, like someone working a hand pump. Up and down, up and down. The man grunted and the speed increased, just slightly. Stopped, then a burst of much faster pumping. Faster still, then he stopped again. He grunted and lay still for a moment Ward concentrated on the breathing The cocaine was making him want to jump up and walk around, but of course he couldn't. The other stood up instead and came over to Ward's side of the cell and Ward's little dais He sat beside him, and put Ward's hand over his balls, then the pumping started again Ward tried not to look, but despite himself caught the odd glimpse, a long, thick, brown thing, slickly reflective of what little light there was, glossy, like well-worn leather, ridged and contoured. There was one particularly prominent vein, and, again despite himself, Ward became fascinated by it, by its thickness and its pulsing as the hand moved back and forth over it. He looked away in time to miss the culmination of this work, and tried to rub his hand clean against the tough, glossy material of the dais. The other man sat still for a second, then returned to his own side.

'Yeah, well, thanks a lot, pal, know what I mean,' Ward said finally, and slumped back against the wall.

There was quiet for a while, the breathing was quiet and regular, and Ward was fairly confident that he had gone to sleep, and was even starting to believe that it might be possible for him to do the same in about eight hours, if he could just stop itching long enough, when the gravel voice drifted over like wood smoke

'Time for another little nose. Wouldn't you say, *pal*?'

tidying up

Marina saw the broken glass on the pavement outside the window as she turned the corner into the street She'd been out with Carola, trying to buy a wedding present for one of Carola's innumerable friends. It had been exhausting and strange but, Marina realized, the best fun she'd had in months. They had fingered every brass nightlight holder and generic-ethnic papier-mâché pointy bird thing in town. She had even briefly hankered after a leopard-skin painted teapot and Carola, in all seriousness, had offered to buy it for her. They had compromised finally on a hinged box made, it said on the bottom, of alabaster, though neither of them liked it. It was, they agreed, a perfect present, anonymous and purposeless and coolly opulent. Afterwards they had gone to Burger King, which Carola claimed to be an entirely new experience for her She had looked surprised and interested as she ate. Out of nowhere Carola had asked Marina if she wanted to come and live in her new flat next term.

Marina stood in front of the house and surveyed the wreckage Someone from over the road was standing at her door looking at her looking at the house, and she filled Marina in on the details. Marina hesitated outside, then with dread in her heart turned the key and went upstairs She found Ward's note. 'Arrested (Not drug related) Do nothing till return. W '

She almost laughed That was it, then. First Steve, then Kel, finally Ward had crumbled, after all his desperate holding out. The cocaine had won.

'Yeah, well, that's what you think, maybe.'

She went from room to room, looking at things. She found Kelvin's cocaine-use graph, all marked out, with the four coloured lines starting at zero. At some stage someone, and she knew who she suspected, had continued one of the lines and turned it into one of those primitive cock and balls cartoons with the little drops of sperm coming out of the tip. Someone else had written rude words on it, and 'Kelvin is a girl ' She thought she knew who that might have been as well She smiled at it for a minute

She went round with an ASDA bag looking for cocaine. There were a great number of secret little stashes here and there, still an awful lot of it around, not including Ward's great wall and she threw it all in the bag. It seemed a shame to destroy something as well made as the wall, and she contemplated it for a minute or two before scooping it all up and dumping it into the bag.

When she'd finished she examined the contents. Actually, she thought, there wasn't quite as much here as she'd expected She couldn't account for it, but there certainly seemed to be a shortfall. She tried to work it out: deduct the amounts lost by Kelvin and Steve, knock off, say, as much as a kilogram to cover what they'd used, and there still wasn't enough left Even so, there was sufficient here for years, if you were just able to be a bit respectful of it. Not go off your head like Ward, not throw it all away like Kelvin, not bloody lose it all like Steve. She had been weaning herself off it for several weeks now, cutting it back, having a bit less a bit less often She hadn't had as much as a smell of it for four days now. Better off without it, the whole lot of it It was bad news, she'd known it would be all along

She opened all the windows and let the wind blow through the place She opened the curtains and was astonished to see how grubby everything looked. Her parents had agreed to pay off her overdraft, so she'd be going back to university in the autumn. She didn't know what to do about Kelvin. He really had to pull himself together.

She took a wrap out of the ASDA bag on her lap and looked at it. It was going to be her last one, she'd decided, her last one ever. The air was soft through the window.

'Well,' she said out loud, 'really I should save it for later.'

She fingered it, traced the edges and the corners with her fingernail.

'Or, I could have it now.' Unless she had two lots, some now, some later. Why not? She stamped down hard on this piece of cocaine thinking.

She debated internally, looking at the options in order. She played with the wrap, turned it over and over in her fingers.

'OK, look, I'll toss it. One side's heads, other side's tails. Heads I have it now, tails I have it later, and if it lands on its side . . '

She put it on her thumb and flicked it up It twisted and rotated, landed on the carpet by her feet. Tails. Nob.

Best of three, then. Heads this time. Also nob.

She picked it up again, held it to her nose. She could smell the acrid powder through the paper; her throat clenched slightly at the thought of it. She could feel it fizzing and snapping its way along the neurons, the lights clicking on, the buoyancy. The sheer pleasure. She held it in the palm of her hand. It was such a nice little package, neat and tight and tidy.

'Sod it.'

She flicked it out of the open window. It sailed delicately through the summer air, twisting and turning as it fell She was, she realized, sick to death of it Sick of chemically enhanced sex and distorted priorities. It was too much like hard work. She got her denim jacket out of the kitchen and stuffed the ASDA bag into her beaded cloth bag and went out into the air. It was mild and breezy; the leaves stirred in the trees and people walked heavily and slowly and smiled She sat upstairs in a seafront bar, at an open window with a panoramic view of the Channel, and watched the sun go down. It was lovely.

*

231

Later she stood on the beach in the coloured glare of the pier lights, the reflections brilliant and jagged on the waves. The wind was freshening. Her bag was cradled in her arms. Now was the time.

But still she was regretful. If only you could just have it or leave it alone. If only it would just give you the thrill and not bother you afterwards. If only it wasn't cocaine.

She unzipped it, pulled out the ASDA bag inside, and rummaged about in it. She pulled out a fistful of wraps.

Powdered joy It ought to be the best thing on earth, the universal antidote to all boredom and disappointment and despair, the panacea. It ought to heal, console, delight, astonish. Instead it just sat down and ate you from the inside, every shiny grain a little tooth, while at the same time telling you you were invincible. It made you greedy, stupid, obsessive, vain and, worst of all, boring She remembered Kelvin saying, 'Marina, if this is not your definition of a gift from the gods . . . ' She saw him now, sitting bleakly on his hospital bed with his bleak little pictures around him. She saw Steve pitting his skinny frame against some bonehead bouncer, goading, needling She saw Ward pushing the wanker's head under the water, she saw him turned into a paper-folding machine, holding out, staring the cocaine down, defying it ferociously, finally flinging his rage and frustration out into the street. She saw herself, even, watching with a cool abstraction as everyone around her fell apart Idling her time away with Ward's body hair. No more.

Still she hesitated. The terrible waste of what she was about to do fell on her and took the strength from her arm Just because they had all failed so completely to get any benefit from it, did that mean no one else should have a try? You could say, she thought, that we just genuinely don't know how to enjoy ourselves. Don't actually know how to do it. Someone else, on the other hand . . A shadowy notion formed in her head if instead of destroying it, she could just put it somewhere, somewhere no one would ever think of looking. Then if anyone did happen to find it, it would be up to them what they did. They could decide for themselves.

After all, she told herself again, it wasn't actually hers to destroy. Not really. It really wasn't her decision to make.

She clenched the wraps tightly. She drew back her hand to throw them. Her arm wouldn't work

Terrible to just waste it, she thought. And it is *so* expensive. And it isn't mine. And it is incredibly good, my God, it was good. (Anyway, I know how to handle it now, not like the others. It's not me that's got the problem with it. And I could sneak back from time to time and get a little bit. Just a little bit. Ooh aah.)

The waves lapped at her feet as a gust of wind came off the sea and she shuddered. It was the cocaine talking to her, whispering to her, cajoling, persuading, seducing, charming, it told her it needed her, without her it was nothing, it would give her anything she wanted, a whole world of mastery and sweetness, only don't leave me, it whispered, don't leave me, don't –

The wraps gleamed like bones as they tumbled through the black air over the sea. They flashed and somersaulted, a gleeful trajectory, as if possessed of some kind of vital energy, before they dropped flat on the waves, floated for a while, circled, then sank. Fish food. She held the ASDA bags over the water and flung the whole lot out, watched as it was swept up and away and finally out of sight. Enough.

three weeks later...

the flower of british manhood

'Ref-er-ee!'

The shout went up from the opposition goalmouth, where Marina was standing with Carola. Steve and Darren, the coat-check man, stood close by. Not arm in arm, though they were certainly shoulder to shoulder Darren's left hand was out of sight. Steve was smiling. Just a little bit of physio, Darren explained Oh, Marina said, I didn't realize he'd injured himself there.

'Oh, and by the way,' Steve had said when Marina told him what she'd done with the cocaine, 'next time you plan to get rid of tens of thousands of pounds' worth of one of the world's most hotly desired commodities, just let me know first and I'll kill you '

'I told you I was getting rid of it,' she said, and Steve with some precision clarified the difference between 'getting rid' (selling it) and just getting rid.

'If I'd had any idea,' he said ominously.

(Prewarned of her intentions, and in agreement with Ward, he had of course stashed away a good half-kilogram against future need, now nestling like some exotic parasitic pupa

237

back inside Seaman Staines's trousers. He was thus able to take a relaxed view)

Kelvin was out now, still grim round the eyes and inclined to mirthless laughter, but out. He was with his parents in Ipswich. Marina went there for weekends and had even started to like his mother, who referred in stage whispers to 'Kelvin's spot of bother' and refused to be told anything about what had happened. 'Now I want you to know that we don't blame you. No one's blaming you for anything. Not at all. I don't want to know what's been happening,' she said. 'I don't care, as long as he's all right now.' Marina suspected that there might be just the teeniest bit of what Carola might have called denial going on Marina found her watching Kelvin rather closely at times, but he didn't seem to notice His dad circled round him, helpless, hearty, devastated. Marina went for short, grim walks with Kelvin and responded as fully as she could to his rather abstract comments about trees and cloud formations Once he asked her, quite casually, if she had any gear with her Oh, of course, Kel, pockets stuffed full of it, obviously She told him what she'd done with it and he shrugged. He didn't care; he didn't care about anything, just at the moment. He was drawing a great deal, though not well. He did a portrait of her, and she couldn't conceal her horror when he showed it to her. it was all toothy grin and wide-awake eyes 'This is bollocks, Kel,' she told him. 'I look like one of those suburban brood-mares out of an Escort ad.' He added fangs and a big festering wound on the cheek They agreed not to discuss it any further.

One Sunday they all drove out to some castle and sat on a blanket in the sun and ate gala pie, potato salad, bitter droopy lettuce. It was the quietest picnic Marina ever wanted to participate in, the undisputed highlight being a discussion about the best way back to the car. She was hugely relieved to get home to Brighton, and spent an hour on the phone to Kel from a phone box (he called her back) She told him she missed him, she'd been missing him for weeks, months even. From well before his 'spot of bother'. He said he'd missed her too, he missed everyone. He was crying, which made her cry too. But he was in no rush to come back to Brighton. Well, all right, she said, I'll come to you, but no more picnics, Kel, I mean it. Didn't you enjoy it, he said, and he was genuinely surprised. You didn't enjoy it?'

'But there is no referee,' Darren said, incredulous, and was duly ignored. Ward came thundering past, chasing an impossible ball, and fell over of course. He was due in court in February, though the charges were criminal damage rather than assault, since the driver of the van had been uninjured. More than anything, he'd been surprised to find himself sharing a cab with a virgin. Ward had tried to present it as some kind of one in a million accident. He'd been cleaning the tank, he said, emptying it out of the window, and it had just slipped. There was a picture of the Madonna in it, because. Because – well, he hadn't got the whole thing figured out just yet. He and Steve spent long hours tidying up the details.

He still refused to forgive Marina for destroying the cocaine, refused to understand why she'd done it, saw no need for it. He refused, in fact, to believe that she really had. He'd never had any trouble with it, he said, and it was hardly his fault if the rest of them were some kind of lightweights. Carola had drifted away since their aborted encounter, and Ward was inclined to blame Marina for this as well, even though he had no serious intentions towards her. He was drinking a bit too much, but he was mostly better. And he'd shown the cocaine who had the bollocks round here, as he never tired of telling people It was all to do with the triumph of the will, he said. (The fact that he had shares in Steve's stash allowed him to be philosophical.) He was still restless though, fidgety, bored, inclined to quick anger. Marina thought this wasn't entirely a bad thing· at least it gave the sofa a rest from him from time to time. She was keeping on at him about repeating his first year And he was reading Evelyn Waugh instead of Nietzsche, which could only be good in her opinion. She never did find out what had happened to *The Satanic Verses*, though.

Bazza came charging up behind him, crimson-faced.

'Hi, Barry,' Marina said, and blushed. Dammit! She cursed herself. A grown woman! He stood in front of them, hands on hips, gasping. Steve glanced over to her. She was trying desperately to look anywhere other than at Bazza's shorts, as she had promised to do She had no desire whatsoever to look at Bazza, not at any part of him, or at any item of clothing pertaining to him. It had all been agreed, in a long and rather tortured phone call with Kelvin last night. She scanned the sky, gazed at nearby sunbathers, studied the horizon The grass. Steve and Darren, on the other hand, had no such scruples.

'Hi, Baz,' Darren said, and gave him a slap on the neck. 'What you doing later?'

tourists, you know what they're like

Jez sat in the quiet gloom of the Fishing Museum and watched the crowds parading up and down outside. He felt lonelier than he could ever remember feeling before in his life.

It was the first day of his 'placement'. The maniac Claire had finally got her way and talked the reluctant councillor into opening up again, her sole motive seeming to be a gimlet-eyed belief in the importance of stopping the unemployed from just sitting about all day. Jez had no idea what he was supposed to do. He hadn't brought anything to read with him. So he just sat there, all day.

Then, mid-afternoon, a group of four piled hysterically in, Germans, two men and two women They smelled of dough-nuts and beer. They laughed at everything, were delighted with Jez, wanted to climb into the boat.

'You will take our picture?' one of the men asked. They weren't supposed to go in the boat, but Jez sought deep within himself and found that, somehow or other, he didn't have it in him to care.

The four all climbed over the little rope and sat in the bows, two on either side of the serenely unconcerned sailor. One of the men put his arm round him, and they all settled themselves

'OK. Now we are ready.'

Jez raised the camera to his eye and counted down: 'Three. Two.'

On 'one', the man with his arm round the sailor's shoulders suddenly yanked him up and threw him out.

'Man overboard!' he yelled, and everyone laughed with an intensity that reverberated round the dark little cave and made Jez wince slightly. He guessed they had this much fun wherever they went in the world. He sighed.

They all shook his hand and apologized and laughed and took a picture of him, and went off to enjoy themselves even more somewhere else.

Quiet again. He poked about and found a broom cupboard. The dummy was leaking white powder for some reason He chivvied it all up and brushed it out of the door on to the esplanade, feeling oddly proprietorial. He squinted into the ferocious light for a moment, then ducked back inside, into the quiet and the gloom.

Simon Nolan lives in Hove, Sussex.
As Good As It Gets is his first novel.